# Discords of The Mind Vol. 3
## The Final Collection of Short Stories

Stories By BC. Neon, Edited By Sean Ailshie

An imprint of BC. Neon

ISBN 978-1-9543-8907-6 (Soft Cover)
ISBN 978-1-9543-8906-9 (Hard Cover)
ISBN 978-1-9543-8908-3 (eBook)

ISBN 978-1-954389-06-9

52499

9 781954 389069

# About The Cover

The Burning Ship is yet another variation on the Mandelbrot Set, another mathematical figure. The Burning Ship is calculated by taking the absolute value, making a number always positive, of each complex number after each iteration. The new equation $f(x) = |z^2| + c$ is otherwise rendered the same as the Mandelbrot Set. The rendition on the cover is zoomed into the value $1.75 + i0$.

Similar to the rendition on the cover, my writing style lacks the fine descriptions and details you may find in other books and stories (or other Burning Ships, Filled Julia Sets, and Mandelbrot Sets) so that you may imagine the fine details of the following stories for yourself and experience the stories in your own unique way.

Please Enjoy.

# Table Of Contents

# Bananas

✠ ◎ ✠

IT ALL went down in a single day; the earth cracked open and molten rock and sulfur consumed all the land, ocean, and even the last Blockbusters, who we thought would've been a safe place during the apocalypse.

In a last-ditch effort, the princess of the late Californian Empire had built a massive airship, colored pink and white, and modeled after a chimp. I barely made it onboard during the panic, right before the wave of destruction hit.

I remember the sight of it, the Earth's crust cracking open to be being swallowed up by molten rock, and exploding as the last stash of VCRs on the entirety of the green, now glowing orange, earth.

And just like that, this floating chimp head is flying above a destroyed continent. The only thing they had to eat on board was thousands of pounds of birthday cake mix, and all other ingredients to make said birthday cakes.

We flew for weeks to find land that wasn't overflowing with molten rock. At last, though, we found an island just large enough to land on. Once we landed, we all kissed the ground, the sweet white sand, like it was sugar.

I went exploring on the small island, and I found a little cave with what could only be described as a gift from the heavens: a banana. Or more specifically, a single banana tree with a single, ripe, ready to eat banana hanging from it.

I ate thereof, and the taste was the best thing to happen to my mouth in my life. The months prior of solid cake with sprinkles on the giant cake pan that was the private cake-pan of the princess had my bowels running not-so-smoothly, but this banana was a godsend.

But I kept it a secret. Using my supreme knowledge of banana farming, I cultivated countless bananas in secret, but not secretive enough. I caught the attention of the princess, hiding in her chimp-shaped rainbow-barf airship. She knew one of her subjects was up to something to upset her from her all-powerful place as royalty among peasants.

She was so incredibly distraught about this possible threat, she confronted me herself in the midst of my fruity empire. But we struck a deal instead. I provide bananas to make a new product to propel the survivors into a new age of food! The Banana Bread Era was born on this small little island.

As more of the island was revealed by receding shorelines of an evaporating ocean, we cultivated several more crops, like kiwi and coconuts!

Chaos, Will, And An Unwavering Soul

✦ ◎ ✦

**T**HE COALS in the fire dance with flames, and crackle about, dancing and singing the song of warmth. I hear the women quietly singing to the children the songs of our ancestors. Life, I feel, is too simple for me; living beneath a million trees, being chased by the beasts of Xoac. My eyes have seemed to wander off into the fire, thinking of what lies beyond the horizon; maybe other tribes?

The chief smacks the back of my head, "You're dreaming again. That's a dangerous habit you have."

"I-I—"

"*You*," he points his finger at me, "Have no idea what lies beyond the light of this fire."

"Maybe I want to learn!" I raise my voice, but he just smacks my head again.

"I protect this tribe from the outside world—"

"Father, please," his son intervenes between us, "He's just a boy."

"He's an idiot, son," he says, "He puts us all in danger."

An ungodly roar shakes the forest trees and even stops the flames from their dance for a brief moment. The chief smacks my head again as I get lost in the flames. "That is what I protect you from," he whispers. The chief walks to his tent and releases the cover for his own privacy.

His son walks closer to me, "It's time, Andega." He leans close and pushes one of his father's swords into my hand. "It's time, you can save us, go!" he whispers into my ear.

I tighten my grip on the weapon; I've admired these weapons for a long time. A single handle and guard, glowing light blue in the night, was forged by the ancients before the beasts of Xoac roamed. I start away from my tribe, step by step, increasing in pace as I run off into the night. Faster into the trees I go, the blue glow of the *halbinger*, the bladeless sword, becoming my only light as the fire disappears in the night, until I run out of breath.

I wave the sword around, looking for a place to sit and catch my breath. "What am I doing?" I say to myself.

A voice in my head replies, "It's too late to go back. You'll be cast out, devoured by the monsters in the forest. You're an outcast."

Before I know it, the sun begins to rise and the sky glows a deep red on the horizon, then: *THUD, THUD.*

Fear washes over me like a raging river down my spine. Footsteps, they're footsteps of a monster. I hear the beast bellowing, like laughter.

I see a large spike slam into the ground, a few bits away from me. I look up to see this monster, reflective black armor with countless legs. It turns to look at me and I hear it laugh and continues walking. I tighten my grip on the sword, whispering to myself, trying to remember the spell to activate it, but the words escape my mind.

◀◀⊙▶▶

The words finally come to my mouth, and the sword ignites; a bright blue energetic blade summoned out of the hilt. But it's too late; the beast is gone towards the sunrise.

"What am I doing," I banish the blade back, "I haven't got an idea of what I can do."

I begin to walk off back into the forest into my new destiny of the unknown. The forest is the same through and through, dense and unrelenting in the landscape.

I finally come across a patch of sky and I see a great mountain in the distance. The beasts of Xoac are dormant during the day, I know that much. Their armor is stronger than stone, but they can be harmed using ancient techniques.

Some branches snap and leaves crumble under some footsteps, but it's not a monster just another person dressed in tattered red and brown clothes. I don't recognize it as tribal.

"Who goes there?" I ask aloud.

"Don't attack," I hear a man reply, "I'm just a man."

I whisper the words to summon the sword and begin to cut away the thick foliage around me. "I said don't attack!" he shouts, "I'm just—"

I cut a thick branch and it reveals the hidden voice to be as he said: just a man.

"Who are you?" I ask, catching my breath.

"My name is Samael," he tells me, raising his hands, a spear in one.

"You have a weapon of the ancients?" I ask him, signaling to the spear.

"I guess you could say that," he replies, "I, uh, found it lying around the forest, so to say."

I retract the sword and sigh, "Well, where are you going?"

"I, uh, I'm going towards the mountain."

"Why?" I ask.

"Sightseeing," he replies, "Why don't you come with me?"

"I'm going to kill the monsters—"

"In the mountain?"

"If that's where they are, yes."

He fastens the spear to his back. "Yes, that's exactly where they are, I'm collecting data, so to speak."

I fasten the *halbinger* to my belt. "You're a shifty fellow, aren't you?"

"You could say that," he holds out his hand, "come with me, I know this forest like the back of my hand."

I grab his hand and embrace it. "Where are you from?"

"The other side of the mountain, actually."

"You're a long way from home—"

"*Home* is relative," he says, "come this way, I know a trail." he motions me to follow. We walk, and we come to a large boulder, blocking the path.

"Over this way is the trail," he leans on the boulder, "Where are you from, buddy?"

"I'm from a tribe a little ways toward the sunrise," I reply.

"I recognize the blue in your clothes," he remarks, twiddles his fingers, "the embroidery."

"They're moving towards the coast, to escape the beasts."

"From what I hear, there are monsters everywhere. You running away or something?"

"You could say that," I look up at the boulder, trying to think of a way to climb it.

"If you can't get over, I know a way around it."

◂◂ ⊙ ▸▸

"I can do it," I persist, "Just give me a mo—" I jump up to grab the top of the boulder, but I slip and fall down on my bottom.

"This is a test, *Soko* man," he says, "If you can't climb this boulder, then you'll never survive the mountain. Last time I was there, I barely escaped with my life."

I look at him and pull out my weapon; I summon the blade and begin my attack on the boulder. *CRACK!* I swing the sword and the energetic blade slices through the boulder, leaving broken, blackened stone.

"Forget it, we'll—"

*CRACK! CRACK!* The boulder must be larger than what's showing "Dude, we'll go around—"

*KRAKOOM!* I swing down hard, straight down, splitting the boulder and flinging stones everywhere. "There, now I can get over," I tell him, grabbing the top and pulling myself over.

"That's one way," he replies, "I like it." He walks beside the boulder and uncovers a set of steps made of mud all the way up. We walk up the mound and I follow, see the blazed trail leading further into the forest.

"You've must've made your way around a lot of places?" I ask, "Have you seen other tribes?"

"Oh, yes," he says moving some branches out of the way, "I've encountered many tribes, moving in all directions."

The sun dances across the sky, and he stops me, "You have to be silent from here on out, understand? We're in beast territory." I nod and we continue on. We pass by what looks to be a sleeping beast; massive, covered in black armor with three sets of legs.

He covers my mouth, and holds a finger to his, reminding me to be silent. The beast's eyes are uncovered, almost looking at us with a deep, soulless abyss. We're soon in a clearing, filled with dead, sleeping, and dismembered beasts lying around the clearing. The trees have been obliterated or eaten and there's nothing left except rotten soil.

But we trek on through the path regardless. I've never felt more dread and fear than I do right now, it's like I'm in a boiling cauldron.

⊶ ⊙ ⊷

"Okay, we're in the clear—"

"What in the name of the gods," I pull out the *halbinger*.

"Hey, hey, hey," he backs up with his hand up, "We're alive aren't we, and you wanted to get to the mountain; well, this is the way."

I stop to think, and he's right. Something else occurs to me: that one monster was headed east, towards my home tribe. "No," I start running back, but he grabs hold of me, driving me to the ground in a hold.

"The suns almost down, we need to get to a safe spot," he tells me, "If you go running off back home, you'll never make it before they wake up and kill you!"

"But the monsters of the night will murder—"

"*And* they'll kill you too!" he restrains me further. Against his mighty strength, I attempt to grab the *halbinger*. Right before my fingers get purchase of my weapon, he says, "Alright, you've lost your awake-privileges—" before striking me on the head.

I then find myself in a dark cave with the feeling of an ax in my skull. "Where... where am I?" I ask in my confused daze.

"A safe spot," he whispers, motioning that I do the same, "Now: *you're* going to stay right there for the rest of the night."

"My people—"

"Are not worth worrying about right now," he interrupts me, "There's nothing you can do until morning."

My vision clears, and I see the cave we're in, almost pitch-black. The ground is hard, and the ceiling is smooth, unlike the stories I've been told of caverns in the past. A small opening in the far side of the room shows the moonlight shining through.

I reach for the *halbinger* for some illumination in the dark night, but I'm unable to find it on my person. "Don't worry; I hid it so it doesn't attract any harm."

I focus on his silhouette, seeing an utterly black shape by his side. "What's that?"

"Oh this?" he lifts it up, "It's a piece of Xoac armor I used as a sled to haul you up here. I'm going to retrofit it as a shield—I lost mine a while back."

"A shield? I've never seen one," I tell him, "Our tribe leader used to tell stories of ancient warriors."

"Yeah, your tribe was probably the most remote of the ones I've seen.

"Get some sleep," he says, "It's dangerous to not be on your toes."

◀◀⊙▶▶

The sun peeps through the opening of the cave, and I finally come to my full wakefulness. He tosses the *halbinger*, and I fumble around and grab hold. We crawl out the cave I have to raise a hand to shade myself from the sun.

The mountain is off in the distance with the sun to the right of it, illuminating the landscape. "*Now, if you wish, you can run off into the forest, I'll offer to wait here if you wish.*"

I tighten my grip on my weapon, and set off, running as fast as I can down the mound. I start sliding partway down, but I keep my balance. The clearing has changed with new monsters, but I'm unfazed and keep running.

A felled tree blocks the path, seemingly knocked down from a passing beast. I summon the bladeless sword and slash the tree twain and continue on my way. The sun dances its way through the sky as I run down this path through the woods.

I arrive at the location I first rested, marked with the step markings of the beast that was moving. Nonetheless, I go onward. The sun begins to set, and I come across the camp from the night I left.

I see the tracks of monster all about, but I don't see anything they left behind. After hours of looking, and the sun setting, I finally find a migration trail, which told me that they escaped. The moon rises into the sky and shines its faint glow upon the forest.

The *halbinger* activates and glows a blue light, giving me some guidance on where I should go. The trail leads off into the same direction as they've been traveling. I start seeing footsteps, and I diligently follow.

Roars scatter the night, sending shivers down my spine; what kind of monsters guard the mountain, or chase the various tribes scattered about the land. Finally, I arrive at tonight's camp, but it's not what I wanted to find.

◄◄ ⊙ ►►

"No," I whisper to myself, looking upon the carnage that was left behind. That beast annihilated the tribe, limbs scattered about with insides between them. No survivors.

*THUD!* I hear the steps of a beast. *THUD!* I ready myself to attack with the *halbinger*, trying to extrapolate where the sound is coming from between the echoes between the surviving trees. "They put up a fight, they did," I hear the ungodly sound of the beast's intelligent voice. It comes from the shadows, revealing the scars and gouges marked all over its body. "But they *all* died in the end, they did."

I scream, running after it, jumping up and slashing against its toughened armor, to no avail. It slaps me with its leg, sending me flying to the ground. I see the twin to the *halbinger* on the ground, held by a severed hand.

I get to my feet and make my way toward the weapon, but I'm knocked away into a mound of tent pieces. I take my weapon and ready an attack. It starts laughing, "You will die, you will."

"I'll kill you!" I shout, running at it, dodging its leg, slashing on its underside. Another one of its legs slaps me away, sending me flying ever closer to the twin weapon.

I land hard, and crawl to the weapon, rolling to avoid the legs slamming into the ground, narrowly avoiding certain death. My feet find purchase on the ground, and I bounce up and start running to the weapon.

One of its legs slams down on the weapon, releasing an explosion of blue light, and cracking the creature's armor against the protective spells left over by the ancients. I dive into a roll, avoiding another leg, and grab hold of the weapon, activating both simultaneously, and I'm ready to fight. The two energetic, lightning blue blades brighten up the battlefield.

I scream in rage, and run towards the beast, slashing up and down its legs and underside. Slash after slash, the beast begins to bleed, spewing black blood everywhere and on me. It moans in pain. The blades' power quickens me, possessing me with the power of all those who wielded the weapons before me.

I take both weapons and hold them side by side; doing a flip and cutting a leg clean off. Blood flows and pools onto the soil, soaking the spirit of this fight into the earth. The beast cries out as I dodge leg after leg, slashing and cutting the beast like a hunter would his prey.

I roll out from underneath it, coming face to face. The soulless abyss of its eyes stares into mine. The blade brightens with my willpower and I charge headfirst at the face of certain death. *KRAKOOM!* The blades slice through its head and cleave it twain and the beast falls dead, and I'm left alone in the night, covered in black fluid.

⊹⊙⊹

The night was sleepless and long, and I traveled in the forest of death through the night and until the sun rose once more. Only then do I find the path up to the cave and see a familiar face poking out the entrance.

He waves as I climb up the mound. "Do what you need to do?" he asks, eyeing the blood that covered me, "That's actually quite the technique there, the beasts of Xoac hate the smell of their own blood."

"Let's just get to the top of the mountain," I command, "I'm killing every last one of those creatures."

He pops out of the hole, and we start our trek back into the forest, up a trail. The sun dances its dance and sets below the horizon as he guides me to another safe spot where the beasts cannot reach us, where we rest and go off in the morning.

We find another clearing with resting beasts, but my companion has his spear out and his shield by his side, ready to fight as the sun sets on the horizon. "We'll have to make our way through the night if we want to get any closer."

The sun disappears and the beasts awaken. A smaller one reveals itself, no higher than my knees, but long as three men. He keeps his spear pointed at it, whilst I summon my weapons and the blue light illuminates the landscape.

The beast turns its attention to me and rushes to attack, but I take both blades and slice it in two with a fantastic sound. He comes and takes the still end and begins painting himself in its blood, and takes his spear and drives it into the head of the writhing end.

"I don't think that's the one we have to worry about," he says.

A larger beast, not quite as large as the one I battled, crawls out of the night. One of its legs swings and slams my companion's his shield, knocking him back into a tree.

I take my two weapons and begin to quicken, slashing the legs and its underside, but it seems to ignore me, traveling overhead. "No," I whisper to myself, seeing the beast going after him.

I run as fast as I can, slashing at its legs, but I see the monster go in for a bite against his shield; he drives the spear into its mouth, but the monster rips the spear in two along with his left arm. I cry out, spinning around and slicing a leg clean off its body. But it's too late.

The monster falters on its steps, allowing me to go in for a killing blow, slicing through its neck. The beast collapses with me narrowly dodging the mass.

"This isn't good," he says, holding his missing limb. Thinking quickly, I tear off some cloth from my clothing and tie it tightly around the wound. "This is what I—," he coughs a little, "What I get for knocking on the devil's door with you."

I tie the knot and help him up to his feet. "Let's get going, might as well help you before I die," he says as we march onward into the forest.

⸬ ⊙ ⸬

Days pass, and we alternate between hiding in small caves and hiking up the mountain. The landscape is steep as we've come to the base of the mountain. There are trails blazed by the monsters themselves, sleeping on the side. The beasts of Xoac are bugs, burrowing in and out of the mountain as they crawl out of the womb.

My companion falls to his knees, weak from the travel and trauma. "Hey, are you alright?" I stop and go to his aid.

"No—" he whispers, wincing in pain, "This is as far as I go, Andega."

"Hey now, that's no talk—"

"What use am I going to be if I continue up the mountain," he continues batting my hand away, "Leave me here, so I can get a nice view of the sunset one last time. Please."

I accept his fate, "Very well, my friend."

"Kill every last one, you understand me?" he begs, falling to the ground.

"I will," I take the remnants of his spear and make a shrine from it as his last resting place, and I go up the mountain. The trails turn into cliffs as I climb, hold by hold all the way to the top.

⊷⊙⊶

I pull myself up to the summit, barely having enough strength left after climbing this nearly vertical shear. The sun is nearly set, and the view from here is absolutely breathtaking; the forest seems to be infinite, extending beyond the horizon. It was a fool's errand to try to escape this; we were all doomed from the beginning.

I look all around and see nothing but trees and scattered clearings with dots of black. A cool wind makes its way to me, despair washing over.

The mountain rumbles as the beasts of Xoac awaken. *THUD!* I activate the *halbinger* and its twin weapon. I pour all of my willpower into the weapons. The blades burn with power, almost overflowing. The beasts show themselves, surrounding me. They are huge, hulking masses, larger than I've ever seen; they must guard this mountain as their birthplace.

I spiral around, slashing back and forth; delivering killing blows with my rage and will. *KRAKOOM!* I slice a beast in two, and it falls down the mountain, shaking the ground as it tumbles its way down. I scream in pain, everything is lost, always was.

I fight until the sun rises, and its view is as beautiful as the sunset. The monsters keep coming and keep coming bigger and bigger. But they fall as the stubble they are.

The sun isn't stopping them. "Eordenburg!" I cry out to the gods, but they are silent.

I scream, *KRAKOOM!* slamming the twin blades into the ground, cutting a beast in half and cracking the very earth, creating a landslide, taking even more monsters with it.

I fall to my knees, unable to complete my mission and ready to accept death. I look at the weapons, drained of power, and the reservoir is cracked on the twin sword. The beasts swarm above me, closing in on me as I'm unable to fight back. Suddenly a pillar of light surrounds me from the sun overhead.

⊶ ⊙ ⊷

"Here he is, my lord," I hear a man say.

I see a white landscape against my knees, "Am I dead?"

A gentle hand lifts up my head, and I see a beautiful woman, with a young child with black hair and pale skin holding her hand at her side. Another man, dressed in white with a weapon in hand, and a single, arced blade atop the weapon.

"In a way," the woman tells me, lifting me up to my feet, even as I drop my two broken blades. "I pulled you from your dying moment to be here."

I take a look at the landscape: pure white as far as the eye can see; an endless escape with no sun. The ground is a pure white soil with a single leafed, green sapling growing from the ground with a few little sprouts growing from the stem.

"Why am I here?" I ask, confused about this landscape.

"I need someone to remove a burden from me," she says further explaining, "I'm the guardian of all there is, but I can't do it alone, I need you to fulfill a higher purpose; to be the *master of time*."

I look to the small plant growing from this white soil, something so strange, so fragile. "Why me?"

"The requirements are too much to explain," she tells me, "but essentially, you will care for that infant shrub, which represents all possible outcomes of creation."

"It's so small—"

"Because creation is young," she leaves the child, so she sucks on her finger in patience. She kneels by the plant and holds one of its leaves. "This branch represents all possibilities your reality holds-"

"Destroy it!" I shout, "Nothing good will ever come of it!"

The small girl laughs a little, but her presence becomes ever so sinister. "Become the master of time, and it'll be within your power."

"Then I accept!" I rush to the opportunity.

"Very well," the woman gets back to her feet and walks up to me, resting her palm on my chest. I feel a *THUMP* and it feels like lightning in my blood. I fall to my knees, feeling enough power running through my body to erupt.

Something begins to materialize in front of me. A creased piece of leather appears from nothing, painting itself magnificent colors and patterns so fine as if it were drawn with a single hair. Thin surfaces begin growing from between the creases, writing themselves in black, creating symbols and pictographs.

The two sides close together and this item descends into my hand. "What is this?" I ask, mesmerized by it as the power within me dissipates.

"It's called a book," this woman says, "In time, you will learn what's held within, and master the magic it contains.

"The only person in the universe able to read it is you."

I've finally mastered all this book has to offer, after what feels like eternity. The bush has sprouted some more, giving life to timelines flowing forth from the stem. But I see it differently now; I see the handiwork of God.

I kneel beside the growing bush and see that, what was once my home has become nothing but a scourge. The branches only produce more despair and pain. No matter how many chances I give that branch of time to bring forth something good, it remains a source of evil.

"Are you sure you want to do that, Andega?" she asks me under the stars in the sky we crafted together, "There's no going back, and you know what happens with all those souls."

"I'll see to it that they're placed elsewhere." I place my fingers on the base of this stem and pluck it from the bush. I witness worlds whittle away into nothingness, and the mighty beasts of Xoac become no more, fulfilling my promise. The souls, I sense, return to the creator, and I say a prayer over them that they might be given another chance.

# Council of Dragons

IN THE DAYS OF CREATION, Xoac laid the foundations for new life amongst the virgin universe. He sowed a seed deep within planets, only to sprout when man began to walk their home worlds and sown their own seeds of good and evil.

In one such place, named Earth, was the first for men to walk upon. The branches of time began growing, flowing in all directions. The deeds of men in one such branch spawned the legendary dragon, beasts renowned throughout the heavens. When the first dragon slithered from the depths of the Earth, it split into nine beasts that went out to guard the lands against destruction, begetting more dragons in their own likeness.

When man discovered magic for themselves, the elder dragons gathered for the first time since their conception. They gathered on the mount in which they were conceived: Mount Nefu, as called by man.

◄◄ ⦿ ►►

"Tannin, you're first to arrive," I, the dragon of the western land, say to my brother.

Tannin slithers around a stone, perching upon it, "I am the closest to Nefu." I stand atop the mount, ready to guide the meeting between all of us. I sent my children out to all the ends of the Earth, and all but one returned with a message from each of the elder dragons.

Shou and Ryu are off on the horizon, far enough apart as to not be in each other's view. Their rivalry goes back to the beginning when we first hatched from our eggs. I was first, Tannin was second, and the next two both broke through at the exact same moment, marking their battle for birthright. Storm clouds surround them both, as they are dragons of lightning and thunder, and their destinies are intertwined.

Tannin closes his eyes, resting from his long travels. Asking all of the elder dragons to gather is a momentous occasion. Hasha should be next to arrive, after the storm dragons. I sense Urda is swimming and will likely not arrive on time. They are dragons of earth and water, and rule mightily upon their lands.

The sun is near setting, and I suppose I should take advice from my brother and rest some before the others arrive. Naga is far from us, and Kukal even farther. I expect them to come when the sun rises, if they are diligent in their travels.

◀◀⊙▶▶

I'm awoken by the squabble between Shou and Ryu. I open my eyes and see the two standing off, crying, and expelling energies at one another. "Are you two not wise enough to put your differences aside?" I ask in a thunderous voice, "I've called you here for a council."

They back away from one another and Ryu wraps her tail around herself, curling up in a protective shell. Urda is close by, walking her way, as she was born without wings, Hasha with her. They are the opposite of Shou and Ryu; they are the best of siblings.

"Why is it you called us here?" Ryu shouts out.

"I will tell you when we all are here," I reply, "Be patient."

Tannin opens his eye to look upon his brothers and sister who are here, "Perhaps I will stay at this mount; it is a nice resting place. The desert is harsh and hot, and this mount is soft and cool."

"We were born to watch over the world, to keep her alive and the life that walks her surface," I tell him, "It is our sworn duty."

"Yes, yes, I know," he closes his eyes once more, "But the work is tiresome."

I suddenly sense Naga's presence, rushing up from behind the mountain. She slides quickly up into the sky; her wings outstretched and as long as her body. She is the largest of us all, and she is mighty. She comes down from the sky and slams into the ground, spewing dust in the air. "My brothers and sister," she says, "I have arrived."

I blow some air away, "I've become excessively aware of your presence. You've come quickly; I wasn't expecting you this soon."

"I left as soon as your messenger came, and decided to be leisurely about my travel," she finds a large enough stone and perches upon it, "If I am here, Kukal is not far behind. Is Drako going to bother to make an appearance?"

"I do not know," I say, "My child who was sent to him found him in a deep slumber beneath a mountain of ice."

Shou scoffs, "Very much like him to neglect his duties as an elder dragon."

I chastise him, "Do not talk so about our youngest brother. He is the mightiest of us all and could end us all."

"He's lazy, and neglecting his sworn duty—" Shou continues.

"Silence!" my voice booms and crashes like a mighty wave on the shore, "Have some respect!" Shou cowers, curling around himself.

Kukal's presence also sneaks up on me; he appears on the other side of the summit. "Hello, Lohi," he whispers to me. He was also born without wings but mastered flight using the natural magics we command. He was banished to the otherworld for his mischief, "It's been too long."

"Kukal," I greet him, "It's been a long time."

"Yes," he perches on the ground, "It has been."

The only ones missing are Urda and Hasha. I should expect them by sundown.

◄►⊙◄►

Kukal raises his head, looking around, "Ah, yes. They are here."

He is right; Urda and Hasha are at the base of the mountain. They are walking along the earth, not in the air like all the others which is why I didn't sense their presence. I listen closely to the air and hear the whistle of the wind rushing over Hasha's wings and the gentle steps of Urda's feet upon the soil.

Soon they arrive on the summit of Mount Nefu, our birthplace so long ago that the soil that blankets the mountain is not the same that we first step foot on when Xoac first gave us life. Even the rock and stone do not resemble what we first hatched out of.

Urda and Hasha perch themselves on opposite stones, and in unison, say, "We are here, what did you call us for?"

"I suppose Drako will not be coming," I say, "That is a shame."

"I've gathered everyone here to express concern of the humans; I've witnessed a tribe of men harness magic for the first time since the days of Adam."

"Impossible!" Kukal cries out, "Legend says Adam cut off his species from magic; once a bloodline is cut off, it's impossible to heal!"

Ryu comments, "Yes, it's true. I've witnessed humans on my island cast spells."

"Impossible!" Kukal cries out. Ryu strikes him with lightning and hisses to quiet the heretic. Kukal rises back up, "You've gathered us here for naught!"

"I am the eldest dragon, and it is my sworn duty to protect the world," I announce over the other, "I do not lie when I say this could become a problem for us.

"Humans have always been devious. Allowing them to harness magic once again could mean certain doom."

Ryu stands up tall, "I've already witnessed the humans ruling over each other with their magic. The magic they use, it's unnatural."

"Yes," I say, "It is unnatural."

Kukal shutters, "It's unbelievable. Men were cut off! I've been summoned from across this world for nothing!"

Shou hisses at our banished brother, "Quiet, and have some respect." Shou turns back to me, "What is to be done?"

"I should consider this to lead to our own demise; humans are not to be expected to be peaceful."

Naga speaks up, "Should we kill them?"

"No, without them the world would have no purpose; the world was made for them, and we were made for the world; we are her lifeblood," I explain.

I awoke with a certain knowledge of the world. I first emerged and witnessed the humans, already established and migrating throughout the world. I was a product of those first humans. At the time, they banded closely together to survive the harsh environment. But that soon changed when there were more of them, they became numerous; they became expendable to one another and their hearts turned to something else.

Is it our destiny to die by the hands of men as men do? "Be diligent," I say, "Men are crafty, and they may try to end our species—"

"I'll take my chance, Lohi," Kukal retorts, "The humans in the otherworld are one with nature, and they worship me and my children. They would never turn against me."

"Given enough time, they will all turn on each other," Naga says, "My people travel the seas and invade each other at every instance they have."

Kukal flies away, swirling about in the sky to start his journey home. "Be diligent, my brothers and sisters; heed my warning: humanity will one day turn against us, against nature."

◀▌⊙▐▶

I lay upon my mount, in the midst of a field of flowers and trees. The humans have approached me for the first time in centuries. The offer me things and ask for things. They think me benevolent, but my purpose is to be the lifeblood of the world.

Their magic continues to advance beyond my understanding. The humans have bent magic to their own will. There have been great magicians, but they rise and fall. One of my children relayed to me that there is a great magician who unlocked the secret to attaching souls to physical objects, a concept I could barely understand.

I sense one of the trickster dragon's children approaching fast. I sense fear and pain, something unlike his kind. He comes and crashes down in the field of flowers, wounded. "M-my name is Kualk, and I bring grave news!" he says, laboring for breath, "Kukal has been slain!"

My predictions were true, after all this time. This is grave news. "Thank you for coming all this way to tell me," I tell him, "Rest as much as you need, I will send word to the other elder dragons."

I sense a storm dragon coming this way as well. I look into the distance and see a wisp swirling through the air to me. I suppose both Ryu's and Shou's children are without wings and rely on such magics to fly in the air, though I don't sense the same fear and pain in this one.

They arrive and I see they are of Shou's lineage, "My uncle, the firstborn of the elder dragons," he says very formally, "I am the messenger sent by the next of kin of Shou's lineage. I've come to tell you that Shou and many other dragons have been slain."

"As I predicted so long ago," I tell the two, "Rest as long as you need, I will go and send a message to the other elder dragons about this."

"What shall we do?" Kualk begs, "The humans struck my forefather down with powerful magic! I didn't know they were so capable of destruction."

The storm dragons adds, "Humans will taste power and hunger for ultimate demise."

"So they do," I repeat, "Be diligent, and be privy to their actions." I come to my feet and begin my journey to my stronghold located in a magical location that existed nearly separately from the world on an island off the mainland. Humans rarely stumble upon it, mostly by accident.

This marks the end of an era for us. There is no telling what is in store for us, but the humans have marked the beginning of their war on the universe. Without us, magic will dry up and the world will begin to die. It's not our place to bring down judgment on the humans, but they will lead themselves down a dark path.

# Demons

## An Alternate Ending

⊪ ◎ ⊪

WHAT IF I had prepared for this betrayal? What if I had taken a few steps further, or taken initiative to snuff out those who would cause harm to the innocent. A few steps to the right, or the left, or if I had said something right instead of wrong.

BANG! The sound echoes in the hall. Martta stops and puts her hand over her chest, seemingly scratching it. Blood starts leaking from her hand. "Dammit, I missed—I mean, these things have hearts right?" Rick boasts, "Start exec. triple—"

BANG! I fire my pistol, landing a shot between Rick's eyes. Henry comes bursting out of the war room, brandishing his rifle. Everything stops. Everyone is standing still in shock; I've just killed a man.

Rick's body just lays there, lifeless eyes staring into the sky. Martta falls to the ground, bleeding out. "Henry, help her," I command him, "What the hell were you guys planning?"

The others snap out of it, but thinking quickly, I fire another shot BANG! A gun is knocked from the hand of one of the traitors. Trevor raises both his hands, "I'm just following the orders I was given!"

Henry starts patching up Martta from the supplies in his bag. "What orders, and who gave them?" I begin the interrogation.

"Mr. Free gave us 'Executive 6-6-6' to start extermination—" Trevor begins to say, before stopping. The two other traitors drop their guns, and one of them continues to stop Trevor from reaching for his gun again.

Martta begins whispering to herself, "I knew I couldn't trust any of you—"

King Borro stands there by the door; looks like he's thinking. "Borro, do you have any rope?" I ask him.

He waves his hands and some of the demons start running out, presumably to get some rope. "I had my suspicions about all of you, including you, James," King Borro tells me, "But mine about you have been put to rest."

"Henry?" I turn around to see him caring for Martta, "Were you given the same orders?"

"We all were, except you," he replies, "I was on the fence about it, though."

"You're all court-martialed," I place my gun away, "Give me all your guns." I look around to see the remaining demon soldiers having their spears out.

Henry hands them to me, and I remove all the bullets and stuff the magazines into my own bag. I hold out the two pieces of war-making, motioning one of the demon soldiers to take it. Someone walks up slowly and awkwardly takes them.

I make my rounds taking everything from the others, stuffing all the ammunition in my bag. Finally, it comes to taking the gun from Rick's dead hands. I grasp the custom pistol and pull, almost feeling resistance from his fingers.

Some electronic whispers begin originating from Rick. I kneel down to get a better listen, following the noise to his chest. I get my fingers to purchase his armor and begin to peel it away from his clothes, seeing some covert electronics hidden underneath. I pinch a connector and turn it off.

"How many of you have coms?" I demand to know.

"Only Rick," Trevor confesses.

But I persist, "All of you take off your armor."

King Borro starts laughing a little, quietly in the back, "You've become a fierce leader in the midst of betrayal."

One by one, they start removing their brown armor pieces and tossing them to the floor. I notice Martta is passed out from the bullet wound on the ground, from the look of it, it grazed her heart and punctured the lung, which means she might be drowning in blood.

"Borro—" I clear my throat and remember his status, "*King Borro*, would you send some of your soldiers with me to escort them to the portal?"

"Of course," he motions his hand to somebody, and they go inside the war room and return with all the people inside, readying their weapons. Borro begins speaking in his native language.

"You three," I point to people standing over Rick's body, "Drag the body back home." People return and I have them tie up the true traitors, with Henry gladly going along in the back.

This new caravan, I lead them all the way back to the portal. When we arrive, I see Mr. Free, standing there on the other side, looking like he's had enough of my crap. But I've had enough of his.

◀⊙▶

I march up to the portal and take a step through as fast as I can. "I thought you weren't supposed to return until a clear success, failure —"

"Cut the bull crap, Free," I tell him, motioning the other side to send the boys over.

"Why is Rick—oh," he sees the body with a bullet hole being carried over.

All the people running around stop, looking at the lot of us. Everything falls silent as I stand off with Mr. Free. "Rick attempted to kill me on *your* order, but I shot first."

One of the other people in charge of this facility steps forward, in his loose-fitting suit and black glasses. "Free, explain," he commands.

"No, I don't answer to you—" I pull out my pistol and aim for the head, but he doesn't even flinch.

He just takes off his glasses, revealing those cold, blue eyes. "You've sabotaged the mission, Free," I say, "But even still, I succeeded in forming an alliance between human and *Euintae*."

Mr. H starts giving out orders, taking care of Henry, Trevor, and the others. And some scientists take Rick's body and move it over. "Bring down somebody to arrest Free," I hear him say.

"Mr. H," I ask, "Rick fired a shot at one of the natives, and she needs medical attention for it."

Kiira and one of the natives stand there, unsure whether to cross the threshold. I wave my hand in, beckoning them to come. Mr. H looks past me, "Oh this is precious."

Kiira steps through with Martta's unconscious body, flinching from the sensation of passing through. Mr. Free dawns an upset look, watching his plan to fall apart.

Finally, another soldier comes running through the doors, following orders and arrests Mr. Free. More people start funneling through the door with a couple of stretchers to carry the people.

The get Rick first, finally closing his eyes and covering the body, then getting Martta on the stretcher. "Kiira," I place my gun away and turn to look at her. She's looking around, in awe, probably form being here and not getting shot at for the first time. "Can you go with Martta to calm her down when she wakes up?"

"Yes," she says, being stopped by someone, but Mr. H lets her go.

"So, a *partial* success?" Mr. H asks.

"Yes, and we've uncovered a substantial amount of information about their government and geography.

"Their leader is someone named King Borro; filename *Icon of Sin*," I start explaining.

"Write a report, will you?" he asks.

"Yessir!" I say, beginning my walk to the office.

◀◀ ⊙ ▶▶

The four who went on the mission with me, and survived, have been arrested for their crimes and imprisoned somewhere on location. I've been stuck for the past week being examined left and right, writing a report in the downtime.

Martta remained unconscious for days with Kiira by her side. I was notified when she woke up, but I was unsure about visiting her. She attempted to claw out somebody's throat as soon as she awoke.

I finally mustered the strength to go see her in my spare time today. Another soldier is leading me through the twists and turns to the other side of the facility, which I've never been to. He says we've arrived, and beyond the doors are the two demons.

He slides his key card and the door opens, revealing Martta in a hospital bed, strapped in by her legs and waist. Kiira is sitting in the chair next to her, wings draped over her shoulders. They both seem to be watching the television.

But my presence is announced by the door hissing as it closes. "Oh great," Martta retorts, looking away from me. Kiira almost doesn't notice me, glued to the TV.

"Enjoying the television?" I try to make small talk, looking to see what's on.

"How is this possible, James?" Kiira asks me, pointing to the screen, "How are there tiny people inside something so thin?"

"There aren't any people in there," I try to think of some way to explain television, "It's like the map, but it changes extremely quickly."

"Glad you're doing well, Martta," I say.

"Since when do you go by 'James'," She twitches her head back at me, eyebrow furled.

"It's a long story—"

"Why am I even here?" she interrupts me, "I have a war to make."

"You were shot in the lung, it was filling up with blood," I explain, but I don't think she understands, "Why were you even at war?"

"Prela formed an alliance with Borro, so they fight together across the sea against Greth," Kiira says, finally looking away from the TV.

"But what started the conflict?"

"Prela needed more farmland for her people, but there wasn't any fertile land left in her borders," she explains.

"So she invaded?" I piece together the story, "We can teach you better farming techniques that will double your crop yield—you don't have to invade for more land."

"Double?" they both look at me like I was a prophet.

"Yeah, we can get an agricultural expert over ASAP if that's what you need," I tell them.

The door opens again, revealing the doctor, "Oh hey! Glad you're here, I didn't want to go near her while she's awake.

"You're free to go," he turns to Martta, "But you *need* to take it easy, understand?"

"We're warriors," Kiira interjects, "There's no 'taking it easy.'"

The doctor raises his hands and pinches his finger, "If you pop those stitches, you'll bleed out without immediate care!"

Martta folds her arms and looks away. The doctor pushes me closer, wanting me to release her from the straps. I get closer and release the claws on her feet which have been trimmed back.

I remove the straps from her feet, but she doesn't kick me like I thought she would. The waist strap goes off next, but she just sits there, staring off. I chuckle, "Comfortable?"

She thrusts her fingers up unto my chin, scratching me a little with the nubbed nails, but she quickly pulls back before getting back to her feet. She walks to the other side of the room, removing her robe.

"Good lord, Martta!" I cover my eyes and the doctor and I turn around, "Have some decency!"

"Then don't look!" she shouts back. I plug my ears, so I don't have to listen to a lady get dressed. Soon after, something taps my shoulder. I look to see Kiira. "Take me back home," Martta demands.

The doctor points, "You better not injure yourself!"

Martta hisses back, and I move between them.

The doctor swipes his card and opens the door. Martta pushes me forward, eager to leave. I see the soldier standing guard and tell him to lead us back to the portal.

⊷ ⊙ ⊶

We all enter the portal room, surrounded by scientists working tirelessly on computers reading out information. Mr. H comes walking up, "I see the doctor finally released them. Go with them, finish your reports later."

"Thank you, sir," I reply, "I may need you to have a farmer on standby when I return."

"Is that what they're requesting?"

"I'll explain when I get back." I look to see the two already beyond the portal's threshold to *Ouauoa*, Kiira supporting a weak Martta. I start running after them, rushing through the portal, feeling the brief burning sensation.

"Wait!" I call out as they walk down the path. Most of the equipment has been pulled back through, with a few things left behind, including Trevor's ukulele lying on the ground next to the drone computer. It's still flying up in the sky somewhere. On my way to them, I swipe the instrument up in my hands.

"Go away—"

"I'm under orders! I'm sure you understand!" I shout back, slowly catching up to them.

We walk in silence all the way to the stone building, with Borro conversing with someone with something I can't see in their hand. We approach, and I see a mushroomed bullet between their fingers.

"Welcome back," Borro turns to us, "I see you're back on your feet."

"James, what is this *thing?*" He asks, pointing to the bullet, "This is what pierced my prized general; we dug it up from the ground."

"It's called a 'bullet', it's made from different metals," I explain.

"Metal? I'm familiar with the word."

"It's a material you have to refine from the ground," I try to say.

Martta turns to Kiira, "Take me to my tent." and they go off.

"King Borro," I address the hulking mass of a person, "I understand you and *Prela* have been at war with someone over farmland."

"Yes, her people have grown numerous, and there's not enough food to go around."

"We can help with that," I tell him, "We can teach you things it took humans thousands of years to learn."

"A thousand years?" I can tell he's trying to comprehend that amount of time, "I accept; I will send word to Prela."

⊷⊙⊶

I've finally finished a complete report on the mission. I've made several trips between our two Earths, and finally, we're at peace. My superiors have arranged for other expeditions to survey the land, and they've made contact with Prela's village, helping them with growing food, and stopping the conflict over the lake.

But I've been stuck with paperwork. Someone told Borro the recipe for paper, and we've had scientists help them create concrete. And I've seen pictures of the landscape, nearly untouched by technology; it's beautiful.

The trees at the base of the plateau look just like oak trees, and the grass extends for so far. More drones have been launched with more sophisticated sensors, taking atmospheric data. There are even plans for building a telescope.

Every time I come over to make plans with professionals and leaders of the alien people, Martta is nowhere to be found, she's absolutely avoiding me.

I finish a meeting with Borro and Prela, coordinating their food issues. "King Borro, one of our scientists wants to meet with someone wise in your language," I ask of him, rolling up my documents and placing them back into my bag, "They want to document your language."

"How so?" he stands up, towering over me.

"We have books called 'Dictionaries', which document all the words that are spoken," I tell him, "It'll help us communicate with your people."

"Of course, then."

"One more question," I start making my way to the outside, "Where is Martta?"

"I knew when I first saw you, you had come here for love," he laughs, his laugh echoing in the war room.

"The last thing she did all that time ago was kiss me in a cloud of smoke and run off through time and space," I reminisce, "But she's been so hostile to me."

"Kiss? I'm familiar with the word," he questions me about yet another human term.

"I'm not going to explain that one to you, you'll have to ask someone else," I chuckle.

"She is coping in her private abode," he informs me.

"I guess I'll have to give her space then." I open the door and leave to walk back through the portal. Every time I pass through back to Earth, I'm scanned and prodded to make sure such trips are healthy to make.

"About this *instrument* you've allowed into my possession," he reminds me of Trevor's ukulele, "I've passed it onto a youngling in the village who was entrapped by it."

"Good, I hope they enjoy it." I smile, leaving. The air is so incredibly clean and a true pleasure just breathing it in. I hear the strumming of the instrument off in the distance and decide to follow it; after all, I'm running early on my watch.

For the first time, I've strolled into the paths leading into the tent village. Some eyes are turned, but I've been cleared of most suspicion. I find a small group listening to the strumming of the instruments by a young girl, whose skin is covered in splotches coloring reddish and dark brown. Her horns are small and look like a buffalo's.

She looks up and stops, frozen in fear. "Keep going," I say, "Don't mind me."

⊲⊹ ⊙ ⊹⊳

I've been ordered to check on the farming specialist who went down to Prela's village. The path down the plateau towards the village was steep, but not dangerously so. The tallgrass was littered with boulders and I saw a few trees on the path down.

Once I came to flat ground, I found a still river flowing by with clay on its banks. The grass became less prevalent down here and oak-like trees dotted the land beside the river. From the directions I was given when the farming specialist radioed back, I'm on the right path and it's somewhere down the river.

I wander down and see a deer-like animal, but without any signs of antlers or the third set of appendages. Now thinking about it, the *Yousi* doesn't have six limbs either, just two sets of wings like an old dinosaur, and neither did that rabbit thing Rick would shoot at.

The animal looks at me and hisses, revealing two sets of fangs on its top jaw. I wasn't told whether to look out for these. I march up anyways, thinking to myself that it's probably tame like a normal deer.

But this thing starts charging me, hissing as it runs at me. I get ready to wrestle with it, squatting and planting my feet down. I get under its head and tackle this thing and toss it into the river, hissing. Although, this seems to have scared it off and it prances away.

A couple of hours later, totaling maybe six hours of walking, I see the village, dotted with tents also with a clay and stone building to match. "Doctor Jillian!" I shout out, disrupting the silence of the demons going about their lives.

There are few hybrids here if any, so it's unlikely any of them speak English. I get to the hustle and bustle of the people going around, carrying goods and crops left and right, a far cry from Borro's village.

They don't seem to mind me here, walking around looking for the farming specialist. "Doctor!" I shout out again. There are trees in between the tents bearing fruit. There must be a field nearby where they grow food. From what I've seen of the drone images, there's Prela's food source, and Borro's, on opposite sides of the plateau.

I arrive at the stone building and find Prela's palanquin besides the building. The farming specialist shouts back at me, "I'm further down!"

I pick up a jog and run further down. Then, I see the fields. They're all stalks covered with buds and flowers. I see the doctor poke his head from the field, "You must be James."

"Yes," I confirm, "I've been ordered to check on your progress and if you were, in fact, still alive."

"Oh yes, I'm still alive and kicking," he twists and turns out of the field, coming to talk to me, "I've been doing a lot of onsite research on the flora of this world. They in fact convert the solo nitrogen in the air to N-O and N-2—"

"Doctor, I'm not interested with sciency information," I stop him; "I'm just here to make sure you're alive, you haven't radioed in weeks."

"Oh, I've been busy with-" he pauses, "*stuff*."

"How's food production coming?" I persist on my agenda.

"I've been conducting experiments on easily obtainable fertilizer compatible with the flora-"

"But *how* is it going, doctor?"

"I've found a good candidate, it's a mix of compost and manure from an animal, they tell me is, called *Bolori*," he replies, "My plants with that mixture are growing faster and more importantly have more yield. I've been trying to convey terracing to them, but they do not understand the concept.

"This stuff they grow is wild, it grows all year round!" doctor Jillian begins trailing off on the nerdy stuff, "I've been looking at other options—try to diversify, ya know?"

"I can see you're doing just fine, doctor," I turn around to look at the townspeople, "Do you have a translator?"

"Yes, a nice young man named Diddo," he informs me, "But he's off gathering some local things for me."

"Can you start radioing in every week?" I ask him.

"I can make an effort to, yes," he finally caves.

"What's a *Bolori*, again? I'm rusty on the manual."

"They're aggressive, dear-like animals, but without the antlers," he informs me, "They hiss and are likely to bite, and from what I know, they're carnivorous."

"Yeah, I ran into one of those on my way here," I walk up to one of the stalks growing from the ground. The flowers are fragrant and the stalk is hardy, almost to that of sugarcane.

‹‹‹ ⊙ ›››

Another meeting ends with my superiors and Mr. H, the new head of this operation, officially replacing Mr. Free. I seem to be the one doing most of the diplomatic work, not what I expected when they first forced me into the military. I close my folder and approach Mr. H.

"Sir! I have a particularly specific question," I formally ask him, thinking about an artifact that used to be buried by my old house.

"Ask away, James—Ostin? Which do you prefer, I suppose your secret got out one way or another," he responds, collecting his things.

"I'll have to think on that, sir," I reply, regarding my name, "There was an artifact buried by my father's old home and at the time, it seemed fairly urgent for the *Euintae* to retrieve."

"Oh yes, we have that in storage," he informs me, "All the files on it are classified, so normally you wouldn't know about that; I do suppose we're done studying it, so I guess you can take it back."

"What exactly was the artifact?"

He scratched his chin, "It was a skull that was fossilized and turned into a chalice. I believe they used it as part of a coronation ceremony."

"That seems like it'd be important to them," I remark. Mr. H motions that I follow him out the door. I never did understand why they wear loos fitting suits and sunglasses inside the facility, but that's just the nature of these people.

"I'll show you the artifact if you'd like," he proposes, "To see it for yourself."

"Sure."

He starts leading me through the twists and turns and through a door, "This is one of the storage rooms, I think it's in here." Mr. H pulls along a computer on wheels and starts typing furiously on the keyboard, not even looking at the screen.

Suddenly he stops typing and a green light appears, and he walks over, opening a small locker. He pulls out a medium case and hands it to me, "Go ahead and take this over, will you?"

"Yessir!" I say. I turn around and start heading for the portal.

I finally get to the portal room after getting lost. It wouldn't be too much of a pain to put signs up on the corners or label the rooms. One of the scientists stops me, asking, "Where did you get that?"

"Mr. H instructed me to bring it back to King Borro—"

"*The Crucible* is Free's prized—"

"Free *is in* prison," I remind him, pushing forward and going through the portal, traveling the blazed path all the way to Borro's *hut, war room, sleeping arrangements*? I never see him outside of this building, does he even sleep?

I see Harru standing guard; it's been a while since I've seen him around. "Harru," I call out to him. He lifts his head and locks eyes with me, "I have something for King Borro."

I walk past him on the way in and see Borro sitting on his throne, staring off into space. He looks down on me and says, "That used to be very important to our people, it was in fact the first thing they stole from us."

"You may not believe it, but this was buried right next to my house, and I suppose Martta and Kiira were looking for it and that's the beginning of this whole story," I explain.

"Really?" he smiles, "Then it was what you call destiny, what we believe to be *Lotta Dillo* or the *Mother's Guidance*."

I flip open the case and reveal a skull, about the size of an adult, the top cut off with a ring of small horns, just like Borro's. Hesitantly I pick it out and look at it, empty sockets looking back. "I suppose this is yours," I say, handing him the skull.

He takes it and looks at it; it's been decades since he's seen it. *CRACK!* He crushes it in his hands, "Something I learned when your people first came was that I wasn't special; I had been raised being told I was special, I was descendant from the *Lotta*, but their arrival showed me I was nothing.

"But please, excuse my rambling," he gets back on track, "That was nothing more than a relic of an archaic past, we have been ushered into a new era."

⊰⊙⊱

There's a language-anthropology expert working with locals on documenting their language and behaviors. One of my trips I catch a glimpse of some asymmetrical horns and I take a detour from my path, "Martta!"

I start running after her, making sure it is in fact her. She turns right around and slugs me in the face, knocking me to the ground. I completely forgot how strong she is, even recovering from a bullet wound to the lung. I come back to the real world and look back up to see her one her way beside Kiira, "Dammit, Martta—"

"Go away," he says quietly, continuing on her path.

I rush up to my feet and start chasing after her, "Why are you avoiding me?!"

She turns back around, opening up her wings and standing off against me, but I'm not afraid. In fact, I see this image in my head and find it powerful and beautiful. "Every time you show up in my life, you take away my purpose for living," she says, just loud enough for me to hear, "I was *born* for a sole purpose, and the moment you show up and screw that up."

"Martta, maybe it's because you're worth more than just being a soldier-"

"I go to war for the good of my people!" she starts marching up to me, screaming, "And you show up again and end the war! You think I'm worth more than just being a soldier, what about you? All you do is follow orders."

She pivots back around, wrapping herself with her wings and going back on her way. Kiira rests her hand on her shoulder, and they keep walking. "Martta!" I march up to her, but Kiira flashes me an angry look. "Martta, I did my best to come back for you. I know it took years to happen, but I did *my* best. I had to fight the long fight against my authority, and despite all odds, I did come back, and things happened, but we're finally at peace. Why can't you be happy with this?"

I follow behind them in silence, all the way to the edge of their village. The grass becomes less consistent, as there's less travel here. There's no trail cut in and the grass is patchy. I look around and see clear signs there's been soil dug up. This is a graveyard.

I sober myself up and try to have respect for their dead and stop and wait for them to come back. I have so many questions right now, but right now, at this moment, I'm shutting up.

I watch them find a spot and kneel down, holding their own hands. They start whispering something to themselves in unison, probably a prayer. They finish and stand back up. When I see her face, blood-red tears are running down her cheeks.

They start walking back to me and Martta quietly asks, "Did you know your mother?"

"No, actually," I admit, "I never met her, or know anything about her."

"Then I take pity on you," she remarks, going on their way.

"Did you?" I ask back.

"Yes, she was gentle and taught me her language," she begins, "She died one day when she was sick from eating a now forbidden fruit."

"I'm sorry," I try to be sensitive, but my father was nothing close to gentle.

"Kiira, leave us," she commands, followed by Kiira walking off into the distance. Martta kneels down and sits down in the tall grass. I sit down beside her, and I see her stare off into the sky, dotted with a single cloud on the green skyscape. "You want to talk, so talk," she says in a passive-aggressive tone.

I take a breath in and out, thinking. "Why do you hate me so much?"

"You abandoned me," she whispers, "I left thinking it was the right thing to do, but I longed for you and waited for your return because it was bound to happen. But you never came back for me; instead, I went from one stupid war to another."

"I had to fight off the entire bureaucracy just to be here, I never once forgot about you," I reach into my bag and pull out her horn. She turns her head to look at it, "I kept this on me at all times, because I knew what my government was doing was wrong, and I wanted to make peace."

"And now you're here, and you think what? That all is forgiven?" she persists.

"I'm here *now*."

"But *now* isn't when I needed you," she turns her head back away from me.

"What can I do, *now*, to make you forgive and forget?"

"*Stay*." Her tears begin flowing again, dripping down red onto her clothing. "I'm always feeling *so* alone, and the only time I didn't is when I was with you, so *stay*."

I start awkwardly scooching over to get closer, probably ruining the moment. But I get right next to her and attempt to wipe her tears away, but she bats my hand away. "It's okay to cry sometimes," she tells me, getting back to her feet, beginning the trail back.

I follow behind her, but she's walking fast. We pass by one of the scientists helping a native with a concrete experiment, building cinder blocks with nearby materials, being supervised by Borro, who seems enthralled by the miracle materials.

◄◄ ⊙ ►►

"Mr. H, sir?" I approach him and stand at attention, "May I request something?"

"Depends? Walk with me," he closes a laptop and starts walking to the other side of the portal room, "This alliance you've brought on is providing us with some of the most important information in human history, once we build an actual facility on their planet, who knows the answers we'll unlock?"

"I'd actually like some leave," I admit, "Enough time to do some traveling on the other side."

"Leave?" he turns to me, confused, "You haven't asked for leave since you started with us; speaking of which, how much time have you spent with us? I know you're on a special agreement, but your time should be up." Mr. H sounds frantic as he looks at all the readouts, pushing past workers to look at their work.

"I've been reenlisted twice, sir, its part of my deal that I serve until otherwise considered unable."

"Oh right," he turns to me, "Well consider this your last enlistment. And write a formal request for leave and I'll go over it. Dismissed."

He just set me free, in another year that is, but I'm now free from this. Mr. Free held this tenure over my head for the beginning of my adult life. "Oh," I pause to take in that news, "Thank you, sir. I'll get right on that leave request when I finish my current report."

"Good," he simply replies, "Go do your report. How did they like the crucible back?"

"Borro actually crushed it with his own hands," I tell him, "Said it was a relic of the past and was no longer needed."

"Interesting, I would've liked to keep it then."

I start on my way back to the office where I've been working. The office is empty this time of day, so I sit down and open the computer, beginning my report.

I get sidetracked and open up a group of reports from the anthropologists doing fieldwork. The managed to document most of the everyday words from an elder in the village named *Serri* who apparently was alive when Borro first took power and human contact was first made. The portion of the document, that I'm assuming, was documenting their first human contact is censored. Interesting nonetheless.

I finish up my report on my interactions with Borro and start my filing for my leave. I only get to see the Earth's sky in the portal room, and nowhere else. My only freedoms are on *Ouauoa*, but that could change now.

⊷ ⊙ ⊶

My leave was approved and I walk through the portal with no mission in mind. I thought I might propose going hiking with Martta. I get past the burning of the journey and begin walking. They completely tore down the structure that originally surrounded the portal and I see they've cleared a lot of the grass to maybe build something more permanent to secure the portal from the elements.

The weather is almost always temperate, there's no orbital data yet, but I know we're above most clouds on the plateau. Not many animals are up this high either.

I make my way into the village and find a concrete hut that's been extended to Borro's stone building. I see one of the scientists, covered in dirt, standing proud next to it along with some hybrids.

"Looks good!" I shout, waving.

"Hard-ass work!" he shouts back.

"I'm looking for the one with the uneven horns, named Martta," I walk up the group. The other native standing next to him is a muscular one, not wearing any coverings on his chest with horns that shoot backward and not up.

I hear that girl practicing on Trevor's ukulele in the distance. All 4 of them are serving time in military prison, along with the cold-blooded Mr. Free. Though, I'd like to believe Trevor would approve of that girl having it.

I point my fingers and place them on my head, one lower than the other. The native says something in their language, and the scientist says, "I think he said she's in her tent."

"I need to start reading the partial-dictionary," I tell myself.

I wander into the tent area of the village and start calling out for her. I come across the crowd and the girl and her instrument, and she's getting pretty good after all this practice. "Martta!" I call out again.

Someone points me to a certain tent, and I go to it. I point the tent and the native shakes their head, which I think is 'yes'. Carefully, I open the flap, which appears to be animal skin. I catch a glimpse inside and I see Martta changing her shirt. "Dammit, Martta," I quickly avert my eyes and close the tent.

"Maybe if you weren't so damn childish, Ostin!" she shouts back. The flaps burst open and stands there without a shirt, staring me down as I cower away,

"Martta!" I shout, turning a full 180 to not look at her, "Have some decency!"

She screams and rushes back into her tent. I feel the eyes of the villager silently judging me as I stand there with my back to her. Soon after, her hand bursts out and pulls me in from behind. "What'd you want?" she demands.

I sit down in the low ceiling in the dimly lit tent. No windows, no candlelight, just the stream of light from the door. "You told me to stay, I got some time off; I was thinking maybe we could go hiking?"

"What's 'hiking'?"

"It's when you walk to a scenic location," I explain.

But she gets a confused look on her face, "But why would you do that?"

"To enjoy nature?"

She starts moving her head trying to understand, "There are wild animals that'll attack you, like a *Bolori*, or you could get lost— Why would you do something like that?"

"Martta, I have a gun for protection, and we have a drone in the sky that connects to my compass," I try to convince her, "Why don't you show me around?"

"Around where?"

"Don't you have a favorite spot to go to?"

"You're sitting in it," she snarks. I look around to get a good look at her living space. Just a single blanket, and a pile of folded laundry, very quaint.

"This is literally your favorite place in the entire world?" I laugh a little, "Nowhere on this planet that you'd rather be?"

"No."

"Okay, what would *you* rather do?" I ask, trying to get her to budge on an activity so my time off doesn't go to waste. Mr. H only gave me four days leave. But she just sits there in silence, probably reminiscing on something.

"When I was with your doctors, there was a *thing*," she begins, "They called it a *TV*, and the people inside—"

"You want to finish your show?" I start laughing after all this time, it's television that's going to change her mind.

"Why are you laughing at me?" she reels back.

"Sorry, I'm not laughing at you," I stop and apologize, "I just think it ironic that *that's* what you want—" She picks up a wad of dirt and chucks it at me, smacking me right in the face.

"You don't need to be a jerk!" she shouts at me.

I wipe the dirt off my face and stand back up, being careful to not hit the ceiling, "Well then let's go watch some TV, I'm sure I can get that episode you were watching." I reach out my hand, and to my surprise, she grabs hold and lifts herself up.

◄◄ ⊙ ►►

My tenure in the military is done, complete. My deal with the United States government has been shredded by the hands of Mr. H, and I am free from this; although, I fully expect to go back. I wish to further my people's relationship with the *Euintae.*, and most importantly, my friend Martta.

But today, I'm going to visit my old comrades, the ones who betrayed me and the human race. The workers let me through the doors and I see the four of them in a shared cell. I'm conflicted on my feelings towards them. We are soldiers, and we follow orders, but at any time we can just say no and do the right thing.

"Good afternoon, I think," Trevor greets me.

"Hello," I say back, "Trevor, I thought I'd tell you, your ukulele was given to a young native girl, he's getting pretty good."

"At least it's not in the trash," he remarks, "That was a gift from my aunt, so I'm glad it's not trash."

"But I have a question for all of you," I get to my business, "Why start another war?"

"It's not like we wanted to, James," Henry speaks up, "I sure didn't, but Mr. Free was a monster."

"At *any* time, you could've done the right thing," I say, "At *any* time you could've warned me, disobeyed the *wrong* order."

"So I'm a monster, eh?" I hear a familiar hollow voice.

"Absolutely!" one of them shouts, throwing a metal cup at the wall.

"We can all agree on that," I say, looking past the wall and seeing the sharp, cold blue eyes that all the men in loose-fitting suits share. But he was marked by the scars Martta left on his face; after that, no one could mistake him.

This is a sad and ironic sight of him, hair no longer clean-cut, but overgrown and falling into his face. He's clad in orange and sitting in the corner. "You all made your choices, and here are your consequences," I say.

"And you're the one with a smokin' demon girlfriend," Trevor chuckles, "We can't all have happy endings."

"You could've," I turn away and leave.

My last stop before going back home, or what used to be so long ago. Anger is boiling inside of me. This man didn't even bother to come to my fake funeral. I raise my knuckles to knock on the door, but I second guess myself. The house has a faint smell of booze.

I back up and kick the door down as hard as I can, smashing the lock and bursting it open. I march in, ready to face him, but what I find is just a drunk, angry man staring me with a bottle in his hand. All my anger washes away seeing him.

"The hell you want," he snarks.

"Is that the first thing you have to say to your son?" I reply.

"You're no son of mine."

"Damn right—"

He throws the bottle at me, spilling whatever was left inside on the ground. Nothing's clean here, nothing neat. I catch the bottle and hold it tight.

"Ya'know, I came here with the sole purpose to repay you for every bruise, every drop of blood from my mouth," I pause, strongly considering smashing the bottle over his head. But I'm not angry, seeing all this, so I set the bottle down on the table. "But it looks like you did that yourself."

"You think *I'm* the failure of the family?"

"Yes!" I shout, "You work at a second-hand dentistry and you're an alcoholic! I at least have a military career."

He stands up, stumbling a little, and walks up to me, backhanding me. But I'm the bigger man, always have been. "You're weak, fight back!"

I recoil from the hit and look at him, eye to eye, "You've never been worth it." I walk away and leave. I hear him throw that bottle at the wall and it shatters on my way out. I open the door to the blacked-out limousine and leave to return to the facility. I have work to do on *Ouauoa.*

# A Demon's Lamentations

◄◄ ◎ ►►

I TAKE A STONE arrowhead, and dig into my first nail, slowly slicing through it and pulling off the sliver that remains. I'm not doing this for *him*; I'm doing this for my dear mother. How dare I think that? He abandoned me. I watched them reopen that doorway, and he wasn't there, no, he was nowhere to be found. The only thing I saw were the monsters sending their machines over.

I cut through the next nail, being more careful to cut it in a nicer curve, just like her gentle hands. The *Euintae* are just as bad. The moment Prela thinks there's not enough food to go around, she invaded over the Grand Sea. The moment Borro suspected they were hostile; he invaded, forcing me to spy and fight. He forced me away from my mother, and when I returned? She was gone.

Nail after nail was trimmed down until my right hand is finished. The blood I shed with them, I don't want to fight anymore, but what does Borro do? Make an alliance with Prela and send me out to fight once more. He's no noble king. When I return, he forms another alliance with the very enemy that wanted our extermination.

And who do I find? *Him!* He abandoned me, and after all this time he thinks he can just walk on *our* land and make nice? Goes by a different name, and for what? Kiira was a traitor, just like him. She thought peace was always an option, and look at what she lost for it: an eye and her pride.

But what if he really did come back for me? No, he's surrounded by warmongerers too. Kiira trusts him. But that means nothing; she'll trust a *Goso* to feed on grass.

I look at my left hand, free from my natural offenses. Is *he* really here to stay? Are they really here for peace? All they carry is empty promises, but he was always different from the rest of them. He went out of my way to help when I was stranded; he was there to comfort my troubles. But he waited all this time, and now it's too late. But is it too late because of what I consider?

I bring my wings close and feel the scar and lumps on one of them, from when his abusive father realigned the broken bones. He risked so much just for that.

I look out the small opening of the tent to see the two setting suns in the sky, giving it that lovely color.

# An Explorer's Note

◄◄ ◎ ►►

I OPEN MY eyes, looking up at the blue sky. *What is this place?* I first think to myself. But the more important question is: *Who am I?* I sit up and look out at the ocean, calm and serene. Thankfully, I'm still clothed, but they're completely tattered. I try to take in my surroundings; grasslands, with trees dotting the landscape, and a hill in the distance, with all kinds of animals grazing.

I also find a small booklet hiding in the sand. I take it and look through the pages. They're all instructions for making items. But most of the book is empty, perhaps waiting for me to fill in the rest. I close the booklet and slide it into my near-ruined pocket. I rise to my feet, supposing I'll have to go and make sense of this world. I look out over the landscape and pull out the booklet again. It has instructions for creating rudimentary tools out of wood, which I supposed I must do by hand. *What a mysterious world*, I think to myself.

I march forward into this new world and spend the day harvesting sticks that I'll need for these tools. It says in the booklet, to make wooden tools first, and then acquire stones to make better tools. Stone is obtained by mining from caverns or the rock beneath the soil by a mere pickaxe. I see no reason why I shouldn't just go right to stone.

The sun begins lowering in the sky and I fashion a pickaxe from the sticks I've obtained. Then it was time to go and find some stone. I suppose I could dig in the dirt until I hit some, as the booklet says. I begin wandering, reading through the booklet, staring at a blank page, when suddenly, as I march through some grass, instructions on how to cultivate the grass into food writes itself on the parchment.

— An Explorer's Note —

I kneel down and pick out some seeds from the grass, as the book instructs, and put them in my pocket. The sun begins to set, my first night in this mystery world. I fear for what it contains. The darkness dawns on the land and red lights begin popping up everywhere. I look closely at a set of glowing red eyes, and eight long legs start moving. Chills travel down my spine, and I start running. There are spiders everywhere, and I swear I just ran past a standing skeleton.

⊷⊙⊷

It's been fifteen days since I've arrived. After my first night, it became apparent that shelter was going to have to be my top priority. I spent the following days cutting trees and constructing a hut. Instructions for doors appeared in the handbook as well. Armed with shelter, I was struck with hunger and began planting the seeds.

But after these two weeks, I had secured food and shelter, and I was safe from the monsters that roam the night. The more things I discover, the more becomes written in the book, it's of curious workmanship. When I sat down in my hut, safe from the outside, I looked through the new items that had appeared. A bed was next on my list to make, but also more tools, as mine have been considerably worn down.

The sun rises on another desolate day. Thoughts on my existence and whether or not I'm alone are always pressing on my mind. I close the door behind me, and ready to find some *sheep*. It says they provide food and wool, used to make decorative things, but most importantly a bed to sleep in.

I unsheathe my blade, made from broken stones I fastened to a stick, and prepare myself mentally to do what I have to this animal I'm going to find. I scour the local area of animals. I find a hill nearby with some pigs and chickens. Finally, I see a sheep with poorer luck than me grazing away on some grass. Since I am the only person in this landscape, I'm sure it's not as scared of me as much as I fear those night monsters.

◄╫⊙╫►

I've successfully built a bed to rest on and had my first enjoyable meal… ever. The sheep's meat was delectable when cooked over a wood fire on my furnace, which doubled in producing heat for me to pleasantly sleep to as well. The next thing on the mental list I've made from the overwhelming amount of entries magically writing themselves in my handbook is a resource called iron, which I find in the ground at depths greater than I've gone before, as well as something called coal, fuel for lighting and cooking.

If I recall correctly, there is a cave opening nearby, that if I'm careful, I could explore it for this iron resource. The things I need iron for? It says here that it can be used to create protection for my person, which I deem to be necessary if I'm going to try and traverse the landscape at night.

It took all afternoon, but eventually I found that cave and I start my journey inside, pickaxe in hand. Immediately, I find some coal in the wall, and after a few strikes, it comes loose. I look at the handbook, and a new entry for a torch has appeared. Strictly following the directions, and striking the torch across the wall, I have light for the deeper cave exploring.

The cave is fairly simple, with no deviations or forks, making it easy to remember where I've been. After hours of searching, I find what I think to be iron, and spend the next few hours harvesting the material. I fill up my entire backpack with the fragments from the wall and decide if I need more, I now know where to go. I have the feeling that something is watching me from the shadows and decide to go back to the surface.

It doesn't take nearly as long to get back up as it did coming down, but the sun is nearly set, which means the monsters will be arriving, and I'm ill-equipped to try and defend myself. I march back to where I came and make it back to my home before the night arrives. Following the directions in the handbook, I prepare the fragments in the furnace with the excess coal and go to sleep, waiting for the morning to bring me the iron.

◄◄ ⊙ ►►

It took several days to make just a protective chest piece made of iron, but some protection is better than none. I also set aside enough to forge an iron sword, also for my own protection… and to keep any animals I might have to slaughter from being in too much pain. After the armor, I decided to focus on farming, to cultivate some food storage. It's been about one hundred days since I awoke on these shores. No signs of intelligent life thus far.

I've also expanded my home in this time, making it roomier, giving myself a dedicated room to sleep in, and another for crafting while leaving the main room for eating. I've also cultivated a path from my home to the cave. Exploring the cave has proven difficult. I ran into a living skeleton drawning a weapon. Though I managed to kill it, it proves that not only do they come during the night, but they seem to survive in the darkness.

Coal seems to be more important than I first thought, providing light around my home and the cave system that seems to drive away the monsters. All this time alone has made me think that it might be worthwhile to explore a little, and maybe find life elsewhere instead of waiting around for life to find me. The hill above where the cave is should be a good vantage point for looking for places to go.

I spent a day climbing the mount to the summit and what I saw disappointed me somewhat. I saw an expanse of grass and trees beyond the hill, the ocean from whence I woke, and not much else. But I waited for the sun to set, sword in hand ready to fight my way back home if need be, to wait for the glow of torches to show itself in the darkness.

When the darkness came, I saw light in the distance. Far away, it would take days to get there. But maybe it's worth it?

◀◀⊙▶▶

It's been days of constant travel. I'm tired, exhausted, surviving off of nothing but bread. I've walked over the long nights, placing markers to find my way back. I've come to a dense forest, and it's been a trial just to make it through. But when I arrived at my destination, I was again disappointed.

I walk up to a village, buildings left and right, animals walking around, and worst of all, people. People, but not like me, brown skin and bright green eyes; they spoke, and for the first time, I heard another spoke, but it wasn't anything I could understand. I didn't know what it is I can understand, but it wasn't this. Their writings weren't the same as the handbook. When I tried to talk to one, using my voice for the first time, they didn't understand me, just as how I didn't understand them.

But they could get their point across; they wanted to trade with me, they had diagrams on paper I could see. They appeared to want a green jewel for various things, paper, meat, food, etc. This was a failure. While they weren't looking, I took some of their crops, a carrot and a potato, things I had in my handbook. And so I started my trek back.

◄╫⊙╫►

It's been about 200 days, one hundred days since my trip to the trader village. I've been keeping close counting on the days on a board in the main chamber of my house. Since then, I've been building my residence even further. Not only do I have a functional farm with multiple crops, but I've managed to procure animals, mostly as a hobby to pass the time. I felt that the animals and I could somehow relate to one another.

All I've been doing is surviving, but it's a lonely existence. I wonder if I am alone. Is this world infinite? If not, where does it end and will I ever be brave enough to find out for myself. I built a second layer to my home as well, also collecting things to make paintings to decorate my mundane walls. It's all in the handbook.

I woke up this morning, thinking I should go to the ocean. I pack some bread, draw my sword, and set out. I was running very quickly through the night and I don't remember the path I took here. But I insist on myself. I start on my way, retracing my steps all the way back to the ocean. The sun traverses the sky during my trip until I arrive.

The ocean, the beach, it's beautiful. I didn't get a good look before, but I see what looks to be an island stranded out in the water. If I recall, the handbook has instructions for a boat to row across the waters. I walk across the coast, not really thinking of anything in particular, just enjoying the sand and the water.

But I stop and look down, and what I see is unbelievable: another person, just like me, waiting to wake up on the shore.

# The First And Last Hero

✦ ◎ ✦

I FIND MYSELF SOMEWHERE I didn't intend to be. I simply wanted a change in scenery, I suppose, and opened a bridge to somewhere in the infinite universe. But I *see* where I am. I see all. The pinnacle of my visual ability, I see galaxies in perfect, harmonious detail. It's not enough, I am a god amongst men, as my old friend once told me, as we mutually agreed no one else could compare when he found me practicing in a wasteland.

This planet is nothing out of the ordinary. It's a rocky world, close enough to the sun to support liquid water, but I *see* no life creeping on it. I suppose it's a good place to meditate. I cross my legs and float above the surface, seeking improvement. I'm the strongest. World-Eater is no match for me, he never was. Coronus was defeated with little effort.

I focus my power, time being an irrelevant thought passing by. I forgot how long I've been here. The orbit of this planet is near-perfectly circular, its axial tilt approaching zero, and its rotation retrograde. No seasons, no point of reference. How long has it been? I've grown tired of this soulless rock. I've mastered this ability anyways in my time here. I see *everything*, all, the entire observable universe in my eyes in perfect detail down to the last microbe.

I see life everywhere of varying complexity and ability, even an alien vessel traveling through the stars. But I see something out of the ordinary. Should I explore, what good could come from it, perhaps a sliver of entertainment to fleet away soon? I rest my feet on the ground, stepping through space to find this peculiarity hiding on a forest planet with no intelligent life to be seen.

◀▌⊙▐▶

I see a man, sitting by a fire, roasting a small animal to eat. I step on layers of space fractions above the ground to remain silent. "Another person?" he says, somehow noticing me, "Has humanity evolved to point of interstellar travel, or is it just you?"

"Just me," I reply, moving myself in front him to talk, "Who are you, and how did you end up here?"

He laughs, "These are the first words I've heard spoken in nearly thirty years. People used to refer to me as the Speed Demon."

"Ah, yes," I remember the story from the newspaper when he disappeared, "You fought a battle and you suddenly disappeared when you had victory in your grasp."

"Tell me," he asks, "Did I save those people?"

"Yes, they are still alive," I tell him.

"Finally, I'm at ease. At an early age, I realized I commanded more than just speed, but another unworldly force. But during that battle, I fought hard, and I broke all my limits.

"Before I knew it, I had run across the entire universe, to this desolate place. When I finally stopped, I had no more power left.

"Have you come to save me?" he begs, tears flowing from his eyes, "How is my son?"

"Your son?" I try to recall, "He became a hero as well, taking upon him the name 'Speed Demon'. In fact, he's fighting the greatest foe the world as yet to see as we speak with his comrades."

"That's just like him," he says, "Why are you not fighting alongside him, if the world is in peril, why are you here? Who are you?"

"I was once a hero, the first generation of heroes, actually. But I was locked away, for my abilities being too great. I escaped my captors to try and find enjoyment in the stars."

"Enjoyment?" he grows angry, "You seek enjoyment while my son battles for the sake of the world? Have you no heart?"

"Matter of fact, I have no heart at all. I gave up hope for humanity, being a hero, all of it after I realized that people sealed away their greatest hope."

"Are you supposed to be a savior?" he shouts, "I gave up everything to fight for what was right, and here a supposed god stand before me saying he has no hope for humanity?"

I hear the voice of Might, someone who embodied the hope of humanity in my head, "I fought for what was right; to fight for the innocent, to defeat evil! To go past my limits and raise up the good in people, to be a true hero." It was the first Speed Demon to coin the phrase, to inspire a generation of do-gooders.

"I believed in that once," I confess, looking at the battle taking place. My old apprentice has just fused for the first time to create a being to fight the great World-Eater, but it won't be enough. "But I stopped when they sealed me away and drove this foe to what he is now."

"*Heroes make sacrifices*," I hear the voice of my apprentice in my head as well as he speaks, "If you're a god amongst men, then do what a god does, and protect his people!

"If you won't do it, then send me there right now, and let me fight and die!" he shouts.

"This foe is too great, even for the best of heroes," I tell him, "You'd be killed in an instant without your abilities."

86

He then says something that strikes even me to my core and shakes who I am. Something no else could've said because he lived and died a hero, to save people. But I'm only dead inside because I chose to turn my back, wash my hands of my responsibility. Perhaps I was wrong to think they're beyond saving.

"Where is this battle?" he persists.

"It's in a remote mountain range in Russia," I tell him, seeing this combined hero fail to defeat him and fall apart, powerless. I open a bridge for him to walk through. "You're useless," I say, "This portal will take you to the outside of a police station where you originally fought."

He looks in his freedom, seeing a car drive by, it brings him to tears. He looks at me. "Be a true hero," he says, "And save them." I move the portal around him and send him on his way.

I look at the fire and extinguish the flame to not burn down this planet. I reflect on my life, and maybe I was wrong to think the way I did.

I step through a bridge to the scene where my old apprentice has failed and the World-Eater is rebuilding his body once more. "You did good kid," I say to her as she protects her friends and all of humanity.

# 0-0-1 The Gate Guardian

## Future

⇥ ◎ ⇤

"Yeah, yeah," the merchant snarks, "This'll easily see a squirrel at 12,000 yards, *no problem!*"

"This thing's a piece of junk!" I shout, opening my *good* eye and analyzing the thing. My Æ-12 processor picks up a smudged off bar code, *something-9142*; this thing was manufactured nearly eighty years ago, "This thing is ancient, don't you have anything newer?"

"If I had anything newer, it would've been sold!" he shakes the scope around, trying to make me lose clear sight of it. The crowds of people are rushing by behind me on the market; someone bumps into me, lightly snagging my back pocket for a wallet, which I keep in my breast pocket for that exact reason.

I snatch the scope from him, "Fine! I'll buy it, you cheapskate. What's it gonna cost me?"

He snatches it back, "I'll let it go for 3,000 credits?"

"Credits?!" I cry out, "What happened to dollars? Don't tell me this is black market stuff!"

"So what if it is?" he grabs my coat and pulls me close, "Dollars are tracked, and besides, you're not goin' to find something of this caliber anywhere else, this is military surplus, ya'know."

"Fine," I cave, reaching into my breast pocket and pulling out my wallet, "Take your damn credits, 2,600 and I'll consider not reporting it."

"2,800," he haggles.

"2,650," I dangle my payment card, "And I'll *consider* not reporting it."

His face wrinkles in disgust, snatching my card and inserting it into an *illegal* payment reader. The light flashes green and tosses the card back to me. "What are you even doing that requires 12,000 yards?"

"None of you're busy-ness," I take the scope, holding it to my *bad* eye, switching it on, the image zooms in and stabilizes on something: a pimple on a cook's sweaty forehead over at the Chinese food truck way on the other side of Freemont. Distance: 1,500 yards. "This'll do," I say to myself. I turn back to the merchant, "Don't spend all the credits at once."

I stuff the scope in my coat pocket and start on my merry way. That was almost all the credits I had saved up. I was expecting it to be in dollars, good 'ol digital cash. Ever since Ameria swooped in to save the crippled Europan economy the Euro crashed, and if you had a physical coin, it belonged to a museum. Of course, that's what dear 'ol Greg says, I definitely wasn't alive 120 years ago to see it happen.

Geez, I hope that credit drain was worth it. I start a call with my Æ-12, trying to contact my homie, Cynthia. That stupid ringtone the Æ-12 came with start ringing in my ear. That ringtone is by far the worst thing about this implant, and I needed a new one bad, but the shiny Æ-13 wasn't due for another 2 months. Who in their right mind puts binaural ringtones on something like this anyways?

A hottie walks by, distracting me while the phone answers. His jaw looks like it's a titanium implant—damn that's good-looking. Cynth's voice starts chattering in my head, "Hell-o?!"

"Sorry, C," I answer with my thought, "He's—I mean, did you get your end of the deal?"

"Oh, yeah, I got the deets," she laughs. She doesn't have to worry about leaking her thoughts over the phone, but since my implant is directly wired to language processing, I have to stay careful, "I found a nice guy who full-times at the Foundation."

"You didn't bone him, did you? He could have some *unnatural* hazard, given his job," I say, "Like, what was it? 13-63?

"No, just a nice kiss on the cheek, and he was ready to talk," she giggles.

"Let's meet up with the others, and we can discuss stuff in person." I'm a little hungry, but that Chinese truck is all the way down Freemont. This side of the road has street merchants, and I'd rather not spend all that time walking. *And* I ate my last protein bar earlier, so I guess I have no choice.

I join the crowd and keep my head low. Lots of police sitting around, but whether or not they'd do something is a coin toss. On one hand, you'll have that new guy who's all, 'by the book!' and on the other, you'll have the sellout, and I guess on a third hand, you'll have that old guy who doesn't care; three hands aren't common, but that's also a bad analogy.

The street is always busy, but I make my way. I get in line for the food truck and the guy's handing out Jianbing for a good price. My good eye sees heat signatures of a few people in the truck, cooks working tirelessly to get some dollars. They work quickly enough and in a few minutes, I get up. "*Yige qing,*" I say, pulling out my payment chip and tapping it against the reader, giving up the required thirteen dollars.

The cashier shouts at the cooks, and they pass around the ingredients, eventually making its way to my hands. I grab it from the guy and it's hot, fresh off the stove. I'm famished; I've been searching all day for that scope and haven't eaten since this morning.

I take a bite, walking back into the crowd. I should catch a cab, then a bus to try and get to the next city over and meet up with the rest of the crew. This job is promising 7,000 dollars and 14,000 credits for information on the subject of the Foundation's greatest historical embarrassments. It's a government censored story that run's in my family: the mighty Torwächter. I've heard it a thousand times.

I finish up the Jianbing and get to the curb. This part of Freemont actually connects to the bridge and road system. Cars, motorbikes, expensive hovervehicles, you'll see everything on the road these days. The bridge up above is vibrating from all the high-speed traffic, sounding out a constant, annoying hum.

My arm holds out, waving for a cab that's decent enough to pick up a low value looking customer like me. I'm not wearing anything fancy, just slacks and a coat; they'll probably think I'm homeless by the look. But one does stop for me, and it's a rundown, rusted yellow car. I open the door, and the unpleasant stench from the cushions in the back makes me second guess the cab, but I get in anyways.

"Where to?" he says, in Jermaine, I think. My left ear, the side with the Æ-12, the chip will auto-translate, but my right ear is unaffected. It was jarring at first, but I got used to it.

"I need to hit up the expressway, so take me to the bus station that'll take me there," I respond, "What's your rate?"

"Five dollars per kilometer," he says. It's always more money for the life of a near-vagabond such as myself, "You got some major bags under your eyes, you sure you don't want to go to a hotel?"

"Just drive," I say, but he's right, I haven't slept right in two days, but I'll catch some shuteye on the bus, it's a long ride.

⊣⊢⊙⊣⊢

Cynthia is waiting for me outside the meeting place. Thankfully she's wearing some actual clothes this time, something that covers her chest and neck, in black. "Charlie!" she shouts, calling me by my middle name.

"Cynthia, is everyone inside?" I ask, my good eye being shut off by some EM interference. Every time we have a meeting on this job, they jam as many electronics as possible. My bad eye is starting to get dry; the rest on the bus wasn't enough.

"No, just the boss," she opens the door for me, and we walk inside. It's just the backroom to the laundromat the boss runs. I'm for certain he's laundering credits through this place, but who cares?

The lights are on, shining on a table, I see the boss and a teenager wearing the uniform to the place. The teen is eating a sandwich. The door closes, cutting me off from the sunlight. "Lunch break's over Jenine," The boss says.

"But sir, I get thirty minutes since I'm on an eight hour shift today," she retorts. She's right though.

The boss roles his green eyes, "Then eat in the— just—" he facepalms because he's been in hot water before about breaking the law. "Put in your earbuds and don't pay attention."

"Alright, Mr. Masson," she says, looking back at us. Just puts in some wires and I can hear the music she's turned up. It's an Amerian boyband that's been popular, I think.

"I got the scope, cost me 2,700 credits," I say, opening one of my coat flaps to show him, "12,000 yards, just like you asked for."

Cynthia smiles, "And I got the exact location of the Foundation's facility in Turk."

"How *exactly* did you manage that?" Mr. Masson asks, skeptical.

"Oh, I found a high *enough* ranking Foundation guard," he giggles, "Kissed on the cheek after more than a few drinks, and he was ready to talk all about it."

"And you got the location in Turk?" he raises is brow.

"Well, a little truth-juice never hurt anyone," he says, "The guy said the exact long-lat of the facility and the target shouldn't be too far, and it's not like it's invisible either, right, Charlie?"

"Story has it as a silver man, about the height of two Jermaine clock towers," I say, "That's all the story says though."

"Charlie, I want you to get some rest before you guys go to Turk," he tells me. The teenager sneezes and closes her lunchbox.

"I'm fine, I sleep when I'm tired, and I'm not—"

I look over to see Cynthia mouthing the words, "I'll sneak her some Trazzies."

"I'm fine! Really!" I raise my voice.

"You look like you have black eyes," he persists.

The teenager stands up and says loudly, "I'm going back to work, Mr. Masson!" She clearly can't hear herself. She walks out and closes the door behind her.

"Where'd you even find her?" I ask sarcastically, "Is she saving up for a car or somethin'?"

"She's part-timing after school to save up for concert tickets," he replies, "She's a hard worker."

I take the scope and slide it on the table, "It's the best I could find, the seller claims it's military surplus."

"From what era?" he picks it up, inspecting it closely.

"It's new enough to be digital, and it has image stabilization," I explain.

"Full-spectrum?" he asks.

"Didn't check," I say, "You gonna cover it?"

"If you don't want to keep it," he laughs, setting it back on the table, "Somebody like you could use to see 12,000 yards."

"I don't sling like that anymore and you know it," I point my finger at him. The teenager walks back in again, pausing in the doorway, looking at my confrontation.

"Oh, I forgot the—the key to the register," she rushes real fast and grabs a set of keys that was left on the table, before rushing back out. She's not an idiot, and probably understands the laundromat is a money-laundering scheme. This is one of the few places that still accept Euro. Credits buy Euro, Euro trades in for Dollars and Credits.

"She's a good employee," I say, retracting my finger, "You pay her well?"

"Two above minimum," he replies, "She's good with the money register."

"Well," Cynthia interrupts, reaching over past me to put a piece of paper on the table, "The, uh, coordinates."

"Really, where did you find a guy that knew this?" he's still skeptical of the information.

"Oh, you can find plenty of Foundations employees at bars," she explains, placing her finger on her cheek, "They're actually hiring part-time, I was thinking of applying, maybe getting close to seventy-three."

I twitch my head at her proposition, "You realize they hire part-time because people die left and right, right?" I turn my head, but I'm barely able to make out fine details with my bad eye; everything's blurry from exhaustion. I should have some eye drops at Cynth's place.

"It'd be *fun* though!" she squeals.

"Alright, you two go home," Mr. Masson interjects us, "I'll pass it onto the client. Get some rest; I can't have a restless slinger."

"Yeah, whatever," I say, grabbing Cynthia, "Cynth, I'm crashing at your place." I push the door open and pull my friend along to the outside. My good eye comes back online and the whole Æ-12 system boots up.

Cynthia catches up to me and gets right beside me. "My bike's over here, ya'know."

"Hey, do you still have my eye drops and medicine?" I ask, "I left some in your fridge."

"I think so, it might be old by now though," she responds, tugging my coat in the direction of her motorbike, "When was the last time you got a good night's sleep?"

"'Good' night's sleep?" I laugh at the proposition, "I even don't think I slept in the womb. I manage to get a little shuteye on the bus over here."

"A little?" She scoffs. I see her bike and we walk over to it. She gets in front and I mount in the back. "How much is a little?"

"Nine minutes and thirty-four seconds," I quote. She turns the key, but the bike is silent. It's electric, so there are no pistons making the constant explosions. It's fast too, but she knows I get nauseous at high speed.

We start on our way, her apartment's about ten minutes out from here, and she knows the roads like the human psyche that she exploits on the reg. "Nine minutes isn't enough, Charlie," she says, the wind obscuring her voice.

◂◂ ⊙ ▸▸

The door closes to the apartment and it's almost exactly like it was last time I was here a few months ago; that same 'ol couch with the spring supports beneath the cushions. I've spent too many nights on that couch to know that it'll make you wake up feeling like one of your vertebrae is out of place. Lots of memories on that couch, but I really hope she'll replace it.

"I'll go get you a pillow and blanket," she says, "You can look in the fridge to see if your stuff is still in there." She hangs up her keys on one of the holders magnetized to the side of the fridge and walks off into her bedroom.

I go to the fridge, opening it up and seeing some actual groceries. I'm on the move so much, I barely know what a carton of milk looks like, much less any brand or even how much one costs. "Do you really drink enough milk to buy a whole gallon?" I shout across the apartment, "Doesn't it expire in a week or two?"

"I love me some damn milk!" she shouts back, coming back out with a pillow and blanket in hand. My vision is disorienting, my bad eye is dry and blurry, but with my good eye, I manage to see my stuff in the fridge door: my eye drops and an anti-dream medicine I buy on the black market for when I need to knock out for eight hours. I unscrew my eye drops and put them in both eyes. My good eye also gets dry since there's ceramic on flesh and not much in terms of excretion in there.

I blink a few times to get the drops all around and feel a little relief. The other is a vial with an injectable anti-dream. I'm sure I left a bag of needles here too... and yup, it's in the butter compartment in the fridge, only no butter. "I'm gonna do my drugs in the bathroom," I grab the vial and the bag of needles, going to the bathroom. This place is kind of dirty, I mean, it's clean enough, but she has something about keeping the bathroom pristine clean.

I close the door behind me and the room has a faint smell of cleaning agent. I pull out a needle from the bag and slide into the vial, extracting about the 1/10 milliliter required for me. I pull down my shirt just enough and continue to inject the medicine into my upper breast. It'll kick in a few minutes.

I take a nice good look at myself in the mirror. I do look like I have black eyes, aside from my literally black metal eye. My hair's a little long too; I could use a few inches off. One of these days, I should take a spa day and clean myself up.

I feel the anti-dream medicine kick in. My mind becomes foggy, and I should probably go to sleep before my lobes completely shut down. I open the door again and close it behind me, seeing Cynthia with a glass of milk. If it's for me, she most definitely has snuck a sleeping pill in there.

"I poured you a glass," she covers her mouth and giggles, "I already drank up mine!"

"Of course you did," I remark, "You slipped a trazzy in there didn't you?"

"Look, if you're not going to drink it, I will," she gets defensive, snatching the glass of milk and cradles it.

"Go ahead and drink your own medicine," I say, plopping down on the couch, "You really should consider getting a new couch."

She scoffs, chugging the milk in one go, all the way. A little bit of milk drips from the side of her lips and continues to rinse out the cup in the sink. My brain starts shutting down and I close my eyes, drifting off. But no dreams, no terrible things for me to see.

Almost without delay, I open my eyes back up and look around, reorienting myself in the real world. I see the time in my good eye, I slept for about six hours, a little less than usual, but it'll have to be good enough. The meds are expensive, illegal, and highly effective.

I start lightly slapping myself repeatedly to fully wake up, eventually sitting up and taking in a deep breath. There's an artificial window on the wall next to the bathroom door. There's nothing but bathroom behind that wall, but she usually has it set to some painting she ripped off from the 1900s. I've even seen a landscape for Hister himself.

I stand up, stretching my sore back. It definitely doesn't hurt as much as I thought it would. My bad eye isn't blurry or dry anymore, but my whole face hurts like someone punched me with all their might, and the bruise is starting to reveal itself.

Milk actually sounds pretty good right now, so I make my way to the fridge, pulling out the gallon and a glass from the cupboard. I watch the white liquid flow down into the glass, splashing on the sides and swirling and eventually settling down in a collection of white.

I take a swig and think to myself, *Damn, this is good.* No doubt Cynth is still asleep, it's about 5 in the morning, and I don't even think the sun is up. I keep drinking the milk and lean on the counter, trying to relax, my heart rate is up. I have no idea what my brain sees when I'm asleep with the anti-dream, but I know it's not any good. The glass is empty, and I'm left looking at the bottom of a glass with a film of milk dripping to the lowest point of the cup. It's almost hypnotizing.

I set the glass down and ping my bank accounts and check on my funds. Still there, but I'm running low, I should pick up a job for dollars soon, and I'm running low enough where my current lifestyle might be affected. What to do, though, what to do? I'll have to pay a visit to a nearby bounty club to look for high paying stuff.

I go to rinse out my cup and I realize something as I get a whiff of my own scent. I smell like sweat and oil. Maybe I should take a shower? But then my clothes are just as dirty too. Geez, have I smelled like this all this time? I'm going to go stop by a clothing store and get something to eat.

◀◀ ⊙ ▶▶

I walk out with a new set of undergarments, pants, shirt in a shopping bag. This place happened to carry my exact size and the brand of jeans I like. People would turn away and walk through the other aisle rather than to be near me. Do I really look that bad, or smell that bad? Sure I might look a little rough; I have a tough-guy looking coat and I got a few tears and holes in my clothes, but it's not like I have a crazy piercing or scars or, heaven forbid, a gaudy face tattoo. Maybe it's just the smell, I do smell pretty bad.

The jeans are almost the exact same, but I'll go back to Cynthia's, there's no way she's still asleep at this time of day with a trazzy. I'll pick up some fast food to bring to her to pay for the night's sleep. She really likes Amerian food, and there's a decent burger place nearby. I hate the grease; like who pairs ground beef with tomato and lettuce? I'm *mostly* vegetarian, like seventy percent of the time. Rice and potates are my go-to, but bread, beef, and lettuce, in one abomination?

It's not long until I find the place I'm thinking of. The line's outside again, just like last time. Cynth must be lying about how it's 'never busy', because every time I stop by, the line's outside. Either way, I find what looks like the end and just stand there, the people inching forward. I start playing some music in my head to pass the time.

Then some dickhead steps right in front of me. I'm shocked that people are always like this. I grab his shoulder and say, "I'm in line, get behind me."

He turns and pushes away my hand, "Make me." I take a step back to recollect myself and put myself in the right distance for what I'm about to do. I wear steel-toe for a reason and this man is about to regret this. I swing up my foot right into his crotch. I feel my boot go all the way and hit his pelvis, and he just drops to his knees, holding his testicles for dear life. I thought I heard a little gasp for air as well.

Someone laughs a little behind me, and the guy falls over, crawling away. That'll probably be the last time he tries to cut in front of me. I step over him as the line keeps inching along until, after probably an hour of listening to whatever music I could think of, I get to the front and order Cynthia a burger, and some fries for me to eat. If Amerians know one thing, it's how to make fries.

Some more time and music pass, and they hand me a paper bag full of food with grease practically dripping from the bottom, it's disgusting. But I take it and make my way back to her apartment. I should've gotten a drink, but oh well to that. There's not a cloud in the sky right now, and the springtime sun is beating down on me. The coat is a little warm, and there's not a breeze to cool me down or make me look bad ass while walking.

The thought of getting a gun pops into my head. Not necessarily illegal, but hard to obtain under the imposed rule of Ameria and the bent-over-backwards government of the Statin Empire. If I got caught with one bought with credits, I'd land myself in prison. Although, I'm pretty sure a badass katana would be fine bought with credits. Maybe if I were to get one with a hyperbeam edge?

I find her complex amongst the numerous buildings reaching up into the sky. In and up the stairs I go. Everything is painted an ugly brown or green to try and match up with the grass and mountainous rock that once stood around these parts hundreds of years ago. The inside lady knows me and lets me walk right through.

The foyer is full of fake plants and a hologram that constantly repeats the rules and regulations of the building. Holograms are expensive, and I don't see why they decided to splurge on them, although they're everywhere in the big cities. The Freemont down the border almost has none, since it's usually vendors going in and out, they'd rather save their money.

I find the door to be locked, so I bang on it a few times, "C! I got a burger!" I hear her footsteps click-clack on the ground all the way up. I see the light disappear from the peephole in the door, her just making sure it's me.

The door swings open, and she pulls me in by the arm. Closing the door quickly behind me. She's paranoid during the day someone will find her here, so she'll only come in and out at night, "What'd you get me?"

"Food? I don't know," I say, "I said burger and the guy handed me a bag." I hold up the greasy paper bag, and she takes it, looking inside.

"Oh, fries," She exclaims, walking over the counter and pulling out the container with *my* fries. I reach over and snatch them away from her, but she just digs through and pulls out the napkins and eventually the food.

"My fries," I say, sliding a salty, fried potato cut into my mouth. She starts eating her food, pulling out a chair, and sitting down. "I'm going to down to a bounty club and pick up a job."

"Masson is probably going to contact tonight," she reminds me. Mr. Masson is pretty good about doing things in a timely manner.

"But," I rebut, "I'm not gettin' paid yet. Things aren't cheap."

Suddenly, Cynth's phone pings. It's in her pocket this time. I just stare at her, waiting for her to pull it out of her pocket and look at the message. But she just sits there, biting into her burger, locking eyes with me. And she just takes another bite, and I keep waiting. "Are you not going to answer that?" I finally break down and ask.

"No," she says, mouth full of food. She just keeps chewing for an excessive amount of time, swallows and takes another bite.

"But," I try to say, "Your phone rang."

"I know," she says again with a mouth full of food. She just sits there, staring me down as she eats. So I take a fry and slide it into my mouth, then another. All this waiting, with locked eyes. She finally finishes and crunches all the paper up, stuffing it back into the bag it came in.

"Are you going to answer it now?" I ask, "It's been like six minutes and forty-one seconds."

"I need to wash—"

"Answer the damn phone!" I shout, "Or let me do it!"

She kicks up her leg, pointing it at me to keep me from getting closer. And she just balances on one foot, whilst simultaneously keeping me at a distance and washing her hands from the oil. "It's probably Masson sending us to Turk," she remarks, flicking the water from her fingers.

"Then answer it!" I shout out. The suspense is killing me!

Finally, she picks out the phone from her pocket and lowers her leg. "Yeah, it's just Masson, he sent me a, uh," she pauses looking closely at the phone, "A green finger-snapping and bird emoji."

⊶⊙⊷

I've been awake for two days straight in the back of a truck smuggling us past the borders all the way to Turk, a lawless country that collapsed in the late 2080s. I'm sitting on the passenger's side of the back of a beat-up truck. Cynth is sitting on the driver's side, and there's a third coming with us. His name is Geoff, and we've met before on another job from Masson. He's more machine than man and has got two real good eyes; full-spectrum, 100x zoom, even a low light mode. I know he has some newer model of the Æ chip. Dressed in gigablack clothes, he disappears in the dark and reflects all infrared light. I have to close my good eye just to look at him.

Geoff, if I recall, can hit the bottle cap of a soda from seventy-five yards single-handed with a pistol. He's good, and he's here for protection if something goes wrong, not that it will; Cynth and I are among the best slingers. You need something, even information, from point A to point B? We'll do it any way you want.

I decided to take a dose of classical music on repeat on my Æ-12. Something about rivers and souls, but it's peaceful and helps clear my racing mind. My bad eye is drying up and I forgot my eye drops yet again. It's the dead of night, and this driver is going at it on the dirt road to get past whatever's left of Turk border patrol. The music is only in my left ear, so I hear every rock flying past us in the right.

I think to myself, *This is one helluva job.* We're collecting information on the Foundation's biggest screw up, and the personal legacy of my family: the Torwächter, the Gate Guardian, the silver man, whatever you want to call it. The driver is going to get us all the way to the outer gate. It won't be unusual, people come to see foundation compounds all the time, this one included, but never once has the exact location been leaked.

The GPS in my Æ-12 says we're approaching the compound in about an hour. C is dead asleep, and Geoff is in 'rest mode'. Come to think of it, he could be a drone from Anderson's or some other robotics company. That company usually keeps to themselves, but sometimes things get out, although other companies do sell drones all the time, for about 2.3 million dollars starting.

"Geoff?" I say, barely above the wind.

His eyes open up and the optics in his eyes recalibrate. "Yes?" he grunts. He's not very social.

"We're arriving in about forty-three minutes and thirty-one seconds," I say, "Tell me something if you would."

"What?"

"Nevermind," I stop myself from asking about whether or not he's a drone, I don't want to get on any bad side he might have, "Do you know anything about Hister's secret weapon he used in World War II?"

"I know that it's the thing you've been sent here to collect information on. Otherwise, my memory is blank," he says, his voice is static, unemotional. I really think he's a robot from Anderson's. I wonder if there are any real human parts to him.

His head tilts back down and closes his eyes, going back to 'rest mode'. And I'm left with myself in the dark, again, like most of my life. A life with no sleep is pretty dull, despite what you might believe. You're either working until you collapse or you find yourself staring at a brick wall in an alleyway until the sun rises and snaps you out of the exhaustion.

The piano music keeps playing, and I catch myself dozing off, slapping myself as hard as I can to wake back up. The sound wakes up Cynthia, and she lifts her head, looking at me. I get a little taste of blood on my tongue, as I probably just cut myself on my silver tooth. Just another reminder of *that* bad decision.

It's not long that we get to the drop off point. Geoff wakes up and Cynthia comes to cognition. It's about 1:32 in the morning when it's easiest to get in. There's a small haze in the distance. I wonder what kind of containment they're using to keep such a force to be reckoned with. I hop out of the truck. I knock on the window, and the driver lifts his chin to me, pulling out a flask full of alcohol.

I pull open the door and fetch the camouflage for the truck. It should make it look like a boulder, which people tend not to recognize. Geoff locks and loads his pistol. The letters J.A.K.O.B. carefully carved and etched into the black and silver steel housing. My good eye links up to my Æ-12 and draws a line, the trajectory of the bullet if it were fired as long as it's my line of vision. I paid hella extra for that feature.

Cynth and I cover the camouflage over the truck. The fabric is specially designed to look like a rock on all spectra, a special meta-material like Geoff's clothes. We pin down the cloth and, yup, it's a rock.

Geoff goes forward and starts snipping the fence open with his fingers. His *damn* bare fingers. He's a drone, for sure, or at least has robotic arms. Those are fairly common, especially for war vets.

He stretches out the opening to the fence and Cynthia crawls through. I get down on the ground and start my crawl. Haven't done this since I was a kid, crawling through a hole. But I get through, jumping back up to my feet. Lastly, Geoff gets through and holds out his gun.

The satellite blocks out about 26,000 acres, so this compound is huge. There's a fence surrounding the entire place, and then three layers of quickbuild walls. Guard towers are scarce though, there's simply not enough manpower to spread out over the world *and* secure this place, it's huge!

We sneak along, and I see no heat signatures. The walls are semi-transparent in that spectrum, and no one is even close to us. Something is a bright spot on my good eye though, and it's in the direction of the haze. It's just a white spot, the temperature is unreadable, but it's through three walls of quickbuild. We keep going until we find a door going through the wall.

Locked, of course. Cynthia pulls out her special lock-picking hairpins. She begins to go at it on the lock. "This thing hasn't been changed since 1957 when the war ended," she remarks, "Fantastically clean though."

I shush her, trying to keep her from making any more noise. The lock slides around and the door squeaks as it opens wide enough for us to make it through. Luckily enough there seems to be another door in a line to the center. The bright spot in my vision is even brighter now that there's one less wall in the way. Whatever this thing is, it's extremely hot. My good eye can detect temperatures up to 10,000 degrees. I have no clue what it is they're keeping here.

Cynthia picks open the next door, and I don't see anyone on the other. This place is stretched real thin, I reckon. The door opens, and we walk through into the next area. My good eye sees a dark spot in the shape of a building. That must be the main complex.

The final door opens and the light spot overexposes my good eye, blinding me. I feel a sting in the back of my eye socket, forcing me to cover my eye and take a step back. It's just as bright in my other eye. I pull out that scope I bought just for this.

I look over and see the Foundation's compound. Just a big, square building. A few guard towers standing about. I hold up the scope to my good eye because it can still see clearly at this stage of sleep deprivation.

"Holy shit," I whisper to myself.

⊷⊙⊶

There's no silver man here. The figure off in the distance looks like raging flames. Flaming auras reach out from behind, laddering down in two lanes. And his hands, they're wrapped around something that burning even hotter. It looks like a sword, but the blade is ever-changing. He looks to be guarding a huge archway with a grove on the other side, full of lush trees and grass; like nothing I've ever seen before.

Most petrifying of all, there's no face, and yet I *feel* its gaze. "What do you see?" Cynthia whispers to me, snapping me out of it, "is that like an infinite bonfire?"

"No, it's worse," I say, "So much worse. There's no silver man here, we must've gotten wrong information—Masson and his buyer, they're going to be pissed."

"Silver man?" she asks herself, "My informant never said anything about a silver man; he said it's more like a flaming seraph. Although, he was under truth juice."

"No, the stories in my family say a silver man, silver like the metal- nothing ever said anything about flames," I start going off.

"You've never seen it until now, Charlie," she tries to calm me down, "Thing's get long in translation-"

"My great-grandparents were there! They watched the thing destroy Londen and Ledivberg—they were literally there!" I start getting loud, realizing, and shutting up.

I go back to looking through the scope. Chills travel down my spine as the Torwächter turns his head towards me. My mind flashbacks to my night terrors as a child. Sirens start going off, red lights flashing all about. Do they know we're here? I doubt it. I look back and see Geoff, cool as a cucumber.

"Activity levels detected!" sirens repeat over and over. The lights keep flashing, and the sound keeps echoing between the walls surrounding us.

We keep camping out. That *thing* and I are locked in a gaze. For once in my life, I'm actually scared of something. I'm uneasy with this. How do I know what truth and what lies in all these stories? My ancestors watched a silver man obliterate city after city, but here I am looking at a flaming angel guarding a grove of trees.

I switch my scope to the compound. Personnel dressed in white and black start funneling out, brandishing guns of all kinds, like that'll do anything to the Torwächter. They all start lining up and trucks start exiting the compound, equipped with rockets, powerful ones I'm sure.

Geoff remains ready to fire at will and Cynthia begins to slouch on the wall while I just stare at him. "When do I get to look at it?" she cries out.

"Right now," I demand, "I'm sick of this thing staring at me." I hand her the scope and turn and slouch on the wall.

"You said it was looking at you?" she says, "It looks like it's facing off into the distance."

I notice the sky begins to get lighter as the sun rises on the Turk landscape. I start playing that river song in my left ear and try to calm my nerves. "Cynth? What else do you know about this thing?" I ask.

"The guy said that they stay around ten kilometers away from it and that they stopped running experiments in the 2010s," she explains, "I tried to bait more out of him, but that's all he had to say."

"Geoff, you know anything about it?" I ask him.

"My memory is blank on the subject," he responds unemotionally.

"Yeah, I'd say a flaming seraph was an accurate description," she says, "I've gotten a feel for the facility, should be enough for Masson's buyer. This thing is rated for 12,000 yards, right?"

"That's what the guy said, and the readout for the Torwächter is roughly 12,000, so I guess he's right," I reply, thinking about those credits I used to buy the thing.

"That means this whole facility is about fourteen miles circular, with the compound located about, uh," she pauses to look and take a measurement, "about six miles from the Gate Guardian."

"What's the buyer even going to do with the information?" I ask aloud, just thinking and ranting.

"You know the code, we don't ask," she replies, "Here you can have this back and go back to your staring contest."

The sirens stop and the lights stop flashing, the siren saying, "Activity nonthreatening."

She tosses me the scope and I lay back down on my stomach, peering back through to the Torwächter. The scope focuses on the target and his head turns back to me. Chills go up and down my spine as his faceless head looks at me.

The sky is blue, signaling we should leave before someone sees us. I get up to my feet and put the scope back in my coat. I start marching back through and Cynth closes the doors. "Aren't you going to relock the door?"

"No, these ones are permanently locked," she remarks as we make our way back to the truck.

"Geoff," I call out, "What do you reckon these walls are for?"

"Spectra-analysis points to them being fire-resistant," he replies.

"So these are to—" I turn back to the Torwächter's bright spot on my good eye, "keep an outburst under control. This thing's a bomb."

"Possibly," she says, closing the second door behind us, "I know this thing has been basically inert since they stopped testing."

"But, the story goes it has a 'ray of death', that's what the story says-" I start getting worked up again, "But this one has a sword."

"Charlie!" she grabs my shoulder, "You're out of sleep and you're being manic. Calm down."

I stop my rant and try to calm myself, shaking my head in agreement. We get through the last door and crawl through the opening in the gate, Geoff crawling through last. We look back to see him reattaching the cut wires with, again, his bare fingers.

I go ahead and march up to the truck, pulling all the camouflage off and scrunching it up in frustration. This could all be a bust and all that money and time down the drain. I open the door and the driver is woken up by the sudden noise of me shoving the fabric into the foot area of the passenger's side.

Geoff and Cynthia follow up behind me, jumping into the truck bed. I look back at the bright spot, eventually stopping and following them onto the truck. Cynth taps the window a few times, signaling to take us to the nearest big city with an underwork network.

Masson rarely uses the underwork; I use it all the time for contacting clients about credit-paying jobs, Cynthia will occasionally use it too for her specialties. But this marks an exception for Mr. Masson since other networks of communication are constantly monitored, especially by the Foundation and Ameria.

‹‹ ⊙ ››

"Stay around here!" I command the driver, "Don't talk about anything either!"

"Aye, aye, Captain!" he says, taking a drink from his flask, "Got to go get a refill anyways."

"I'm serious, Mr. Masson doesn't take too lightly about snitches," I reiterate. Cynth, Geoff, and I start walking across the street to a sketchy bar and pub that screams *slingers* and has *bounty* and *underwork* basically written on the walls.

I burst through the door, and see the crowd you'd expect to see. My bad eye is having trouble focusing on it being dry and all. I just continue to march through in between the table all the way to the barman standing behind the counter. But before I arrive, I feel a hand grab my buttocks.

I stop in my tracks and slowly turn around to see who it was that is going to get a double serving of bones served on wheat. It's this fat, bald guy laughing to his friends. There's a specific part of the ear cartilage that when pinched, causes extreme pain. I know exactly where that part of the ear is.

I pinch this guy's ear, and he winces in pain, turning to me. I get a good look at his ugly face; a few eyebrow piercings, a lizard tattoo on the opposing side, and a prosthetic eye. "What the hell, bitch—" he remarks, right before I knuckle him on the bridge of his nose. I feel the bone underneath crack, but not break.

I let go, and he stands up, towering over me by more than a few inches, blood dripping from his nostrils. Geoff pulls out his gun, ready to fire, and says, "Threat Identified." The letters J.A.K.O.B. flash out in front of the whole bar. My eye draws lines to the inner brain, targeting right behind his temple. Geoff is ruthless to be sure.

He looks around at the three of us, Cynthia readying her push knife, and sits back down, turning away and carrying on with his cronies. We all calm down and I continue on my way to the barman. I fish out my underwork token and hold it between my fingers, making sure the barman sees it. "I need a messenger hawk if you wouldn't mind."

He twitches his head to tell me to follow him across the bar to the end, where he pulls out the messenger hawk. It's an older one, but it'll still do. The old ones don't support the encryption and protocols that are mainly used today. These older ones are sometimes tracked and cracked, but I don't have a choice right now.

I insert my token and get my credits payment card ready for the barman. These old ones use a wheel, like phones from the 1900s to dial the twenty-four digit, disposable contact number. These things are built to be dumb, in contrast to the modern tech that surrounds it. No serial numbers, no barcodes, no branding. It's a blank piece of machinery purpose-built for the underwork.

I start moving the wheel back and forth to dial in the number that Mr. Masson gave me before we left. Twenty-four digits are absurdly long on a wheel, but I get to the final digit, and I pick up the speaker and mic. No ringing, you just wait until the other side picks up.

I look over to see Cynth taking a shot and Geoff staring blankly into space. Finally, I hear the voice synthesizer the underwork uses. "What'd you find?" I'm pretty sure it's Mr. Masson on the other side, but the voice synth makes it impossible to know for sure.

"Well, the thing was on fire, didn't expect that," I say.

"You said it was made of silver," he replies.

"I know that, but either my family was wrong, or we got the wrong target."

"What else did you find?"

I look over to Cynthia looking out to the crowd. I hope she isn't drunk already, she can *not* hold her booze. "The target had a sword too, of some kind, also unexpected. The whole facility was an about fourteen mile circle, with the main compound full of heavily armed men."

"A sword?" he questions me.

"And there wasn't a soul within six miles of the thing."

"Good," he says, "Stay in town, I'll give you an update later." he gives the address of the hotel we're supposed to stay at. It's further into the city. Geez, I just hope there's an Intellavision for me to watch. I didn't bring my anti-dream, so I'm pulling a third-day-nighter.

"Alright," I say, "What do we need to do next?"

"I'll need you to go back and get a layout of the compound," he tells me.

Some gears grind in my head, "You want us to infiltrate the compound?"

"Yes," he commands me. I bite my lip; this is more than I signed up for, but I always see the job through.

"Yes, sir," I say, hanging up.

I walk over to Cynthia and pull her arm to get her off the counter; Geoff stands up and follows us. We walk right past the fat bald guy, and he flinches as we go.

Traffic has picked up on the outside, cars, and hovervehicles rushing by. Cynthia lightly starts slapping her face to sober up a little from the shot. I have no idea what she decided to ingest. Alcohol and I don't mix… at all. Last time I had an encounter with booze, I was having terrors the entire time it was in my system.

I see the driver on the other side of the road, leaning on his beat-up truck, enjoying the damn weather. The sun overhead is hurting my bad eye. The traffic stops for a moment, and we, with some others, cross the road. I look down the roadway and see the big city all the way down. Towering skyscrapers shimmer in the air. I see the road split into bridges down the line too.

We get across and I tell the driver where he needs to take us, to the hotel Mr. Masson has paid for us to stay at while we're in the city. We all mount inside the back of the truck, and we go off down the road.

The skyscrapers get closer and closer. I see the faint holograms glowing in the daylight. Cities aren't usually too bright during the day. You see billboards on every space that isn't a window, advertising anything, and I mean *anything*. Outside the urban areas, life hasn't changed much in the past hundred years. But urban life is for me, it makes me at home.

◀◀ ⊙ ▶▶

The driver's sleeping in his car; Cynthia decided to take the bed in the other room. Geoff is lying on the ground behind the couch, *perfectly* still like a corpse… or a drone. Me? I'm sitting on the couch hugging my knees watching a documentary on serial killers. These things fascinate the hell out of people, including me. I actually know one of the people that they were talking about. *Way* back in the day when I was first slinging, I did about anything. I never killed anyone, but I was involved in certain jobs that did. I was young, a teenager who was haunted every night by night terrors.

One day, I did a terrible thing— *I* didn't do it, but I was directly involved. When I was reeling from shock, I made the decision to limit what I would and wouldn't sling. Not that I could just change professions, I had no other applicable skills, unlike that teenager working at Mr. Masson's laundromat. I was younger than her when I first started slinging, but she's got cash register skills, people skills. I've never even been behind a counter, handling money or what little physical cash actually circulates now.

Anyways, the show follows the murders and a few killers and their arrests, one of them killed themselves rather than to serve his sentence. The person I knew that's featured, I did a job with him moving a shipment of illegal medications, like the anti-dream I take now. Not all of it was illicit drugs, most of them were prescriptions that were smuggled or made for other buyers. The guy was assigned on the job for protection, similar to how Geoff is assigned to protect Cynth and me. That job went well, but he was arrested for killing nine people, all sling-related.

A knock on the door brings me out of my haze watching the intellavision. I get up and stretch my back. It's a little warm, so I remove my coat and overhang it on the opposing chair next to the IV. I get to the door, opening to find a hotel staff holding a decently sized box. "Hello, I was told to deliver this package to room 91," she says, holding out the box.

Confused, I take it, shaking it around. It's lightweight, feels like clothes. "Uh, thanks," I say, "I guess." She walks off, and I take the box and toss it to the couch. Moving to my coat, I pull out a pocket knife and go to open the box.

Upon opening it up, I find Foundation uniforms. This means I won't be able to wear my pants during the operation, but maybe I can smuggle my coat in. I see a note stuffed into the box as well. I pick it up and it reads, "ACB: remember to bathe before the job." I do have a habit of not showering for days. There's no set routine for me to remember. I'm up three or five days at a time, and rarely does it occur to me I might smell bad. I should shower now since it's fresh in my mind. A hotel such as this should have hot water.

I made sure to bring some spare clothes on the trip this time, something I often forget to do. I set the stuff back into the box and go to the window. 42nd floor up, and to ruin the view is a ginormous hologram advert back facing the window. A hologram of this size costs millions and thousands to operate. But I disregard the giant ass in the window and go to take a shower, taking one of Cynthia's push knives.

I get the water to a nice warm temperature, and I just stand in the flowing stream a little while to relax and calm my nerves. I'm always so worked up from the lack of sleep. My hair is seriously too long; I'm going to cut it off when I get out. I continue to clean myself, making sure to scrub the stink off.

I get out, drying myself, looking at the foggy mirror. I wipe my hand across the mirror to clear the moisture, but it just fogs back up again. I start pulling my hair back into a tail, making sure there aren't any strands looser than the others. I hold it back with one hand, and take Cynth's push knife in the other, and slice off the excess. A wet clump of hair falls to the ground, and I look at it. *How many times do I do this? When was the last time I went to a hairdresser?*

I continue drying off and get dressed in the clean clothes. My hair is nearly dry and the mirror is clear. I look at myself, seeing my black metal good eye in contrast to my white and blue bad eye. At the time, I thought the black paint job was bad ass. What is it I think about it now? Kind of like a bad tattoo; sure you could get it removed or covered up, but something is stopping you from doing so, some sort of sentiment.

I go back to the main room, seeing blue skies peeking through the window. Day already.

⊷⊙⊶

The driver gets us back to the access point. We cover the truck and Geoff reopens the fence where we first entered. Cynthia reopens the doors, and we get past the second wall, where we start walking to the nearest point to the compound. I see that ever present bright spot on my bad eye. Cynthia got a good layout of the facility and spotted a tunnel leading from the outside to the compound.

We walk in between the third and second wall, passing by a locked door every so often. It took about forty-seven minutes and eleven seconds to find the tunnel that she mentioned. There's no one here, so Cynthia begins opening the door. It swings open and we walk through. The compound is smaller than I had first imagined. I decided to wear my coat over the Foundation uniform, whilst Cynth and Geoff are fully dawned in the clothing that Mr. Masson provided. Geoff, though, has his gun under his arm to conceal it. Any new metal detector would find the weapon, but this place doesn't seem to be that updated.

I feel the Torwächter looking at me. My nerves are excited, and chills constantly blow into my bones; I don't like it here. Still no one in sight, but there's a double door next to the tunnel entrance. I knock a few times and wait. The door swings open, nearly smacking into me. Someone in a uniform. He starts speaking in Turk, but my Æ-12 translates, "What the hell are you three doing out here?"

"I, erm," I clear my throat, "Perimeter is secure."

He rolls his eyes, turning around and speaking in Anglish, "Why were you checking the perimeter?"

"We were told to, sir," I say.

"And where are your firearms for checking the perimeter?" he asks. His accent is thick and barely understandable.

"We were told to leave them behind," I repeat. Cynthia is overly quiet, she must be nervous. Geoff barely speaks anyways, he's level-headed.

"So let me get this straight?" We turn a corner and enter a large room, one side of the room, there's a big scream with readouts and camera views of all spectra. "You were tricked into walking the entire seventy kilometer circumference *without* protection?"

He turns to the crowd of people wading around the room, doing various things, "Who the *hell* did it this time?"

The room falls silent and everything stops. The man just holds his arms out, waiting for a response. "Well if no one is confessing, then you better hope I assign laps again!" he shouts.

Some of the people inside curse, then get back to work. "Hey!" someone calls out to me, "Lose the jacket, if the director sees you wearing it, it'll look bad on all of us."

"Right," I say, removing my coat, and folding it up and holding it.

"Well?" the guy repeats again.

"Yes?" I say, frozen in anxiety and chills.

"Get to work!" he shouts, turning back to the screen, directed at the gate guardian, "Shit, I can't stand new people."

"Give her a break, maybe she's hearing things," someone else says. I turn to see Cynthia sitting in one of the chairs already, and Geoff on another table all looking natural.

"Hey, you!" he calls me out again, "Are you hearing stuff?"

"Well—" I try to say.

"If you are, report imediately to the Director!" he shouts again.

"I'm just a little on edge," I tell him.

He scoffs, and the girl sitting next to him punches his arm, "Get over it, it's not like this is the worst time you could be assigned to watch."

Someone else chimes in, "Yeah, I wish I could just be assigned to contain that cake one I hear about."

"Yeah, 871," the guy laughs, "Yeah, newbie, come check this out."

Slowly I take step after step to him, I see all sorts of camera views watching all sorts of things. I get behind him and bend over to see what he's looking at, "What is it?"

"It's looking directly at the compound," he says, "it happened yesterday too, but this time he was slowly turning his head, and he's completely locked on the compound."

"Strange," I say, knowing that he's looking at me.

"Take over for me," he says.

"I—," the girl next to him interrupts me.

She turns to him, "Quit trying to get out early. You, just go sit down and wait until you're next."

I go sit down next to Cynthia, who's struck up a conversation with someone at the table, talking about some guy named Cain. Cynthia is just wanting so bad to meet him, and the girl she's talking to says that apparently, he's actually fairly nice to be around, if not a little creepy. She heard this from some international guards that paid this site a visit.

"When did you guys start?" she asks us.

Cynthia answers first. She knows I'm on edge and not great at people skills in the first place, "We started recently actually."

"Well, this place is kind of a dud when you think about it," she explains, "No tests are ever run, and aside from that scare yesterday, *nothing* ever happens."

The door bursts open and that guy that led us in here marches in, gun in hand, but finger off the trigger. "Where are the three I led in here?" he demands to know.

I stand up and pull Cynthia up with me. "Here, sir," I manage to say. Geoff stands up; arms folded, and ready to pull out his gun.

"Follow me, the director wants a word with you about your doop," he demands. This is probably a trap, a bad one. We follow him, and he guides us down a series of hallways, covered in various sized doors and panels. We stop at a door labeled 'Directors Room'. The room opens, and we come face to face with an older man. Round glasses looking at a screen mounted on his desk.

Someone sneaks up behind Geoff and jams two bars into his temples, but he doesn't flinch, just stands there, frozen. Cynthia gets the bars jammed into her head too, but she falls down in pain, and she's cuffed by one of the guards.

The door slams shut and the guy holds his gun to the back of my head. The director looks up from his screen and says, "In all my time as director of Site Zero, I've seen many break-in attempts, but none as bad as this.

"What's your name?" he asks.

"I go by Charlie," I say, scared and frozen in fear.

"Why try to break in?" he persists, "Surely you didn't come here to try and steal the o-o-1, you'd need an army and a very powerful explosive device."

"I'm just here—" I stutter, pausing, "To investigate."

I duck down while swing up my leg to get the man in the crotch and dodge any bullets. The gun goes off and barely misses the director. Geoff is frozen in place and I run, letting my instincts kick in. It's fight or flight, and I'm fleeing. I burst through the door and run down the hallway. The walls are partially transparent to my good eye, and I just keep trying to find a way out. A few twists and turns later, I find a set of glass doors leading to the outside, and I burst through the glass, flinging shards everywhere.

I pause to find a way back, but my mind is racing, I can't think clearly. My heart's pounding and I just want to break down and cry, but now's not the time for that.

Sirens and red lights start going off, saying, "Breach!"

Then, everything falls silent for a moment. *Everything*, my heart, the world, my mind. It's serine for a single moment and I hear what seems to be the voice of thousands of people in perfect harmony and synchronization say, "Come to me." I feel a force like a rope start pulling me to the Torwächter. My feet start running by themselves, and It feels I have no control. Real fear and terror strike me down like when I was a child. The brightness of the flaming man overexposes my good eye and I can't look away. My Æ-12 starts frizzing out and shuts down, and my good eye stings from the overexposure.

"You remember me, don't you?" I hear the voice again.

"Yes!" I cry out, tears flowing out my eyes.

"Your ancestors remembered me. I remember them," it says, "I remember all I cast my gaze upon."

I feel like I'm running faster and faster than I could possibly do otherwise. The flaming man grows larger and larger as I come closer. "You've seen me all your life," it says.

128

"Yes!" I cry out, "Every night, I see you!" My hand is pulled up by some force and it feels I'm being pulled along by a chariot.

Roars of the Foundation's vehicles grow ever louder as they chase me. I hear loud sirens call out, "Don't let her reach one kilometer!"

Rapid-fire starts going off, a bullet bites into my left arm that's reaching for something. I see the blood spray and obscure my view for a moment. Suddenly the rain of bullets stops and something explodes, finally stopping me and knocking me to the ground. I tumble and roll and stop shy of a dirt mound that extends out in both directions. A barrier they must've put up.

I roll over to my back and see a truck with a sonic weapon attached to the top. What are they even going to do with that? The screeching of the weapon pierces my ears and it feels like I have a boulder crushing me down. My vision tunnels and all I can think is *don't make me dream.*

⊷⊙⊶

*Where am I?* I think to myself. I look around, something's different. I don't have my good eye or my Æ-12, but I'm not any younger. I'm in a restaurant, a busy one. And there's only one waitress, rushing as fast as she can from table to table.

I look outside the window and see old cars, like *really* old. Not holograms, hovervehicles. There's an old tube IV mounted on the wall with the customers' eyes glued to it.

"Charles!" a woman shouts.

The waitress greets the people with food, "I'm working as fast as I can, Myrtle."

No, it can't be. The waitress is in a red and white uniform, with a fo-corset. I turn to the IV, and see a black and white news reporter, "The Red Army continues their crusade throughout Europan, and experts say that they're going to invade Angland soon, despite public statements from Hister himself saying we're of no interest—"

The ground shakes and half of the restaurant explodes, the patrons turned to dust in a ray of death. I've seen this before. I've seen this many times. It's the silver man from the stories. And that's my ancestor, one of my great-grandmothers, Charlie.

Everyone starts screaming and running away, Charlie is frozen in the gaze of the Torwächter. I look outside the window and see the terrible thing pushing over buildings, and firing his ray of death at anything, in all directions from ninety eyes on its face. Planes appear overhead, the Amerians from the story and their nuclear, world-ending bombs. I've seen this enough times to know every count, every face and thing out of place.

I turn around and the world shifts to a different city. I see Charlie, covered in burns and patches, being lead through a crowd by a Red Army soldier, Charlie's husband Charles. Suddenly the ceiling collapses and bombs start dropping. This time, it's not the Torwächter, just the sad realities of war. I turn and see the crowd disappear.

I'm in a room, an apartment, with Charles and Charlie, and some others—two young girls and an older woman, all sharing a meal over a glass table. I start to walk and run, but I seem to be going in the opposite direction. "What am I supposed to do?!" I cry out, my voice cracking. I'm so scared. I'm full of terror and fear; my legs barely have the strength to stand.

I see her turn to me, and she disappears. I fall to my knees, crying, waiting for someone to come save me. I look up and see Charlie, standing above me with an outstretched hand. But when I reach, another hand grabs her and holds her tight. I see the fear in her eyes.

Behind me is the silver man; I turn and see *him*. His cold gaze, his ray of death burning down an entire Jermaine city. "Look at me!" I hear Charles say, "You're my top priority!"

Some other soldiers flip over the truck and the engine starts up again. He leads her heroically into the truck, and they drive off, leaving me behind. I start running, and everything fades away into blackness.

The ground gives way and I start falling into the void. I slam into the ground and I see the two. Charles walks away into the blackness, and Charlie holds out her hand for me again. I reach out and grasp her hand firmly. "What am I supposed to do?" I whimper, "It's always haunting me."

"Survive!" I hear her voice whisper before she fades away too.

My eyes open back up to reality. I start screaming in fear, not knowing where I am or what's real. I thrash around, but I'm held back by restraints to a hospital bed. I see a machine, reading out my vitals. My good eye and my Æ-12 booting back up and recalibrating.

My vision focuses and I come to see the Director from the compound. "I contacted your mother," he says, "She said you've had night terrors for as long as she can remember. This is why you purchase illegal anti-dream medication? So you don't have them?"

"What do you know?" I scoff, my heart pounding and the heart rate monitor going crazy.

"Your heartbeat is irregular, so I suggest you calm down," I see him putting one leg over the other in a chair opposite the room, "I pulled a very extensive check on you—"

"Where's my coat?!" I demand to know. It was a gift from my late father.

"It's in a locker," he replies, "*and if* you care about your friends, they're currently in containment."

"It's part of the job not to be concerned with others," I say, "What did you learn?"

"Well, I know your full name is Agnes Charlie—"

"Agnese," I correct him, "with an *easy*."

"*Agnese* Charlie Brandt, you're a descendant from Charles and Charlie Adamonte, one of the few people to survive an interaction with item 0-0-1 during the Second World War.

"*You* started slinging in southern Jermaine and Austian country when you were around thirteen, officially registering as a P.I., and might I say, you've been involved in some very *interesting* jobs," he says, "Now let me remind you, I'm not a cop, nor are you even wanted in Turk, so once I've conducted an independent investigation, I won't be able to detain you any longer."

I try to lunge out and attack him, my left arm slipping through the restraints, but when I reach out, I notice my hand is missing. I start screaming, not being able to look away. "What happened!?" I scream.

"During your capture, one of my own decided to open fire, and shot off your hand, but rest assured the Gate Guardian instantaneously obliterated him as one of the bullets went through the one kilometer threshold. We attempted as much repair as we could on the wound."

A guard comes through the door, and comes to release my restraints. One by one I'm set free, and the director says, "We put those on because you were thrashing around quite violently in your sleep.

"You have been classified as an SCP, and you'll be cleaned and prepared for containment at this other site along with Geoff."

I lunge at him, but the guard grabs me and holds me back, dragging me along through the door. I stop because I know it's futile, this guard is roided beyond belief, I doubt I could overpower them. They lead me along through the door and the guard pushes me into a corner and says, "Strip down and you'll be cleaned." It's a woman, a strong one.

⊰⊙⊱

She closes the door and turns away for me to get undressed from my hospital gown. I pull off the gown and go to touch something with my missing hand, reminding me it's gone. I step under the shower head and with my other hand, I guess my bad hand now, turn the knob and ice-cold water starts flowing down. No soap, so I just rinse off the leftover dirt on my face and hair. The water suddenly spurtters out and stops.

The guard turns around, and I cover myself to be decent. "Put these on," she tosses me a *very* ugly orange jumpsuit with a male undergarment.

After getting dressed I'm pulled along down a hallway and through a set of double doors that lead to prison-like hall full of people in orange jumpsuits with a black logo on the right breast. The garments are very comfortable, though. But we don't stop, she leads me further down, and I walk past a guy with a hole about two and an eighth  inches clear through his forehead, among others.

She leads me through another set of doors and to the left, through another door, but this time, it's an office. The guard pushes me inside and closes the door behind her. "Good afternoon, Agnes—"

"Agnese, with an *easy*," I correct him, "And call me Charlie."

"Of course, take a seat," he says, "I'm going to ask you a series of questions—oh, my name is Doctor Hagnes, I'm a researcher here at this site for the Foundation. I'll ask some questions and all you have to do is answer to the fullest of your abilities and you'll be free to go."

"Whatever, fine," I scoff.

"You've been classified as a 'Safe' SCP with the anomalous property of being able to dream memories of your dead ancestor Charlie Adamonte. Could you describe the types of things you see when you dream?" he asks me.

"I have night terrors of a silver man. It ranges from destroying cities to bombings," I explain.

"By the silver man, you mean 0-0-1, the Gate Guardian, or the Torwächter as it's known in Jermaine?" he asks, "These dreams are variations on the destructions of Londen, Angland; Ledivberg, Jermaine; and the bombing of the Lordov Check-in, yes?"

"Yeah, I guess—I don't know," I turn my head, "Why was the Torwächter on fire anyway?"

"Oh, right, you must be confused about the appearance," he leans back in his chair, "You see, Hister invaded Site Zero, he used a nuclear explosive to make 0-0-1 dormant for a small time, and then stole a branch from the tree of good and evil from the gate. When he left, and 0-0-1 woke back up, the gate guardian started walking towards the branch, leaving his sword to guard the grove. When doing this and when not in direct contact with his sword, he loses some divinity and takes the appearance of the 'silver man', or so the theory goes.

"Back to *my* questions," he leans back forward and starts back writing on his papers, "You currently stay awake for as long as possible and take Nevoperin, an illegal market anti-dream drug when you do sleep, yes?"

"Yes, I'm awake three to five days at a time," I say.

"Now, I'll explain to you that this type of anomalous property is fairly common amongst descendants of people who suffer traumatic experiences involving certain types of SCPs," he goes on, "In fact, it's so well studied here at the Foundation, that we have a ninety-five percent success rate of neutralizing such properties—"

I jump up and slam my hand on the table, but I slip on my left nub and fall to the ground, smacking my head on the desk, "You can take this away from me?"

"Yes, it's possible," he says, looking over the desk to me on the ground, holding my missing arm. I climb back up to the chair and situate myself in it. "In fact, we can do it today, we prepared for this while you were asleep.

"A few more questions," he starts again, "Who hired you to break into Site Zero?"

"The code for slinging is don't ask, so I don't know the buyer," I say, cradling my nub.

"Why were you traveling with a drone from the Anderson Robotics Company?"

"I wasn't," I say.

"He's listed as Geoff," he goes further, "He's a highly advanced drone, we're still working through studying him."

"He was assigned for extra protection, he's the best in the business," I tell him, "He's a sharpshooter."

"He's very high tech, so I'm not surprised," he writes some stuff down on the paper, "Last question, which is more of a statement. This one time because you're an SCP yourself, any more infractions against the Foundation, you *will* be tried for your crimes against the SCP Foundation, do you understand?"

"Yes, I understand," I say, *perhaps it's time.*

"Good," he says to me, standing and calling back out through the door, "Take her to the memory chamber!"

What happened after that, I don't remember. I woke up in my own clothes and all my stuff at a train station with nothing but a ticket to my hometown. The train pulled up and I got inside. The ride was nice; I don't think I've ever been on a train. It gave me time to think about how I got to where I am today. I made an early stop and went to Mr. Masson and told him everything I learned, and to tell him I'm done with this job.

"You sure?" he asks, "I'll pay you for your work, of course."

I let out a laugh, "I'm going to spend it all getting a good hand."

"Well, consider it done, I'll have it transferred tonight," he remarks, "You haven't been sleeping again. If what you said is true, then you should have no problem now."

"I'm afraid," I say, "You think you can find me a real job?"

"Whaddya' mean a *real* job?" he snarks.

"I don' know," I lean on the wall, "I'm not working at a laundromat, though. By the way, I haven't seen that girl around, isn't it break time?"

"I transferred her to Betty's," he says. *Betty's,* I think, I recognize that name. "The IRS was getting too close to me, and I didn't want to get her involved."

"Sign me up, I'm sick of slinging."

"Consider it done," he smiles.

"Has Cynthia checked in?" I ask, "Her number changed."

"That question is against code, but I guess you're done with that now," he says, "As far as I know she's in the city, try checking her apartment."

"Aye, aye," I say, popping off the wall, and leaving. Maybe I'll stop by Freemont and hit up that Chinese truck.

⊷⊙⊶

"Welcome to Betty's," I say to the customer walking through the door. I remembered that Betty's was the name of the restaurant Charlie worked at. It's a large franchise in the 1950s and made a resurgence in Europan in the 2050s. The uniform is ugly and clashes with my good eye and good hand; metallic black and red and white stripes don't mix.

Cynthia agreed to let me move in as a roommate as long as I pay half the rent. I finally collapsed from exhaustion on the new couch I bought her that doubles as my bed. I took a chance and decided not to take the anti-dream, and for the first time I can ever remember, I had a good dream. It was about Charlie and Charles' first son, Charles the second, and his first day at school after the war ended. For once in my dreams, I felt at peace.

I take the customer's order, and they go sit down and wait. That teenager that Masson employs, she walks up and sees me struggling with the register. "Ya'know I've heard things about you," she remarks.

I laugh, "Like what?"

"I know you work under the table for Mr. Masson. *I* bet you've seen some pretty cool things!"

"Not anymore, but you don't know the half of it," she points to the button I have to press, "Maybe I'll tell you about it sometime." Another customer walks in and I say, "Welcome to Betty's," and I take their order.

# Notes on 0-0-1 The Gate Guardian

"0-0-1 The Gate Guardian: Future" is based on "SCP-001 Proposal CODENAME: Dr. Clef – The Gate Guardian" By "DrClef": http://scp-wiki.wikidot.com/dr-clef-s-proposal

# The Girl of Forests and Foxes

⏸ ◎ ⏸

THE DOCTOR finishes his final checkup. "She's in otherwise good health," he says, "There're no signs of internal *or* external bleeding, any wounds she may have had have all healed and scarred over."

"That's great," my mother says. I look over to my dear little sister, smiling and kicking around without a care in the world.

"I've been told there's a brand-new treatment for her hemophilia on the horizon," the doctor continues, "It requires a regular injection of blood clotters, and it's on the cusp of being approved."

"That's great news!" my mother says, jiggling my sister's foot, "We were planning a family picnic this weekend, do you think she'll be alright with that."

My little sister twists her head to face the doctor, curious if she'll be able to go out. The doctor thinks for a little bit, "If she wears long clothing and maybe a pair of gloves, I think she'll be alright. She has very gentle skin, just be sure to keep her skin covered. Use plastic utensils, etc; I've told you all that before."

My sister smiles wide, Gigi loves to go out exploring the world. She's such a curious girl. Mom picks her up, and we leave the doctor's office, going home.

◀◀ ⊙ ▶▶

We arrive at my mom's secret spot in the forest outside the city. It's been my mother's favorite spot since she was a child, where she would often go to read and relax in nature. It's a soft clearing covered in grass, and three trees surrounding the clearing, with another tree that had fallen down, obscuring the location somewhat from the path. Over the years, my mother had built and moved small things like benches and tables, but she often came to maintain the grass to make it perfectly soft.

Mom leads Gigi around to look at the flowers and moss on the trees whilst I lay out a thick blanket. We are so very careful with her in the outside world; a single cut, and we could lose her forever. I sit down on the blanket and wait for my mother and sister to stop their lollygagging and sit down with me, so we can spend time in the nice weather and eat.

I hear a nearby animal rustle through some leaves and branches. It doesn't sound like anything dangerous. They both come and sit down, and I start preparing our lunch. Gigi plops down next to me and I hand her a sandwich that was previously prepared. But I hear more rustling in the background. It's more than one animal.

Suddenly, a fox comes crawling out from underneath the fallen tree. It slowly approaches, making chirping noises, crawling to us. There's definitely more than one, walking around; they probably want our food.

Gigi reaches out, but I grab her hand and set it down. The fox pounces towards us, but I reach out my hand to block the animal from biting my sister, and it sinks its teeth into my forearm. But before I notice, another fox is biting down on Gigi's shoulder. *This is bad*, I think to myself.

I toss the animal to the side and pinch the fox's neck to make it release its grip and throw it aside. She *is* bleeding, and my mother is already on her way to retrieve the clotting medicine from the car; she must've forgotten to bring it out here.

Blood starts staining her clothes excessively. Moving her can open the wounds further, but if I wait too long for mom to come back with the medicine, Gigi might bleed out. I say a little prayer in my heart, and pick her up and start running as fast as I can up to the path to try to find my mother and the needed medicine.

# Into The City

WHIP! THE TIPPED leather chords strike me once more. I've found myself trapped again in this forsaken city with a cloned Jennifer, both of us bound to wooden crosses, being marched through the streets and flogged on a timer.

WHIP! The leather strikes Jennifer and me once more. Madam Grenand is nowhere to be found, neither is Sir Lakewell or any of our government officials, but instead, we found something that Omuru had to tell me the word for: Military, jobs whose sole purpose is to enforce the laws of our civilization through violence.

Blood starts dripping from my back as both of us are paraded through the city. "These are the traitors! This is their punishment," the machines shout. WHIP!

I cry out in pain as this last one hit me right across my spine. I see Jennifer cry during all the pain. The people in the crowd are all staring at us, most of them with fear in their eyes. I recognize, even now, the faces of my classmates, my coworkers.

I try and free myself through brute strength alone, but I'm not strong enough to shatter steel, and even if I did, the fall from this height would do some serious damage. What I do know, is that the three of us triple-handedly changed the paradigm of this city *forever*. I hope that that's enough to topple the government, at least in the long run; they can't keep this up forever.

I look down and see some Osheky walk into the middle of the street, dressed in bright blue robes and striking white faces with the runes of 'Order' written on them. They stop in the road and hold out their hands.

The vehicle holding the two of us comes to a halt and a few escorts point their guns at them both. "What do you think you're doing?"

In their Osheky language, they reply, "Release them." They both, in unison, grab the barrels of the guns, crushing them and tossing the devices aside. "Release them," they repeat.

The soldiers pull out some knives, sharp and defined for a certain purpose. But they stop, and the chains holding the both of us up begin to lower us to the ground. "You're being transferred to Osheky custody."

The chains release and we drop to the ground. The small stones in the road dig into my skin. I try to pick myself back up, but I'm too weak, my arms are failing from the intense abuse I've been dealt from the past few days of no food or water.

One of the Osheky picks me up by the arm and starts dragging me along. I look over to see Jennifer, nearly unconscious, being dragged along as well. "You two have been charged with treason and unpermitted contact with an Osheky government official."

Government official? I suppose I didn't know Omuru's past life, or really what he's up to now. He never talked about it and I never asked. I let my feet drag behind me; I'm too weak to walk alongside them.

◀◀ ⊙ ▶▶

I wake up suddenly, frantically looking around to see where I am. I last remember being taken by Osheky from the military. I try to reach out, but straps made of leather hold me back. I see a clean white prison cell. I'm in a chair, and the only other features of the room are a table, and the clear bars making a wall.

"You're awake?" I hear a familiar voice, but I'm alone in this room; where is it coming from? I see Jennifer, alive and well, standing on the other side of the clear bars, dressed in Osheky clothing, a blood-red circle painted across the face. This confuses me more, wasn't her face is pristine now.

"Jennifer?" I come to my senses and see her standing very formally.

"No. You have me confused with Jennifer 91-42," she says, as another Jennifer walks by carrying a tray of food somewhere, "My assigned number is 91-42-31, as I'm the thirty-first successful Osheky hybrid-clone of Jennifer 91-42."

"Jennifer!" I cry out with all my might, my voice breaking.

"91-42-01 is in the cell next to you, no need to shout," she assures me, "She is still asleep and receiving medical assistance as we speak."

The leather that binds me is soft and comfortable, not too tight compared to the steel chains that bound me before. "Where am I?"

"You're in a holding cell in the inner ring, in fact, the first non-government official to enter in so," she explains, "Is there anything you need?"

"How many of you are there?" I demand, "Where's the original?"

"There are 42 Osheky hybrid-clones in service of the Osheky people," she smiles, revealing a perfect set of teeth; the *real* Jennifer had slightly crooked canines, "I personally find it ironic that there are 42 of us, considering our assigned numbers."

The clear bars recede into the ground, and she walks in. I scoot away into the back into my chair, even though I am bound and cannot escape. She pushes something on the wall and a side table pops out. Another Jennifer walks in and sets a plate of food by me, and they both walk out with the bars rising once again to the ceiling. The wall to my left shimmers and becomes clear, and I see the Jennifer, the one who's been traveling with me, sleeping with a tube coming from her arm and a similar-looking plate of food on the table.

I see a clone with a blue square on her face, and another with a brilliant purple rune on her forehead. I stand up, but the restraints are only long enough to reach from the chair and the bed. "Thirty-one?" I ask aloud.

The one with the red circle walks back up, "How may assist you?"

"Why am I locked up, *exactly*?" I ask, seeing if they'll answer my question.

"You're a prisoner of the Osheky people, for treason against your own people, colluding with an Osheky government official, and escaping the wall."

Fair enough, it's all true. "Where is Omuru?"

"He is in an Osheky Prison," she replies.

"Aren't I in prison?"

She smiles, her perfectly straight teeth shining in the light, "You are in a holding cell in the Osheky cloning facility, as Osheky prison cells are not suitable for lesser people, or even Osheky hybrid-clones."

"What," I pause to think, "Is going to happen to the both of us?"

"Oh, well, that has yet to be decided by Sir Lakewell and Minister Kisoro, but for now you'll be held here, in cells designed for inferior life forms."

"I want to speak with Omuru," I demand

"That is not allowed," she replies with a smile.

Either the real Jennifer, or the first clone of her, begins to cough and come back to the land of the living. A clone rushes to her side and attends to her. It occurs to me that I should be in pain, but I'm not. I reach behind me to feel my back only to find bandages. "You were given painkillers prior to your awakening," Thirty-one tells me, "Unless there are any more questions, I have duties to attend to."

"No, I guess I don't," I admit, and Thirty-one walks off.

"Never thought I'd be back here," Jennifer says, lying on the bed on her side, "I honestly thought I was home free."

I remember that the real Jennifer died, and that these are all copies, clones. She may look like Jennifer, and have all her memories, but does that *make* her Jennifer? Even her teeth are the same.

"Do you remember that time that Mr. Otto hit me in class, and after class, you evaded the cameras to talk to me?" I investigate her memory.

She laughs, "I do. I studied the cameras for weeks to figure out the pattern."

"They changed all the cameras shortly after, too. Do you remember that?" I smile, reminiscing.

"Yeah, they were all wide-angle, so that was out of the picture," she chuckles, "What is this? An interview?"

"To be honest?" I think carefully what to say as to not offend her, "Yes. I just don't know if you're really her."

She scoffs, "Of course I'm not, why would anyone ever think that?"

"I'm sensing a little sarcasm," I say, knowing I made a wrong turn in this conversation.

"I *know* I'm not the original, but even still," she goes on, "I have the memories, and I have the habits; Like I still have to flip my fork in a circle before eating, which you gracefully used to criticize me for."

I laugh; I remember when I used to copy her during lunch at school. "I'm sorry," I finally admit, "I shouldn't've brought it up. Is it weird that there are so many clones?"

"A little," she says, "When I first woke up, there were only 2 of us, but that changed over time. They try to refine each generation of clone-hybrids."

I look around through the bars to see a bustling facility. Everything is so pristine and white, with many more clones and several Osheky milling about in their colorful clothing. There's a decently sized open space, with advanced machines and screens. Every single Osheky has runes on their face, but only a select few of the clones do.

I've seen a lot of female Osheky, just as abundant as the men. I haven't heard any of their voices, but from what I can tell, they're all just as strong. No Osheky will talk to me, but occasionally, they'll respond to Jennifer.

"Thirty-one?" I call out, hoping she'll hear me.

A clone stops just in my view, "If you're referring to 91-42-31, she is unavailable." The clone smiles again, with perfectly straight teeth. No face paint to be seen. Her hair is significantly shorter, around her jawline rather than past the shoulders. "I am 91-42-34, how may I assist you?"

The painkillers have worn off for the most part, so I'm feeling the pull of the healing wounds on my back. "How long are we supposed to be in here?"

"You're actually scheduled to meet with Madam Grenand later today," she informs me, "She'll decide ultimately what to do with you."

"Parading us through the city whilst simultaneously whipping us isn't enough?"

"Oh no!" she laughs, "She wants you, in particular, to die!" Her casual laugh is unsettling.

"Lakewell doesn't want to deal with the traitors himself?" I retort.

"No, he has much better things to do," she replies, before walking off.

Hours pass in silence, and I'm unable to rest with the pain from the laceration inflicted on my back. But when I begin to doze off, the bars covering the opening fall down into the ground, and two clones enter, placing a bucket with wheels down on the floor, specific to place it over the threshold of the room. "Please stand in the bucket," one of the clone says, a blue moon on her cheek.

"Why am I going to stand in the bucket?" I ask, confused on the subject of the bucket.

"Traditionally, lesser life forms are not permitted to touch anything that belongs to an Osheky, even the ground," she explains, "Though; this bucket will keep you from touching anything as long as you're diligent."

"Right, that whole thing," I remind myself, it's been so long since I've been in the city, it's rules are now foreign to me.

The blue moon clone comes closer and cuts through the leather cord that tie my hands to the wall, then leads me to the bucket, where I reluctantly step in. "Please keep your hands to yourself while we transport you."

I look over to see them leading Jennifer as well, with nothing but her bare feet and the clothes that they dressed us in. Blood stains her back, and she's still weak, barely able to walk with assistance. But why does she get to touch the sacred floor of the Osheky, and I have to stand in a bucket? I must remind myself that jealousy isn't going to get me anywhere.

"Why doesn't she have to be in a bucket, exactly?" my mind speaks out.

"91-42-01 is an Osheky clone-hybrid, and thus is not a lesser life form," Thirtry-four says with a creepy smile, "As are all 91-42 hybrid-clones."

They drag me along in my bucket through the room and out to a hallway. The walls of the hallway turn from white to stone: the inner wall. The structure of the walls have a tunnel leading from the center all the way out to the Wildlands and is in fact how we managed to reenter the city. There's a meeting room somewhere near the inner wall, and I'll guess that's where they're taking us.

We all take a turn into a door carved into the inner wall. As soon as the door opens, I see Madam Grenand, older and with a gray streak running into a hair bun. She's never been angrier, and she's always looked like there was a deer up her back.

⊣⊢⊙⊣⊢

I'm enthralled. "Did you miss me, *Diane*?" I ask, trying to push her over her edge. This is a battle, and I'm going to win it.

"In fact," she says, definitively, "Yes.

"You see, we are all cogs in a clock, and the hands do not tick without every *single*, tiny, most minute spring or gear."

The clone gestures I step out of the bucket and sit down on the chair. Both Jennifer and I sit down in the chairs opposite of a lone Madam Grenand. The two Osheky and the two clones stand at attention at the door.

"And tell me, what to do with us little gears and springs," I say, "Slot us back into the clock?"

"Oh, no!" she lets out a single laugh, "You've been replaced. But the servicing of the clock loosened the rest of the gears, and there's the ever so slightest give to the entire mechanism that's been quite a pain to keep in check."

The conversation falls silent. If I'm going down, I'm taking as many people with me; rest in peace Henry. "I'll break the clock." Grenand stands up and raises her hand to slap me, but I swiftly catch her hand and punch her straight in the nose, knocking her back in her chair. Blood starts leaking from her nose as she holds her face.

"Well?!" she shouts, I guess at the Osheky, "Do something for shit's sake!"

Thirty-four smiles wide, "The Osheky and Osheky hybrid-clones only answer to Sir Lakewell and Osheky government officials."

"Like Omuru," I remark, but that name makes her steaming. Jennifer is sitting very silent during all this, being very careful.

The door opens and the Osheky and clones stand aside. Omuru steps through the frame and smile, "Just like Omuru." He's in more normal-looking clothes compared to the other Osheky, and his skin is not painted.

"I hate you and your entire species!" Madam Grenand screams, pulling out a knife. I rush to one side of the room and Jennifer to the other.

"Attack me, and you'll unleash the full wrath of the Osheky People upon yourself," he states, but she doesn't back down. He steps, slowly to her. She strikes, but he just catches the blade in his hand, dripping black blood on the ground. With the other hand, he grabs her throat and lifts her to eye level.

"Kill me, and—" her voice become weak as he squeezes, "You'll be —smitten down by—the—"

I see her blood flowing from her eyes now too, and *CRACK!* Her arms fall to her side, and she's dead. "I hate this thing," Omuru says, "91-42, how have you been?" Omuru drops the body and turns to her.

"My back definitely hurts,"

"Ah, yes, I heard," he turns to me, "Scott, my friend. How is *your* back?"

Never once has he ever called me that; he's up to something. "Fine, I guess."

He turns to the other Osheky, "I've been demoted, as you've probably heard, which means I'm no longer an Osheky and barred from entering into the inner ring."

Thirty-four smiles, "This is correct."

"And now that I'm an Oshekai, my dealings are no longer of interest of the Osheky."

"This is correct."

"Good, then let me take these two to the outer ring," he smiles, holding out his hands for us. I slowly walk towards him and see Jennifer already cowering behind him.

"Very well," Thirty-four opens the door, and we just walk out. We walk further to the outer ring. Omuru flips around the knife and slides it into his pants.

⊷ ⊙ ⊶

At least I'm not in a bucket, nor tied to a metal beam being whipped to death. "Omuru, what are you planning," I demand.

"Nothing you need to know about, Scott," he barks back, "Everything is going accordingly to plan. I've *finally* become free from Osheky, and I'm going free you of Lakewell."

We almost get under the open sky once more. The inner ring is much cleaner and kempt than the outer ring. And this tunnel is the most pristine part of the city. The government office is close, though, if I remember correctly. My back is screaming from trying to keep up with Omuru's pace.

People lingering in the tunnel stop and cover their eyes as we walk by, the people are in the dark. He stops at a particular door, made of glass. Omuru rams his fist through the pane, shattering the inch-thick glass into tiny pieces. "Follow," he tells us.

"You're going to kill Lakewell, aren't you?" Jennifer says, and I notice her crying, "Can't you think of other ways than killing people?"

"No, Jennifer, it's what Osheky were born to do. *We* are born as tools of war, and when that terrible war was over, we became bored, and tired of being ruled over.

"So we created the Mystic, stepping through to a fresh world to be rulers ourselves. But I am tired of this; I have become Oshekai, an outcast free to do as I please, free from the world." I see it in his eyes, he's bloodthirsty, but in control.

The hallway leads into a building I've never learned about, Sir Lakewell's main residence that he rarely leaves. He does all his legislation and leadership from here.

The people inside stop and cover their eyes, letting us walk right in. the open space has a chamber made of glass on the second level, where I see our great leader. "Lakewell!" Omuru shouts, so loud it feels like my body is vibrating.

Lakewell turns from his view to us, stopping his entire meeting. The inside of this building is made of clean white walls and floor, with glass all around.

Omuru takes the knife and launches it right at Sir Lakewell, not sparing any strength. It pierces through the glass, missing Lakewell by a hair. He turns and leaves the room. "He's coming," Omuru whispers.

Shortly after, Sir Lakewell appears coming from a door on the other side of the complex. "Leave us," he says, just loud enough to echo, and every soul scatters and runs off as fast as they can.

He comes within talking distance, "Jennifer, How are you feeling?"

Jennifer cowers behind Omuru like a child, but I'm not afraid. I scan him up and down, and I see a sword: the legendary sword of the Lakewell lineage. "I'm not afraid of you," I stand my ground, moving past the pain, and maybe tearing my wounds back open, readying my fists. The natives outside the wall taught me to fight, mostly against prey, but fight regardless.

Lakewell twitches his head, "Scott, is it? I don't expect you to be afraid. I expect you to be *terrified*, quivering in the mud, awaiting slaughter. But you're not, and that is foolish."

Omuru pushes me back, "I am afraid of *nothing*, not even your blade."

"It's time for a history lesson, children," Lakewell rests his hand on the sword, "In civilizations past, there was a concept called IQ, and the most brilliant minds barely broke 200 on the scale. I have a score of 376, and my entire lineage is as such.

"Do you know why the Osheky continually contract with my lineage? It's because *we* are the pinnacle of humanity, the summit of the mountain."

"And yet, here you three stand before me, unafraid and unmoving, and for what? The concept of freedom?"

"The 91-42 clone-hybrid project produces finer stalk than you ever could," Omuru states, "You are my last obstacle."

"You'd strike me down, but then what, Omuru? There'll just be another to take my place, and you'll have to strike them down too. But yet another will take their place; do you see the pattern?"

"You may be an Oshekai now, but you are still very much under contract with my forefathers. In fact, don't you remember the one who basically enslaved your race?"

"I do," Omuru says, "I remember he was the only one of you to outsmart even us."

By now the complex has been evacuated, and we're all alone. "You'll have to fight for the rest of your now shortened life, just to taste true freedom."

In an instant, Lakewell draws the sword, cutting through Omuru's clothing, revealing a backdrop of scars and a gaping laceration of black substance. "Your fighting skills are no match for mine," Lakewell states, dropping into a fighting stance.

⊷⊙⊶

Omuru just marches on, Lakewell strikes again, black blood dripping on the ground. Lakewell loses it, "How dare you bleed on my sacred soil!"

The sword thrusts forward, nut Omuru holds out his hand, getting pierced through with the now equally blackened metal. Omuru, with his other hand, grabs Lakewell by the throat. Jennifer rushes to pull the sword out, leaking more blood on the ground.

"Where is this contract my past people made with your forefathers?" Omuru whispers, "It must be your most guarded asset, your most sacred treasure, *or* the most obvious secret one could hold."

Jennifer is in awe of the blade, holding it as she backs away from the two. I rush to her side, eyeing the sword. The most guarded relic in history.

But she loses it too, striking the ground with the sword, hard. The metal rings out like a bell. Lakewell hears, wrapping his legs around Omuru's arm and *SNAP!* Omuru's arm breaks, dropping him. Thinking fast, the culprit begins to rush us, but Omuru wipes his blood over his face, stopping him instantly.

"The *filth*," Lakewell grits through his teeth, but he begins again to run towards us.

I swipe the sword and swing it at Lakewell, "You think that's filth? What about your entire legacy?"

I swing again, but he dodges. I go back and forth, trying to land a strike, driving him back. And he stops suddenly, Omuru behind him. I swipe the sword through his neck, and Lakewell falls to the ground.

"Give me the sword," Omuru demands; holding out his hand, "I'll shatter this contract between us before his very eyes!"

I give up the sword, and Omuru snaps the blade in half, the metal slowly cracking apart and falling to the ground. "No," I hear Lakewell whisper in his dying breath.

"Father?" a child's voice echoes in the empty room.

"Your father is dead, I killed him," Omuru announces to the young man, "He's a traitor, a liar, a thief; he's a long line of terrors upon his people, and ends with *you*."

"No," the boy says, "My father was a great man—"

"Your father only spawns evil," Omuru begins to walk towards him, but falters and falls to the ground, his black blood slowly pooling around him. But he continues to crawl forward.

"Omuru, I forbid you from touching that boy!" Jennifer cries out, "I'm sick of people dying!" She falls to her knees, crying. Omuru stops in his path, and the boy runs off further into the complex.

The sky is orange from the sunset that I was gifted enough to see in my lifetime. Am I free, free from this civilization? *What's going to happen next,* I think to myself.

Things went on. We waited until the people came back; people just came in and cleaned up the body. They put Omuru on a stretcher and took him away, Thirty-four came with another clone, and they told us to come with them and wait for further instruction.

They escorted us back through the inner wall, no bucket this time. They brought us into a room where we were given Osheky-like clothes and on the way out, Thirty-four painted something on my face. Jennifer in hand, they led us to an empty home and told us just to 'await further instruction.'

They told us Omuru was receiving medical care. After weeks of being inside this home we received a letter, written in Osheky language, detailing that we were to remain in their care/custody and that the contract that bound them to Lakewell was broken after over a hundred years, and the Osheky government decided to give us Osheky titles. It also detailed that the research of the Mystic made a breakthrough, giving them a chance to close the Mystic and open up this city to the rest of the world, which the state of is unknown.

Life isn't perfect here, but I'm with the one I love and that's going to be enough for me, after all this time. And maybe if we wait long enough, we'd be able to see what the rest of the world is like.

# The Keeper

W

HO ART thou, to save me from such a horror in the night. I ran into the mist away from my captors. When I fell to my knees in deep exhaustion, I looked upon thee to see two knights, readying to save a fair maiden. Alas, one swept me up and the other drew his sword upon the heathen monsters who drink the blood of innocents.

They drove them away, and I was brought to town, given board at an inn. The two brave knights hid me in the day, but they did not know my newfound curse would renew my strength. When he who carried me thus removed his helm, he was fair.

The night came and the moon replenished my body. With vigor, I rose in the moonlight and a rage came upon me, and I was powerless to stop myself. My fingers turned to that of a monster and my senses were heightened, but I was trapped, my mind in the body of a beast.

I struck the fair knight down in a savage moment, ending his very life. His brother came and I struck him down too and drank their blood. When I aroused my faculties, I was drowned in guilt and fled back into the forest. Though my strength failed me again, and I became afaced with my captor once more.

He outreached his hand and said, "You have become a sinner, for killing another is the greatest sin of all. Come with me, and we shall live forever, away from the judgment of the divine!" I had no choice but to return with him.

# Legend of The Sands

✦◎✦

I KNEAD the dough back and forth, readying it to be set aside to rise. My dear sister is playing with her doll at the table waiting for the bread to be made. "Jin," my mother addresses me, "go invite the neighbors for supper."

"Yes, mother," I say, abandoning the bread and rinsing my hands.

I dry them with a cloth and begin on my way. Sand is still blowing with the summer wind. It's blowing a little too much for me to see, so I shut the door, and pick up my late father's invention. Something he called 'glass'. It's almost as if you trapped the air you breathe into a rock.

I place the item over my eyes and prepare to brave the elements. Sand starts pouring over me as I make my steps outside. I make my way along this path I've walked countless times.

I twist and turn between the buildings until I'm sure I've arrived. This storm is worse than normal, and I'm positive my mother is arranging me a marriage with this family's daughter. It's obvious that I'll have to remain in their home for several hours until the storm eases.

I knock on their door, and wait for someone to answer. Moments pass and I hear a knock from the other side: the neighbor's daughter trying to be playful while I'm being beaten to death by wind and sand.

"Just let me in, Kiv!" I shout over the wind, before the door opens and I fall through, into a pile of leftover sand at the base of the door.

Kiv pulls me through the door to keep more sand from collecting inside their house. I pull off the glass from my eyes and empty what's collected inside.

"Let me guess, your mother would like us over for dinner, again?" she asks, standing over me.

She helps me to my feet, and I brush off my tunic. "As a matter of fact, yes."

"*Well,*" she fiddles her fingers, "You'll have to stay until the storm dies down."

"Yes, yes," I bow to her parents in respect, "I'm sure that's what my mother had in mind."

I set the glass on the table by the door and give her a hug. "So the storm is fairly bad, huh?" her father asks.

"I thought one of the local masters would've done something already."

"They're all lazy, new, or gone off somewhere else," he replies, offering both of us a seat at the table.

We both sit down, and Kiv leans on my shoulder, not at all hiding her apparent affection for me, while I look in the other direction.

"How's your mother, Jin?" their mother asks.

"She's busy at the market," I say, "She and I will probably have to leave early in the morning to help clear sand from the streets."

"You're a good son," the father tells me, "I hope one day my daughter is as successful as your mother."

"Thank you."

"Perhaps a game of backgammon, while we wait?" he proposes, standing up and going to the shelf.

"My father's gotten better since you two last played," Kiv tells me.

"Is that so?" I ask, "My father was the best, and he taught me well."

"Yes, he was," the father agrees with me, walking back with the game board.

We set up the board and we start playing. Kiv stares deeply at the game as we play, and hours pass until the storm finally dies down. We play two games and I win both; by the time the second game comes to an end, I can no longer hear the wind blowing against the door, and we get ready to walk back to my mother's home.

Sand has piled up against every wall, at every doorstep and in every corner of the city. My footsteps are labored as we trudge through the mounds of sand that had collected in the streets.

The wind is still blowing lightly, but no longer has sand going along with it. Mother's bread should have finished baking by now. We twist and turn through the streets, already seeing the townspeople beginning cleaning, packing sand in buckets and setting them to the side for the local masters to get rid of later.

The sun is almost at the horizon, about three fingers from setting. We arrive at home. I lead them inside, just in time to see the bread taken fresh out of the furnace.

Kiv makes a sound of excitement as I close the door behind them, pushing the sand to and fro. My mother sends the loaves to the table and my dear sister stares intently at them, eager to consume them. We all sit down and pray over the meal, and begin to eat.

⫷ ⊙ ⫸

The asses are fully loaded with sand to be taken out to the desert. I've been working all day, alongside the other men moving the collected sand somewhere else. None of the masters are helping us, which is unusual. The markets are working as intended throughout the day, trading labor and food.

I stretch my back to relieve all the tension built up from the day's labor. "Where're the sorcerers when you need them, ammiright?" somebody says, tapping me on the back.

"I heard they were out hunting beasts," another says.

"It's not like they tell anyone, 'em bastards."

The rider starts leading the asses out of town. I stretch one more time before thinking of heading home, but the rider tugs me along as he goes, "Come on, everyone pays their dues."

I hop on the cart and go for a ride all the way out of town. The sun sets for the day as we reach the destination. Bucket by bucket, we toss the sand out to the side.

"Jin, right? You're Salek's boy," the man asks, "You're a strong, strapping, young man."

"Thank you," I say as I pour out another wooden bucket over the side of the cart.

"I'm Mil," he introduces himself, moving more sand to the pile, "I used to gamble with your father back when we lived in the capital."

"Really? I didn't know he used to live out there."

"Yeah," he sets the bucket down, stretching his back, "We were teenagers back then."

"Small world."

Mil turns around looking out into the night. "I reckon the masters are back."

I move a little to look off into the distance and see a faint glow working towards us. But I keep on with the sand, moving back and forth with the wooden buckets.

Not long after, the caravan of masters arrives on foot. "Here say!" the leader shouts, stopping all of them right beside us. Some of them lift their heads and open their eyes.

"You missed the storm," Mil tells them, "*And* the cleanup."

"I apologize, but we were summoned by the King to the capital," the leader explains. Cold wind begins to blow down from the north.

I look to see that the masters are walking on a stone path, the sand being transformed underneath their feet. "You, boy!" the leader calls out to me, "I see you've been helping with the recovery from the storm. For that, I thank you."

"Yeah, it's no problem," I reply.

"Perhaps, one day, you can study with us," he offers.

But I remember my father was partial against the masters. He didn't talk much about it, but he believed they were only serving the King and not the people. "I'll be alright, thank you."

We bow to each other and continue on their journey back to town. We toil away until all the sand is piled up in a mound outside the town. I stack all the buckets and lay down on the cart, finally resting from the day's labor. We start our way back and I start counting the stars, the smear of beauty stretching from one end of the heavens to the other.

We finally arrive back in town, and everyone is gone, the streets vacant and some homes are being lit by oil. I say farewell to the man and hop off the cart, walking home on my tired feet.

I knock on the door, not seeing any light shining through from the cracks. Finally, the door pushes open, revealing my dear sister opening the door for me. I walk in and fiddle with her hair before lying down on the ground to rest for the night.

I drift off into a dream. I find myself in a field of flowers as far as the eye can see. The aroma is pleasant and the view is incredible. The flowers are colors of every kind, organized in delicate rows.

The sky is blue, and the weather, for once, is temperate. I begin walking through the rows of flowers and pick one. As I inspect it, it's nothing like I've ever seen growing in the desert. I look up from the flower and see a woman, her skin white as the clouds, with hair like pure sand. She looks at me, and I see her eyes, blue like the sky. Her clothes are elaborate layers of cut leather and blue fabric. What a sight to behold, someone so different from me.

I wake up from this dream, looking at the ceiling of my home. I'm greeted with the familiar heat of the desert. When I sit up, I notice on the back of my hands, magical markings drawn on them with soot or something else. One of the masters must have cast this on me during our meeting. I wipe them off on my clothes and continue on with my day.

⊰⊙⊱

My side job today lets me go for the day, toiling in the fields where we grow our food. I've been uncovering the troughs and irrigation ditches from the sand brought by the storm, preparing them for the masters to come and summon water from the well.

My employer tosses me a piece of copper as payment for the day. I wipe the sweat from my brow and set the tools aside, going on my merry way. The town is busy, people trading food and goods. It's a small town, and I'm afraid I'll never get to leave and see what that wonderful landscape I dreamt about is.

I slip the copper into my bag and walk about the city, looking to see if there's anything else I can do for more money. The thought crosses my mind to visit the monastery. It was built to found the town and annex another town into the kingdom.

I find myself wandering down the path to the monastery. I do find it, and it's the first time I've been this close to it. It's made of sandstone forged by the masters themselves, constructing the building right out of the surrounding desert.

I walk around to find the entrance and see there is no door, but the main chamber beyond is empty. "Hello?" I ask aloud, walking into the chamber and crossing the threshold.

The moment my foot contacts the tiles constructing the floor of the monastery, people appear before me from nothing, walking busily about carrying scrolls and books back and forth.

One of them stops for me, turning and saying, "What can I help you with?"

I stop and think, "I was wondering if you could give me a location from one of my dreams?"

"Follow me, if you will." he motions for me, and I follow him through the crowd of people. I never thought there were this many people studying within the monastery.

"I didn't know there were so many people here," I say.

He responds, "Most of the people you see are spells cast from those in practice."

He leads me through a doorway without a door with decorative tiles, creating a geometric pattern on the floor. I notice faint markings of ash on the ground and the walls. "Please, sit," he motions to the floor. The man sets his books and scrolls on the shelf and sits down across from me.

He pulls out a small piece of papyrus, and in a whisper and an instant, it bursts into flames. The ashes fall down in a seemingly random fashion but collect in a circular pattern with markings going in strange tangents. It's incredible.

"Tell me about this dream," he asks.

I tell him about what I saw: the endless flower fields flowing with rivers of color, and the woman with skin as the clouds, hair as the sand, and eyes of the sky with her blue clothing. "When I awoke, I saw patterns such as these on the back of my hands," I tell him, pointing to the ash on the ground.

"Where were you when you fell aslumber?" he asks.

"I was working to clear out the sand from the storm, and a group of masters was returning from the capital."

"I see, one of them must have cast this spell on you." He leans down, placing both hands on either side of this circle and whispers something to it. When he raises his head, he reaches over and touches my forehead. I begin to dream the dream once more, seeing the fields and the woman.

When we arrive back to wakefulness, I see him open his eyes and lean back. "I'm afraid I've read of no such place, not in our library nor the capital's."

"I see," I stand back up, and put my back over my shoulder.

"But people like that do exist," he tells me, "far beyond the desert."

"Have you ever seen somebody like that?" I ask as we walk together towards the exit of the monastery.

"No, I'm afraid not," he replies, seeing me off as I walk out. I step passed the threshold of the spell and all the people inside disappear from view. I make my way home to clean before my mother returns.

⊶⊙⊷

As I'm walking down the street, some merchants come riding into the city on camels, carrying goods originating from all over. They carry scrolls from other desert settlements, fabrics from faraway places, and other miscellaneous items from all over the desert and beyond.

I wave to the traveler, gowned in a cloth covering his face. He raises his hand in return and stops his camel. "Do you wish to buy something?"

"Depends," I say, "Do you have anything from beyond the desert?"

"I have metal from a place called Egyptus, and scrolls from a traveler who came from the east," he tells me, "And trinkets collected from the ocean."

Kiv comes walking up, probably coming from her day's worth of working. "May I see these ocean trinkets?"

The traveler reaches into one of his many bags and pulls out an oddly shaped object, pink in color and ridges forming the main portion. "It's a remnant of a creature that lives in the ocean."

"How much do you want for it?"

"What do you use in this city? Copper, yes?"

"Yes," Kiv, rummages through her satchel and pulls out a few pieces of money, "This is all I have."

"Give me two of the small ones and it's yours."

Kiv gladly hands him the money, and she takes the item, kissing it and placing it in her satchel. She turns to me and waves as the camel continues on its way further into the town, maybe to the monastery. She hops over to me and wraps herself around my arm to publicly claim me amongst the townspeople, not that there's much competition here.

"Walk with me, Jin," she demands.

"Where to?" I ask, going along with it.

"Can't we just admire the sky and the earth?"

"There's not a cloud in the sky, and we're surrounded by sand," I retort as she pulls me along.

"It's all there is, as far as the world extends is sand and sky; forever."

"I had a dream, Kiv," I begin, "of a faraway land with rivers of flowers and people with skin white as the clouds."

"Somewhere like that doesn't exist, Jin," she pats my chest, "The desert gives life to all, and therefore all is desert."

"And what about the ocean?" I ask. We turn a corner to view the setting sun.

"Father says the ocean lies on top of a desert made especially for the creatures of the sea. The desert extends even to Egyptus and beyond the capital," she says, "But one can dream."

She stops me and looks at the red sky painted each night by the setting sun, before kissing my cheek and running off to her home.

I take my time watching the setting sun, as the sky goes from red to purple to black, with stars dotting the heavens. Finally, once the sun is gone, I go home and rest for the night.

◂▸ ⊙ ◂▸

Rains are pouring down, a gift from the gods during this scorching season. All the townspeople are setting out barrels to collect it. I step out of the house and feel the gentle drops falling onto my face. Some of the children are dancing in it.

I look to my left and see a group of masters, swords in hand, heading to the desert. "Where are you going?" I call out.

"We were scrying, when it was revealed to us that beasts are wandering too close during this rain," the leader replies, marching on.

"What kind of beasts?" I persist.

"The great desert wolf!" he incants, being repeated by the others, "Will you come with us boy? Come and earn a title for yourself?"

One of them tosses me a sword, beckoning me to join them. "Why not?" I ask myself, marching along with them, thinking to myself I might get to see some battle magic in action instead of just in stories.

The rains begin to lighten as we leave the city. The pathway begins turning to stone, one step at a time as the masters march further and further.

Sunlight begins to peep from the clouds as the town goes from view. "I sense the beasts," someone alerts us. I ready my sword, cautious now of my surroundings. The wind begins to blow harder, and a vortex begins churning, casting sand up and around.

The sounds of steps in the sand grow loud as a small pack of desert wolves advance towards us. "Momr Kai!" a master shouts, and a bolt of lightning flashes before me, striking one of the beasts. But it stands strong with the shape of lightning sintered on its fur.

The beasts are large, hunched wolves, the color of their fur the same as the desert sand. Black markings draw themselves along the backs of the wolves. A wolf barks, casting a wave of air at the group. A master holds out his hand and sends another wave of air back to negate the attack.

The animals begin running about, swirling more air and sand in a vortex. My visibility is gone, but I'm staying sharp. I swipe my sword through the wind, back and forth, thinking there's something there, but hitting nothing.

The wind picks up, and I begin to be buried from my feet. With my young reflexes, I see the wolf pouncing at me, swipe my sword at it, and remove its right ear. But it's too late, it feels like I'm sinking down into the desert. The sand begins to swallow me whole, grabbing hold of my arms and pulling them down. Finally... black.

I cough myself awake, expelling some sand that collected in my mouth. I'm definitely buried up to my chin, my mouth barely uncovered for air, and I can still feel my sword in my grip. I wiggle my head back and forth to free it from the sand.

The sky is blue as far as the eye can see, empty and void of anything but the sun. I pull my unoccupied arm with all my might, slowly freeing it from the burial.

I get my arm free and pull myself up a little to look around, not immediately recognizing the dunes from the previous day of fighting. Tirelessly I shovel sand away with my loose hand, slowly freeing myself from the desert's grasp.

"The sun," I begin panting, starting to feel the heat. I feel around for my bag. Frantically, I start digging into the sand, looking for it. I spend hours expanding the hole I was trapped in, but I don't find it.

I already feel weak from the sun's power, but it nears the horizon. Giving up on the bag, and the possessions I had inside, I begin walking westward, towards town. I walk for hours into the night.

But nothing, I find nothing. No stone trails made by traveling masters, no glow of civilization. Just the blackness of the night and the stars in the sky. I finally fall to my knees, exhausted and overheating.

"Are you aware of the wolf that's been trailing you?" I hear an old man say to me. I must be hallucinating from dehydration. "You may want to tame the beast before he consumes you."

I turn to see a man sitting on a stone by a fire, but I fall on my chest in doing so. I hear the footsteps of the man coming closer. He turns me over to my back, and I see now he's real. How could I have missed him on my journey?

◀◀ ⊙ ▶▶

He brings a water bladder to my lips and allows me to drink of it, bringing me back from my collapse. "Who-who are you?" I manage to say.

"That is of no worth to you," he helps me to my feet. He magically raises another stone from the ground, constructed of the sand, for me to sit on with him.

"Where are we?" I ask him, "I was in a battle, and I was swallowed up in a storm." I get a good look at the man in the light of the fire. He wears a whip and a blade on the same hip. It's of gray metal, unlike copper we use for money, and the metal from Egyptus.

"*You* seem to be lost in the desert," he says, "*I* am traveling to a certain somewhere."

"Where is the capital, do you know?" I ask him.

"It's a very distant place."

"Where are you traveling?"

He scratches while thinking, "I seek a place known as the *Eternal Storm.*"

"I've never heard of something like that," I confess, "May I travel with you?"

"You might be exactly who I was looking for," he says, "I am tasked with finding champions to save worlds beyond number from certain devastation."

"I am no champion; I'm just the son of a widow."

"And the last one I had chosen was a farmer," he chuckles, "Heroism finds a way in all. Tell me, have you heard the Legend of Obadiah?"

"No, I've never heard of such a legend."

"This is a tale from long ago, as told by my people, passed down from generation to generation, and now I am here to recount it to you. It is one of the many legends of the desert. Are you ready?"

"Yes, I am ready," I reply

"It started in one of the earliest settlements of the desert," he continues on to recount the legend of a master who pioneered the desert, creating the hidden village. He fought valiantly, losing his life to battle with the corrupt king Malik.

"And what then happened to Obadiah?" I ask him, knowing such a powerful master must've not met his final end.

"Thus the legend continues; some say the desert resurrected him from that cavern's grave he rested in," he holds up his finger, "After that battle, their resting place was known as the Grave of Two Masters."

"The Grave of Two Masters?"

"Yes; the catacombs of the ancients." he continues on, telling me how this great master woke with one less arm, and he spent years trying to relearn all that he knew, being chosen once more by this 'Hakim' person.

"Obadiah encountered the Eternal Storm and sought his foe."

"The Eternal Storm?" I inquire.

"This foe summoned a storm from another world to hide himself, building a massive monument to threaten the entire desert."

I've heard of a monument hidden by a storm, "The Hall of Sahar?" he recounts the glorious battle between the three powers, Obadiah, Hakim, and Sahar.

"Some say he's still there, meditating inside the eternal storm amongst the mirrors," he tells me.

"He never left?"

He rubs his face, blowing into them to warm up, "No one really knows."

"Is there any more to this legend?" I insist, invested in the story.

"For now? No," he confesses, "But there is need for another champion, to go inside this eternal storm with me and finally put the enemy and hero to rest.

"You see? Their souls are still trapped inside the storm and I *must* do the hero a favor and free his soul, as my master commands."

The sun begins to paint the sky a different color as it begins its journey up above the horizon. Then I remember the wolf he said that was following me. "What was your name again?" I try to remember.

"My name is Abd al Hakim, servant of the wise," he tells me.

"That's impossible—" I become confused, "That would make you —"

"I'm immortal," he cuts me off, "I serve the gods, and they granted me eternal life to carry out their will."

"I don't understand," I confess, confused by the whole proposition.

He puts his finger on his lips, telling me to stay quiet. Quickly, he rushes around and throws his sword, and I realize it's attached to the end of his whip. It cracks and echoes between the dunes, followed by the whimpers of the wolf.

Step by step, he pulls the animals along from the sand, revealing the beast trapped in a cage of leather. The beast is dragged along all the way to the smoldering fire.

The beast is familiar, the missing ear I removed with my sword. "It would be helpful if you were to tame it."

⊷⊙⊶

He trained me, day after day, year after year. I continually compounded my knowledge, becoming a master in my own right, outside the standardized training of the king's order. I learned battle magic as well as defensive spells. I mastered the art of turning sand to stone first.

After years of mastery, wandering in the desert with no end in sight; alongside my training, I became the master of this great desert wolf; it began to obey my every command.

I began to believe this desert really was infinite, traveling and learning in it after eight years. Finding an oasis was a gift among many. One day, I was practicing spells, and my dream from long ago enters my mind. "Hakim?" I ask, as he summons more water from the air into his waterskin, "Is there a place where there are rivers of flowers of every color, and where people have the skin of the clouds, hair as the sand, and eyes of the sky. Where they wear blue clothing?"

"Yes," he tells me, finally confirming my dream, "But you could never go there."

"Why?" my heart drops.

"Because it doesn't exist yet," he drinks out if the bladder, "it exists thousands of years from now."

"Then how do you know about it?"

"I'm immortal, and a servant to the gods," he gently chides me, "I've seen and learned things beyond mortal knowledge."

"Now, our destination lies ahead in tomorrow's journey."

I beckon my pet to me and rub his face, before we begin our travels once more. I wonder how many travels along these pathways we've made in our eight years of journey, yet we've not come across any other pathways. We travel the whole day long.

◀◀ ⊙ ▶▶

The eternal storm is here, a vortex so great it swallows up the desert and raises the sand to the sky. "It's grown strong since I was last here," Hakim tells me, "You must summon a shield of stone to protect you from the wind; if you do not, you will suffer a thousand cuts and die."

I push my hands together and summon stone from the sand. It begins to grow around me and my great desert wolf. I pull him close as we're encased in rock. I put one of my hands forward and the stone begins to move along with my hand.

We begin our travel into the storm. The sound of small particulates smashing against my barrier envelopes us. The bombardment becomes strong and stronger, going from sand to pebbles. My breathing becomes labored, but I must go on. Suddenly, something big crashes into my stone barrier, cracking it.

Another large stone crashes into my barrier, and it begins to split, with a piece on my right fracturing away, revealing the storm blowing around me. Sand begins to pour in; I look up through the hole and see the heavens overwritten anew, the blue sky and sun being eaten away by a new set of stars and single celestial body overhead.

We make it all the way through to the eye of the storm. My stone barrier falls away, revealing the landscape: a place utterly stripped of sand, a mass of black stone stretching across the entire storm's eye.

"What's wrong with the sky?" I try to say over the wind.

"The storm has worn the barrier between worlds thin," he replies, drawing his weapon from his hip.

I look around to see eroded ruins of two structures. All returns to the desert eventually. I walk further into the ruins. I see the decorative walls, painstakingly carved by the hands of an ancient people, fallen to the ground. There's what appears to be a shrine, worn away to a barely recognizable state, surrounded by an ancient fountain.

And atop the ruins of the ancient Janubii monastery is the monument built by Sahar, with a scar going across the entire landscape. But even that too has been eroded by the storm.

My foot hits something, and I look to see the bones of a man cut perfectly in half. I take a step back and see his remains line up with the scar cutting the monument down.

"I remember this battle," Hakim says.

I allow the barrier that protected our passage here to dissolve and swim to my feet. From the sand, I summon a mace made of stone to use alongside my blade.

The bones of Sahar begin to rattle, the two halves rising to their feet. I feel a dark force dawn on me, seeing the spirit of Sahar gliding through the air to possess the bones. "Have you come to finish the job?!" the dark voice shouts.

Hakim's whip cracks, shattering the skull of the bones with the blade, quickly snapping it back. The pieces fall once more, but remain cracked in all places. Sahar turns to face Hakim and says, "I will escape this storm with your body!"

"My body is a temple, and agents of Death are not welcome!" he shouts, whipping the skulls of other skeletons before they can rise. I swipe my sword and a thin structure of sand travels out, slicing the ghostly being in two.

But the two halves reconnect and turn to face me. "A new champion of yours?" he whispers. Claws begin growing from the fingertips as it approaches. It comes upon me, and I swing up the mace, smashing the bones apart, and then run off before they reform.

I arrange all the sand around the reforming bones and bar it inside a trap. We both begin chanting the same incantation, drawing runes and circles on the sand trap. Symbols and markings burn themselves into the stone, but not before the spirit of Sahar tries to escape.

It's too late for him; the trap is complete as his torso becomes locked in place on the surface of this trap. He struggles but is trapped as long as the runes remain intact, which as a disembodied spirit halfway trapped in stone, he won't be able to do.

◄◄ ⊙ ►►

"Allow us to explore these ruins a little," Hakim pulls out a small yellow trinket, "I must locate Obadiah's body."

"Yes," we start our journey through the ruins. The closer we go, the more deterioration of the surroundings we find. With the sand stripped from underneath, everything crumbled.

I climb a pile of rubble and see a mummy, resting in meditation amongst a few, still standing mirrors. I call out to Hakim, saying, "I've found him!"

Hakim floats himself up to where I am, looking at the mummy. He holds out his yellow trinket and wanders around. I turn to admire the mirrors, some of them still intact. I see someone who isn't me looking back. I see someone oddly familiar, but whom I've never met.

In another mirror, I see my mother, and another I see Kiv, grown in these past years. I see other townspeople in all the mirrors. "What do you see in the mirrors?" he asks.

"I see the townspeople from my home," I reply, seeing the figures copy my every move. "What do you see?"

"I see the pantheon of guardians that employ me to do their bidding," he confesses, still wandering around the room, "Including Death."

"What are these mirrors originally used for?" I ask.

He stops, beginning to incant, and for a brief moment I see a man walking towards him before disappearing. When he stops he turns to me, "Mirrors were used for a multitude of purposes, they had many for the many masters who would study them."

"Who was that man?"

"Obadiah's soul," he slips the trinket into his pocket, "I was instructed to retrieve it."

"Shouldn't you trap Sahar's soul too?" I retort.

"I only have one soul-catcher, and they're notoriously hard to make here," he starts walking the other way, "What do you think we should do with this place?"

"I don't know," I stop to think, about the places that once stood here, "Perhaps we should allow Janubii to become once more?"

"That's quite the idea," he jumps down from the mirror room.

I also jump down and follow Hakim. We walk all the way to the struggling spirit of Sahar. "What should we do with this?" he says, "You'd like to allow this place to be once more, then we should release the eternal storm, and allow the reaper to handle him.

"Incant with me."

He tosses me a scroll, which unravels as it flies through the air. I catch the scroll and read the words, committing the words to memory. I place my hands and fingers in the right orientation, and we start our incantations. The wind howls and becomes chaotic in pattern. Runes and other markings begin burning into the surrounding rock, creating a massive spell. The sky begins to change from the black to the familiar blue.

Finally, in a burst of power, the storm stops and sand begins to fall back down as rain. The ground level begins to rise, and soon is up to my knees. The cool sand is pleasant on my legs, but I work my way out.

"Well," Hakim begins to say, "I suppose you've done all I've asked of you, perhaps you should go back home."

"One thing left." I say, going back to the mirror room. The sand has created a place to walk instead of climbing, so I traipse along the inclined pile of sand.

I put my hands together and begin incanting, taking the grains of the falling sand and organizing them into a spell surrounding the mummy of Obadiah.

The spell is prepared, I kneel down and place a finger on the circle, and cast the spell. A heavenly light begins consuming the mummy and rises like a serpent in the sky. The spell should last for 30 days and 30 nights, acting as a beacon to call for someone, anyone to resurrect this once ancient monastery.

"Now, I shall go home," I tell Hakim. I see him walking and I run after him. When I catch up to him, he points behind me.

"Oh, look," he says, "A camel for you to ride." I turn to see an animal that I know was not there before. I laugh at the old man's games. "Goodbye, Jin. Thank you."

I go to pat him on the back, but I find he's no longer here. He left me yet another gift. I mount the animal and go on my way, looking back at the beacon I've put in place.

◄◄ ⊙ ►►

I arrive in town, the camel taking a slow step onto the hard surfaces. As I walk down the streets, the people start seeing me, staring and gasping. "He's back, he's alive," I hear. I dismount the camel and look around at how little things have changed. There are some new children going about the streets, but all the vendors have remained the same.

I travel about, looking for the stall where my mother would work at, but I think it's moved. The young, familiar girl from the mirror walks up to me. "It's you," we both say, as she jumps forward to wrap her arms around me.

"Jin," she cries, burying her head into my chest. I have no choice but to embrace her back, "I thought you'd never come back!"

It dawns on me that this is my dear sister, all grown from my time away. "Where's mother," I ask.

"This way," she grabs my hand and starts pulling me and my camel along the streets, "Where have you been, Jin? You went out with the masters to fight the beasts and you never came back."

"I became lost in the desert, and I went on an adventure," I tell her, "A great adventure!"

She pulls me along to Kiv's house. My dear sister starts banging on the door while I fasten the camel's lead to the wall. The door finally opens, revealing a grown Kiv. We make immediate eye contact, and she marches up and slaps me.

"Where have you been?!" she shouts, "We've been worried sick for eight years!" But she just wells up in tears and embraces me, and I wrap my arms around her. I see my sister run inside and start telling everyone inside that I've come back.

We all sit down at their table and I tell them about my journey. It's a tall tale, and I don't expect them to believe all of it. Kiv, has already started wrapping herself around my arm, something I hadn't realized I missed so much. I do a little trick of fire to show them I really am a trained master now, to the surprise of my mother, who admitted that my father was against the monastery.

"I must return this sword to the monastery, I'm sure they've missed it," I say, leaving them and walking through these old streets to where the masters are.

I notice the spell that was once here to hide the occupants is gone, and I walk in. Somebody stops to talk to me and says, "What can we do for you?"

"I went to fight a pack of great desert wolves eight years ago, and became lost," I say, holding the sword out to give back, "I am now found and would like to return this blade to you."

"I see, you're Jin," he recognizes me, "We searched for you for days when you disappeared. I'm glad you're back." He takes the sword, and we bow to each other, parting ways.

I spent time with my family following my return. Kiv and I married and had a wonderful ceremony in the monastery. I promised her a life of adventure, and we set off to prove to ourselves the desert was not the only thing to see in our lifetime.

◀‖⊙‖▶

This camel has carried both of us beyond the expanse of the desert, up north where the flora has transformed from oasis to white mountains, where the ground itself is green with threads of life. Trees as I've never seen them, standing tall above the ground with three times the girth of the stem.

We've seen landscapes that only I could dream of, and it takes our breath away. The weather went from eternal heat to a cycle of warm and cold, where the water in collection would harden into glass and return to the water in the pattern of the skies.

We watched the stars move across the sky every night, revealing new dots in the heavens from the north. We stop at a group of people with skin as the clouds, hair as the desert sand and eyes of the sky. They look estranged at us, looking so different from them.

I arrange my hands in a triangle and whisper the spell of tongues. "Who are you, to look so different?" a man asks me. There aren't more than ten of them, wearing hide from animals.

"My name is Jin, and my companion Kiv," I tell them, looking down. "We are travelers coming from a land of sand as far as the eye can see, from the desert in the south."

"I've never heard of such a land," he says, "I've only seen forests and flowers."

"Then we have much to tell each other," I laugh, coming down from the camel, "Allow us to trade knowledge."

And we conversed for days, learning about one another. I taught them to grow crops, and they built a village of their own from the surrounding trees. He showed me a field of flowers of every color in a clearing between trees.

And most of all, I taught him magic. That was the last thing we conversed upon, then Kiv and I traveled once more, to the east where even more secrets lay. The world is in the palm of my hands, its secrets to be mine.

# Mr. Impossibility

⊷ ◎ ⊶

JUST ANOTHER day in this life. I close my eyes to see the other world. I haven't come up with a good name for it in all these years, but when I close my eyes, I see a world similar to this one. It's just people going about there days in a dim haze. They look just like me: two arms with hands and two legs with feet; two eyes and a nose, just like me.

I don't hear their world, and I can't read their lips, but they are just normal people living in a populated world. *My* world is desolate, and as far as I know, I'm the only one. I woke up one day, without a memory in my head, in an empty world. Thankfully, I don't *need* food or water, but it sure does taste good when I find a beverage that isn't bad.

I find things, devices leftover from someone, who left it here. My favorite device by far is a music player, and I find little cassettes to listen to. Sometimes, I just put on my favorite song and close my eyes and pretend I'm *in* the other world. The other world isn't all good though, I see people cry or get hurt by others; it's a terrible thing.

I wonder who's eyes I see through, and whether they see my world when they close their eyes? Questions for the afterlife I suppose. I wander this world, filled with abandoned buildings, stores, even skyscrapers, just like the otherworld. Sometimes they were brought down by some force of nature or weather; sometimes they're overgrown with flora. None of the amusement parks are in working condition, so I'll just sit down, strap into a roller coaster and close my eyes, hoping the person on the other side is doing something amusing.

There are some real kickers when it comes to music that these extinct people left around for me. I have a backpack full of cassettes, and I found a lunchbox that I can organize them in. I'll kick a ball just to see how far I can and look in a mirror and wonder, "Am I really the only one?"

The real fun is when I go to sleep at night and dream. It's the only time I can actually spend in another world, be it a fake, temporary aether in my mind. I'll dream of the animals I see in the other world, cats, dogs; one time, I saw them go to a zoo and I saw some incredible things.

But when I wake up, I forget most of it and go about my mundane life of wandering the wasteland. Maybe I'll find a genie, and he'll grant me a wish. He'll be like, "Ho, wishes three, choose with wisdom," and I'll be like, "I want to go to the other world, and that's all I want."

I remember one time, I stumbled into a library. The doors were locked and the windows were impossible to break, so I busted down that door after a whole day of trying, and what did I find? Books I could spend a lifetime reading.

I hurried to the history section, and I looked through the books to find the most recent thing, and with blistering anticipation, I opened to the first page, and it was scribble. Or maybe a language I just didn't know, but I tore through the next, and it was the same, and the next and the next. It was a total bust. I did find a map in there, but it wasn't any more helpful, because it didn't mark where I was.

And for this day, it comes to an end. I'll go to sleep, dream a dream and rise to see another day in this desolate world... Or will I? One can hope.

◄╫ ◉ ╫►

# My Life As A Vampire Part II

⊷ ◎ ⊶

"**H**EY, BRANDON!" I shout across this new house, hanging up the phone, "Chris and Linda want us over for dinner tonight!"

"Is Julie back from college already?" he asks, appearing in the doorway, "Time flies." He walks up to me and looks at the books by the phone I've been reading. "History books?"

"Yeah," I turn to him, ready to unleash the knowledge I've obtained, "Did you know tanks were invented in World War I?"

"Yes, Sarah," he laughs, "I was there."

"Tell me about it!" I get all starry-eyed, ready to have a first-hand account.

"Well," he trails off, "Erm... I was in England at the time." He pauses and averts his gaze.

"Yes?"

"I was drafted into the English military, fought a few battles," he pauses again, "I remember there was a tank, there was a battle. I was shot and paralyzed, when my American doctor friend bit me, and I was switched to a night platoon."

"And?" I get closer to him, trying to get him to give me more details.

"There were some more tanks, some planes, a lot of trenches; although, after the vampire thing, there were fewer trenches," he counts on his fingers, "A couple of years later, we won the war, and I went back to my family in America."

I sigh and sit back down in the phone chair. There are so many chairs at this house, and everything's brown and overly ornate. "For someone who was there, I'd expect more details."

"It was a long time ago," he persists, "And it was sort of traumatic for me, so I don't like to talk about it."

"But you use it to flirt with vampire girls?" I try to turn it on him, "Speaking of which, do you have vampire friends?"

"What do you mean?" he replies.

"Like when parents have *other* parent-friends?" I take the books I've finished and put them back on the shelf.

"I have a few friends, whom I suppose are also vampires," he trails off, "Goodness golly, look at the time!"

"What is it now?" I retort.

"We should get going to your host family," he said, looking at his bare wrist, but I just stare him down in disbelief. "What? It's a long drive. And I'm sure Julie would like to see you for a bit longer than dinner; she'll be lagged from the flight, so she'll probably sleep early."

"You're right," I lean over and kiss his cheek, "So, about these vampire friends?"

"Friends, erm, acquaintances," he leads me along to the foyer. Gerald has been given more time-off because I don't want to be accustomed to a wealthy, lazy lifestyle. I make Brandon drive more often.

"You don't have any friends—"

"Not true!" he flips off the lights to the room on the way out, "Gerald is my friend—"

"Ha! Gerald is an employee," I wrap myself in my jacket and grab my purse.

"I've known Gerald's family since 1951!" As we get to the main foyer, I see his family portrait at the base of the staircase, wondering where his family went to after all this time.

We both grab our umbrellas and walk out to the setting sun. The grass is starting to turn back to green after the cold winter. The spring flowers are also coming back to bloom. Among the books, I've been reading some gardening books; I'd like to start one.

⊷⊙⊶

The sun is down by the time we get Chris and Linda's. I still recognize their cars sitting in the driveway. I remember all the scents surrounding the house and every single tree on every plot. Brandon parks by the sidewalk and when I open the door, I smell pasta.

We walk all the way up and knock on the door, and I hear every little thing on the other side. The door opens and Linda on the other side. She jumps forward and hugs me, "I was expecting you guys later," she says, welcoming us in.

"Brandon wanted to leave early," I punch his arm, "to avoid my questions."

I see the three girls sitting at the table, Jule laying her head down on the tabletop. "Hey Sarah!" she says, her face smashed on her plate.

"Welcome home!" I sit down with them at the table. Linda goes back into the kitchen, and I realize I don't smell Christopher. "So, you got your degree?"

"Well, not yet," she lifts up her head, "I still need to apply for graduation, but I'm all finished." She raises her hands and yawns.

"And, Tina, you're starting college soon, too, yeah?" I ask, as the realization of how far I'm out of the loop with them hits me, "At the local college?"

"Yup," she gives me two thumbs up, "Full time in the fall."

Lila, I think is in high school. "How was school for you, Lila?"

"Fine," she says quickly, but stops right there.

"Sarah!" Jule grabs my attention once again, "flights are so cool!"

I turn to find Brandon going into the kitchen, "I know, but someone won't tell me about planes!"

"You're up so high, you're like a bird!" she lays back down, "Don't get me wrong, the train rides were super cool, but you can see the entire city!"

Linda comes out with the bowl of home-cooked food and Brandon sits down next to me. "Where's Chris?" I ask her.

"Working late," she replies, "They kept him late since he got there late." she sits down and everyone grabs hands. Brandon finally got used to the idea and manages to be in unison with us.

"Amen," we say.

Jule wakes up and wipes off her plate from the dirt from her face. The pasta is as good as I remember. "So what are you planning on next?" Brandon asks Jule.

"Well, currently, sleep," she laughs, "But I was thinking product design, something along those lines."

"That's a good business," he says, "After I went to school, in the 1920s mind you, I worked at a bank for a lot of years; the one I worked at had this huge mechanical calculator we would use. I think the exact one is in a museum now, but at the bank, I was in charge of designing banners and whatnot."

"Wow, that's legit," Jule says, stuffing her mouth.

"What about you two?" I ask the other girls.

Tina scratches her head to think, "I don't really know yet, I haven't declared a major. I really like my math class though."

Lila remains quiet, just eating her food. I hear a vehicle drive up the driveway and smell Christopher's cologne. The door opens and Chris rushes up to kiss the girls hello, then Linda. "Hey Sarah, Brandon," he works his way around to hug us, "Glad you guys are here." He sits down and starts serving himself. This smells like home, and I missed all this time without realizing it.

Chris suddenly stops and drops his fork on his plate, "Lila, stop giving us such a cold shoulder!" he puts his foot down.

"Whatever—"

"Not whatever!" he raises his voice, "Everyone's home, can't you just enjoy it?"

Brandon leans over to me, planning on going to the kitchen, "This seems like family business."

"You're part of this family now, sit down!" Chris remarks.

"I can't enjoy it knowing everyone is just going to leave again!" she shouts, standing up and putting her hands on the table.

"Hey, *Lily*," Jule turns to look, "I'm staying home for a little while, no need to worry—"

"But you're just going to leave again," Lila starts yelling, "Sarah left, then Tina's going to leave, and then I'm going to have to leave too."

I didn't realize that my leaving was so stressful on them. Lila slams the table and leaves, running up to her room, stomping each step of the way.

"Hey, *I* didn't do it this time," Jule says, eating some more food.

"I'll go talk some sense into her," Linda stands up, but I stand up too.

"Actually, can I?" I ask her.

"Be my guest," she sits back down, while I go chase after my adoptive sister. Each step I take up these stairs is an old memory. I reach my old room, and for some reason, I don't want to open the door. I turn to her room and knock lightly on the door.

"Lila?" I say through the door. I hear some music playing on the other side.

I crack the door open and see her with her MP3 player. Her room has been redecorated with posters and vinyl records. I sit down beside her on her bed, and she pulls out one of her earbuds. "What?" she whispers.

"Talk to me," I tell her.

"I just didn't want things to change," she admits.

"Things are supposed to change—"

"You don't," she barks, "You've stayed the same since dad took you in."

"That's not true," I fight back, "I got married, I'm getting an education—"

"You'll stay the same forever," she starts crying, rolling over on her pillow, "Just bite me already."

I rest my hand on her back, "You're just saying that. You're almost as old as me, did you know that?"

She lets out a chuckle, "Really?"

⊰⊙⊱

I'm sitting here on the floor, waiting for the mail to pop through the door. The clock is ticking, and ticking... and *POP!* The mail is shoved through the little door. I scurry to grab it all and rush over to the side table by the two chairs in the foyers.

"Why are you so excited about the mail; are you expecting something?" he asks me.

"I don't know," I retort, pulling out a fantastic looking letter with a wax seal on it.

But he plucks it from my hand, "You can't read that one—"

I use my speed and rush him, taking the letter back. "Why? What is it, I'm curious." I quickly turn around and open the letter. I skim it down and it reads something about inviting him to the annual conference. It's all very fancy.

"What conference?" I ask, with him rushing me and slipping the paper back into his own hands.

"I'm not going, so it doesn't matter."

"Have you gone before?" I ask.

"I used to," he replies, walking off into the phone room, "It's just a bunch of snobs and snoots."

I start to get suspicious, "*When* was the last time you went?"

"fifty-ish years ago," he tears up the letter into small pieces.

I follow him to the phone room and look at the stack of books I'm on. I've completed one whole shelf of reading. "They're vampires, aren't they?"

"Most of them; there are some government officials who keep tabs on everything."

He turns to face me and I eye him down. "We need to make friends with people," I persist.

He kisses my forehead and walks back to the foyer, "We are *not* going to find any friends there. Some of those people are over 300 years old and just as uptight to match."

I count back the years and try to relate some history to it, "That would mean they were, erm, there for the signing of the Constitution?"

"Yes, now could you please drop it? I don't want to go."

"And what about making adult friends?" I chase after him as he walks into the office.

"Didn't you have any friends outside of your host family?" he asks me, sitting down at his big desk, "You guys went to church, right? That's a great place to make friends."

"We were all concerned I'd burst into flames or melt with the holy water—"

"What? Seriously?" he starts laughing.

"Hey!" I slam my hand on the desk, "It's not like any of us were given a handbook."

"You know what?" he stands up, looking through the shelves of books, combing through each once until he finds what he's looking for and pulls it out, "A replica of a 1698 manual written by the notable Spanish vampire: Peppi Deocampo."

"Ha, Ha," I swipe the book and open it up only to find cursive Spanish. I look up in exasperation and toss the book back at him. "Do you have any vampire history books?"

"Why are you so fixated on this vampire stuff? Can't you be fixated on, like, a video game?" he blurts out.

"Do you have them or not?" I persist, walking up to the shelves and looking for the books myself. So many old books.

"Most of them aren't in English, since most early vampires were European," he explains.

I find a red spined book that reads 'Dracula' with the name Bram Stoker printed beneath it, which I recognize. Abe had gotten me a copy early on, and I read it at least ten times. "Who was Bram Stoker?" I ask, pulling out the book.

"He wasn't a vampire if that's what you're asking. Be careful with that book, it's a gift from my grandfather," he tells me, so I just put the book back on the shelf, "Hey, I was thinking of getting one of those *personal computers*. I really thought they wouldn't take off when I first saw them, but now?"

He pulls out a magazine and flips it to an advert from a superstore nearby, advertising these gray boxes full of holes and buttons. Each one is surrounded by a flashy yellow shape with a few hundred dollars marked as, I'm assuming, the price.

"That's a lot of money," I say, "What does it even do?"

"It does stuff like accessing the internet, spreadsheets, documents," he goes on, "And besides, I, erm, *we* have the money, it's not that much."

"What about a TV?" I ask, getting up and sitting on the desk to Brandon's dismay, "Chris and Linda didn't get one until after Jule left for college for fear of making them stupid."

"I guess, but where would we put it?" he flips to the next page of the magazine, "We don't have an extra room."

There's the bedroom, the phone room, the office, the library, the kitchen, the foyer, the storage room, and the guest bedroom. That's it. "Maybe, put it in the bedroom?" I suggest, "But you know what I really want?"

"What?" he laughs at me, attempting to be suggestive.

"To go to that conference," I demand. He throws his head back and quietly screams in his hands.

◂◂ ⊙ ▸▸

I look out the windows to see a beautiful full moon shining right above the horizon. We left right as the sun went down, but the drive took us all the way to midnight. The landscape this far out is beautiful at night. I see the destination in sight: a huge mansion with its windows glowing in the dark.

"Now, before we get there," Brandon starts, looking out at the building in the distance, "Oh, he swapped the trees— Anyways, this is a neutral zone for all vampires. This is simply a place for vampires to stay up-to-date with current events. You *may* find people there that are, uh, *disagreeable.*"

"What's the worst that can happen?" I retort.

We pull up to the estate and I see countless cars already parked, with three of them having little flags on the front that I should, but don't recognize. We make our way all the way to the doors. They both have huge metal tiger's heads with rings in their mouths.

"Should we knock?" I ask him.

"No, they already know we're here."

I take a careful breath through my nose to try and smell who's on the inside from here, but I'm tired from the drive. I definitely smell other vampires, but I can't make out how many.

One of the doors opens up and a man dressed even finer than Brandon on this occasion. "Brandon," he simply says, walking back inside.

"Sir William," Brandon leads me inside.

"Who is and where'd you find this hick orphan?" he snarks at him as Brandon closes the door. The smells are much more potent inside, and I smell too many to count who has walked through here.

"She's my wife, William," he defends me.

"We're starting soon," he keeps walking through another set of doors, where I know there are people. We follow and I see maybe thirty people standing around and sitting at a large table. There are a few casually dressed people, a few humans in suits, and some others.

"How old is he?" I whisper to Brandon over the commotion.

"I'm 321 years old," Sir William tells me, "I was turned into a vampire when I was the age of 24."

"Wow," I get a little starry-eyed, "You were there for the Revolutionary War."

"I was alive, yes, but I was visiting Germany at the time," he retorts.

"Brandon!" another person shouts, "Who's the broad?"

"My wife, thank you very much," he repeats.

"Wow, I'd never think you'd land someone," the man starts walking up to us. They shake hands and he turns to me. "I don't see your kind here very often."

"What do you mean?" I angrily ask.

"The savage ones are usually in a pen—"

"I'll have you know—" I start to retort, but Brandon shushes me.

We sit down at this table and the man goes off back to his seat. There's a woman with dark hair and sharp eyes sitting across from us. "Let's begin," Sir William says. His voice is so empty, "For those of us who are new, we will go around and quantify any new vampires that have been made, and the governor will record.

"I created zero new vampires in the past year," he says.

The next person says, "I've created one new vampire in the past year."

And one of the casually dressed people is next. He leans back and rests his feet on the table, boasting, "I created 42 new vampires."

They keep going around, most of them saying zero, or maybe one or two. And then it comes to me, and everything falls silent. Brandon nudges me with his elbow. "Um, I created zero new vampires," I quietly say.

"In the—" Brandon pushes me.

"In the past year," I finish off.

Brandon repeats after me, and they finish going around the table, making it all the way back to Sir William. Sir William, still standing, reports, "There were no notable events to happen in the past year."

The next person repeats the same; the next man lets his feet down and says, "Six battles in the past year."

"Casualties?" whom I assume to be the governor asks him.

"Thirty-six," he simply states, before the next person and the next. Some of them report battles and it finally clicks. These people reporting battles are most likely ringmasters, treating poor people like objects.

Without knowing, my teeth begin to sharpen, and my fingertips turn to claws. My vision focuses on that disrespectful man sitting across the table. Brandon rests his hand on mine, calming me down from going into a blind rage, and I notice some people are staring at me, and I recede back in the background.

The announcements go around the table and get to me and Brandon, "There were no notable events in the past year," we both say.

Everyone else goes about telling, the governor stands up, "If there's anything else that's notable, say it now." But no one says anything. The man closes his folder and slips it somewhere underneath the table. "See you ingrates next year," he stands up, with some others in suits following him out of the building.

"Now, you're all welcome to the food in the other room," Sir William and some others walk the other direction to another room. I stand to my feet and march over to that man, the other ringmaster, claws at the ready.

I get within a few feet of his smug look, when suddenly it feels like a weight is crushing down. Items on the table begin clattering and I fall to my knee, with everyone stopping in their tracks. Words begin ringing in my head in the voice of Sir William, "There will be *no* conflict in my home." Forcefully, and painful, my claws and fangs recede back.

The force is released and Sir William continues on into another room. "I know you're new here, but this is a non-aggression zone. If you'd like to lose a fight off his property, I'm glad to go outside—"

Brandon comes rushing to me, bringing me back to my feet and pulling me away. Some of the others leave to the other room where there's food prepared, but others are leaving. He keeps leading me away, saying, "William is aggressively non-violent."

"I cannot sit idly by while there's another ring—"

"This is neither the time, nor the place for this, Sarah." He squeezes my hands and pulls me along to the dining room, "These are elite vampires."

⫷ ⊙ ⫸

Brandon goes to the room where Sir William went, going in. as the door peeks open, I see him sitting in a chair, all alone looking at a fire. The door closes and I rush to go hear what they're talking about. Their voices sound like whispers through this door, but I can vaguely make out the words.

"Congratulations are in order, Brandon, for your marriage," William tells him.

"Thank you."

"What did you come here for?" William asks, "You haven't bothered in fifty years."

"The wife dragged me along."

"She's moxie; I never thought you'd ever settle down."

"I have a question you might be able to answer," Brandon goes on, "What happens to the vampirism of the parent having a child?"

William scoffs, "The child born of a vampire is immune to the parent's strain of vampirism, in your case, to both. A rare occurrence; although, the immunity doesn't carry through generations."

"Thank you, Sir William," Brandon says. I hear his footsteps come further to the door, and I back away a little to give room. Sir William sounds... lonely; perhaps I should invite him over to dinner.

The door opens and he steps out of the room. William reaches out, "Before you leave: thank you for attending."

"I'll come by next year," Brandon caresses my arm and leads me along.

"He sounds so alone," I say as we leave.

"He's over 300 years old, it's a common thing for vampires to be depressed," he explains.

"Maybe we should have him over for dinner," I propose, "Get him out of this mansion sometime—"

"That's not a good idea for him."

We get to the large front doors, Brandon opening one of them for us to leave. "Why not?"

"He had three wives. His first wife refused to become a vampire and died during childbirth. His kid died during the Revolutionary War, which made him flee to Europe" he starts to explain, opening the car door for me, "His second wife divorced him after he tried to convince her to turn their family into vampires."

"What about his third?" I ask as he starts the car.

"Another vampire lord killed her," Brandon starts to drive into the night, "I remember when it happened. He went mad, and it was a war between them. It ended with Sir William tearing out his heart and crucifying him to die in the sunrise. After the event, he took a vow of non-violence and became extremely secluded."

"Wow," I say, shocked.

"Yeah, inviting him over would just dangle those old memories in front of him," he says, "So he drinks and hosts these events."

We drive all throughout the night, and I watch the few stars that I can see here disappear in the sunrise. The windows of the car are fully protected from the sun. I tune in the radio to the classical station and listen to the nice piano.

◀▮⊙▮▶

Lila's back from college, so Linda made an effort to have everyone over for a family dinner. Julie is off with her husband on the other side of the city, but we all made it. Chris decided to order food this time, and he brought Chinese takeout.

"So, I started a new job," Tina announces to us, "I'm working at a nice bank. They hired me almost immediately because of my accounting degree."

"I bet the bank industry has changed since my time," Brandon laughs.

"I, uh, don't mean to overshadow your news," Julie stands up and extends her stomach out and holds it.

"No," Linda gasps.

"We're adopting!" he shouts, letting go of her stomach, but everything falls awkwardly silent. Derick, Julie's husband, starts laughing.

"I thought it was funny, babe," he says.

"That's big news," Chris chimes in, "Do you already have everything going through?"

"We're filing all the paperwork right now," she sits back down.

Linda turns to Brandon, "Why don't we hear anything about your family?"

Brandon turns to me with the 'Oh No' face, "That's because they're all dead. But I have a whole horde of great-grand nieces and nephews."

"But he won't visit them because they wouldn't recognize him," I chime in, "You should hear some of the whacky theories they come up with about their 'space cousin.'"

"That's what they call you?" Tina laughs.

"Oh, Lila," I call out to her, "You'll like this, we know someone who's 321 years old! He's super scary, a real Dracula character."

"Wow! That's super cool," she says, "Hey, is Dracula real?"

I turn to Brandon since he's the one with the history books he won't share, "He was, in fact, a very famous vampire lord, and there was a famous siege against him and his servants in, uh, Bucharest, where he was staked and beheaded."

"Wait," Derick pauses to register.

"Yes, babe," Julie confirms his thoughts, "they're vampires, keep with the program."

Gears start grinding in his head as he tries to comprehend what Brandon and I are. "I thought she's your younger sister?" he asks.

"*Older* sister, did I not mention this?" Julie goes on, patting his back, "We'll talk later." He looks like he broke his brain.

"Can you, like," he pauses, "turn into bats?"

"No, Derick," I shake my head, "We cannot turn into bats. But what I can do is count your eyelashes."

He chuckles, "Cool."

I clear my throat ready to announce the pregnancy, vaguely considering pulling a *Julie*, "This may also be overshadowing some news as well."

"No," Linda gasps, dropping her chopsticks. Tina starts choking on her food and pretends to pass out on the table.

◂◉▸

I turn on the television in the phone room and tune it to some background noise while I read. I managed to convince Sir William to let me borrow an English copy of an old history book on German vampires. The preface is a legend on the first two vampires to ever exist. An unknown year or place of origin and a warlord struck a deal with an archangel to curse him with ultimate power to strike down his enemies in exchange for his entry into heaven. The angel accepted and turned him into the first vampire.

In his first rampage, he decimated a nearby village. A surviving priest struck a deal with the devil, who tricked him into becoming a ravenous beast, being the first savage vampire.

—◉—

"This is a very nice park, Julie," I tell my sister. The summer heat is on the edge of bearable in the long sleeves and umbrella I have to carry around at this time of day.

I drove all the way out to their neighborhood to spend time with them and catch up since get-togethers are few and far between now with everyone's schedules. Derick and Julie recommended a park nearby.

Their adopted child, Asya is currently playing with our daughter in the grass, chasing each other in a game of tag. I remember the girls when they were just a little older than this. I thought I'd be in crisis as they've gotten older whilst I remain in the body of a teenager.

"Yeah, this whole neighborhood is called a 'Master Plan'," she tells me, "Everything's taken care of, everything's in place."

I look back at our husbands talking in the shade of a tree. Derick is currently asking dumb questions and Brandon is trudging along correcting him on things.

"So do you just bite someone, and, *boom*, new vampire?" Derick asks.

I focus closely on their voices, and hear Brandon reply, "No, it's not really like that; it's a whole process." I've never thought about it, making another vampire. I never thought I would want to.

Julie brings me back to our conversation, "Lila's been going off the rails," she admits, "Mom didn't want you to know, but I think you should."

"What do you mean?"

"I had to borrow her laptop for something while I was over there, and I caught a glimpse of her history; vampire this, vampire that; she was going to some dark websites," she informs me, "She's become obsessed. Of course, mom gave her a lecture about it."

My heart sinks. "Why would she be researching that if she could just ask me?"

"Because I don't think you'd approve of her wanting to become one. She's been falling into a slump since Tina and I left. Her grades are falling in college, and she's *so* close to graduation."

I bury my face in my hand. "I should do something," I say, "I'll stop over there tomorrow."

"I would've done something already, but you're the leading authority on that stuff in the family."

⬤

The sun has already set, and I'm walking up the pathway to Linda's house. There's a faint, familiar scent lingering around of another vampire. It's faint, so it's safe to say they aren't close.

On my way up the pathway, I hear Linda shouting. I take my key out and let myself in, only to be greeted by Linda and Lila shouting at each other. Linda storms off up the stairs.

Lila screams and starts rushing towards the door, only to be stopped by me. "Lila, where are you going?" I ask.

"Somewhere," she mutters.

"I can literally smell when you lie. I'll ask again," I persist, "Where are you going?"

"Move out of my way, Sarah," she grits her teeth.

"No," we lock our angry eyes, "I don't know what you think your doing, trying to turn yourself, but I won't have it—"

Lila pulls out a decorative metal crucifix, "Get out of my way!"

"A cross? Those don't—" I rush to swipe it from her hand, but the moment I touch it, my hand starts to burn as if it were in the sun. I release my grip and hide my hand.

"It's silver-plated," she informs me, holding closer to my face as I back away from it.

"I *forbid* you from becoming a vampire," I command, "You have no idea the horrors that come along with it. I'm stuck as a child with no memories! I share no blood with anyone, nothing!"

Lila shoves the cross onto my neck, burning me and driving me away. I scream in pain, falling to my back and holding the wound on my neck as she runs off behind me into the night. Linda comes rushing down the stairs to find me bleeding profusely from my neck with Lila nowhere to be seen.

"What the hell happened here?" she goes into the kitchen to get the first aid kit.

The pain is lingering, and blood is flowing from the wound. If I use my abilities to heal, it'll leave a terrible scar that'll take years to disappear. Linda pulls me in closer as she starts dressing the wound. "How did this happen?" she asks.

"She burned me with a silver cross," I tell her, wincing from the cleaning agent, "She ran off."

"I always kept the silver hidden away because I didn't want this to happen."

"She's about to do something she'll regret forever," I admit, "She doesn't understand—"

"It's not going to be your fault, *she'll* be making that choice," she assures me, applying the final tape on the bandage, "Did Brandon drive you here? Where is he?"

"I actually drove myself," I admit, "For the first time without him."

"That's wonderful, I'm proud."

⊷⊙⊶

I sit down on the couch in the office, while Brandon sits in his office chair caressing a sleeping child. "Silver wounds are particularly nasty, I remember after the war," he begins to tell me a story, "There was a witchhunt in England when I returned from the mainland.

"Thankfully, nobody actually died. But I was wounded fairly badly by a silver bullet that lodged itself in my lung after it bounced off my scapula."

"Why were you being shot at?" I rest my head back.

"I was being chased by the witch-hunting mob to stand trial for dealing with the devil or something. Took four hours for the doctor to remove the bullet."

"Nobody's seen her in four days, I'm worried," I admit, looking at the molding making up the ceiling, "it took Linda an hour just to be transferred to a department that could deal with 'Monsters'; she said it was 'code V'. They said as long as she isn't *turned*, they can report her missing."

"I doubt any of the other vampires are going to cooperate," he admits.

❮❮⊙❯❯

I wake up from my sleep in the dead of night. And for an unknown reason, the voice of my ringmaster says, "I said I wouldn't be the last one."

I become aware of my surroundings and smell someone in the house. I start shaking Brandon until he awakes, and I see in his eyes he's become ready to kill. I start my vampire-trance and silently rush out of the room and into the loft atop the stairs.

The ringmaster from the conference is just standing there by the open door, manually ticking the clock. "Tick tock," he says, "Not only did you kill my direct competitor, but I recently caught wind that you have a child completely immune to vampirism. That pays a lot to the right buyer."

I jump down to the first floor, but before I can move, Brandon rushes him. Brandon attempts to grab him by the throat, but the man kicks him away, twisting around and sideswipes Brandon in the face with a loud *CRACK!*

I draw out my fangs and claws ready to fight him as he approaches me. He claws at my face, but I duck down and deeply lacerate through his leg. Before he falls down to his knee, I thrust my fingers up through his head, bringing him up.

I ready my other hand to pierce through his heart and kill him. But a kitchen knife slices through his forehead; I hear his heart stop and something comes over me, and I ready myself to bite him. I hear my husband try to say something, barely snapping out of it, and I let him drop to the floor. I look at my bloody hand with some bits stuck on the nail and shake it away.

I see Brandon leaning on the doorway with his head bent in a strange direction. He grabs his own head and *POP!* He fixes his neck, falling to the floor. I run over to him and catch him from falling down. "*You* nearly bit him," he whispers.

Something else strikes me; I set him to the side and run as quickly as I can up to the baby room. I burst through the door to find her safe, but awoken and scared from the door flying open. She starts crying and I close the door to keep from scaring her further.

I hurry to the bathroom and begin scrubbing my hands. I focus and release my claws, dropping them into the sink and revealing my regular fingertips. I also feel the wound on my neck completely healed from the incident, but most definitely scarred.

Once I finish, I look in the mirror and peel away the bandage I was letting heal to see what has happened to the cross-shaped burn. There's darkened skin exactly outlining the previous wound, like a permanent stamp on my skin.

"Brandon!" I call out, going back out to the foyer to overlook the mess. My eyes quickly adjust to the darkness, noticing multiple blood sprays all over the antique rug. I see him sitting on the couch, holding the back of his neck. "What are we going to do with the body? I doubt I'll get away with it this time."

"Relax," he says, moving his head around, "This isn't my first rodeo. It was established that vampires aren't human beings, and don't have human rights. They said as long as it doesn't interrupt citizens, we can kill or pillage other vampires."

◀◀ ⊙ ▶▶

I finish off the second layer of my daytime sunscreen to go to a parent-teacher conference at Elizabeth's kindergarten. They wouldn't tell me why but insisted that both Brandon and I go talk to the teacher. This is an unusual event for me to have human contact outside of the family, which concerns me because they might have questions about my age.

We leave and arrive at the school. Today is a particularly sunny day, and we look like idiots with our umbrellas and long sleeves. I manage to pull Brandon along through the school to the room we're supposed to meet in.

I knock on the door, feeling hot from all the natural, ambient light. The door opens and the teacher looks very carefully at us, shocked by our appearance. "Come in, Mr. and Mrs., erm, Ahlborn?"

She leads us in, and we sit down, "Do you mind closing the blinds? My husband and I are sensitive to light."

"Oh," she sounds confused but goes to limit the light. We collapse our umbrellas, and she sits down at the desk, "That mark on your neck, do you mind if I ask where it's from?"

"I do mind, it's a sensitive topic," I reply.

"Your daughter, Elizabeth, turned in an assignment that was very concerning."

She pulls out a paper with a drawing of the cleanup day of men cleaning all the blood from the rugs and walls after that vampire had attacked us. "Wow, she's pretty good," Brandon says, handing me the paper.

"You're missing the point, Brandon," I tell him.

"She drew a very violent scene, and I wanted to know if she was involved in anything recently."

"Yeah, we had an attacker pay us a visit recently and it was a little violent," I tell her, handing the drawing back, "We had to have a cleanup service come by."

"Oh, goodness!" she exclaims, "Is everyone okay?"

"Yeah, everything was just fine," I explain, "Elizabeth was in her room the entire time, she didn't see any of it."

"I see," the teacher puts the paper away in a drawer, "Well, while you're here, your daughter is otherwise doing well academically."

✦⊙✦

The door opens to Sir William's estate, revealing one of the servants. "Come in, he's expecting you," he says, leading us in the servant leads us into the meeting hall where they hold the conference, and I smell something akin to a stray dog. I look and see a burly man, large in stature and moderately covered in black hair. He and Sir William are conversing over wine at the end of the table.

"Oh look," Brandon grits, "a dog!"

"Welcome, Brandon, Sarah," William stands up to greet us, "I thought I'd have Sarah meet with a Lycan, as she's unfamiliar with otherworldly cultures."

I prance up to the man, standing up to see me. I look up as he stands up to a towering height above me. I reach out my hand to shake with him. I pause and ask, "What's a Lycan?"

"Werewolf, I believe is the common term they use in fiction now," Sir William corrects me.

The man grabs my hand, and he's almost as strong as me, "You have quite a grip."

Brandon comes up behind me, and we all sit down, "I had no idea there were Wer— Lycans."

"They're cultists, really," I hear William laugh, a first.

"It's a private, natural worship," the man points his finger, "Not a cult!"

"Might I introduce you two, he's the current archbishop of this region. I figured we should acquaint each other," William takes a sip of his wine.

I turn to my husband, "You never told me there were *others*."

"We're a dying breed," the man says, "There's not nearly as many of us as there used to be. Creating others is a lost art, so we're only created by birth." He taps his neck, signaling to my scar, "Silver scars are nasty, aren't they?"

"Oh," I cover it with my hand. He raises his, showing a scar of his own going across his palm.

"I was helping a friend do dishes during his sick time when I was a teenager, grabbed a solid silver spoon, and the scar's been there ever since," he explains, "Although, I'm sure your story is much more hardcore."

Sir William chimes in, "I, for one, have never sustained a silver wound."

"You also never leave your house," Brandon retorts.

"How old are you?" I ask him.

"I'm about to turn sixty," he replies, "We age about three-fourths of the speed of normal people, while you don't age at all."

Brandon stands up, "William, a word?"

"Of course," they walk off to William's sitting room. Brandon closes the door behind him, and I start listening carefully.

"Do you have any other questions about me?" the man asks.

"Do—do you really transform during a full moon?" I whisper.

He laughs and says, "Normally, but there's been medicine for that for centuries."

I begin to hear the other conversation, "Killian attacked us, we ended up killing him."

"Yes, I heard," William says, "Finally put an end to that scourge."

"Do you know who took over his legion?"

"Actually, I was considering it," William admits, "I've done nothing for our people in hundreds of years. I was considering rehabilitating them.

"Your wife turned out so incredibly well, and is serving as proof that it can be done."

"That's very unlike you," Brandon says.

"Perhaps it's time for a change, wouldn't you agree?"

The man lifts his head to listen. "In all the time my family has known Will, not once have I ever heard of his doing something so against royal vampire culture."

"How long has your family known him?" I ask.

"I come from a long line of bishops, and it was my great-great-grandfather over 150 years ago that established a relation with William," he drinks the last of his wine, "How much do you know of Will?"

"Not a lot," I admit.

"He's about to tell you I've been the reigning authority for 200 years in this state," William opens the door back up, "I remember that man 150 years ago, very proud about his lineage."

"So a Lycan's child isn't immune to it?" I ask him.

"There's a fifty percent chance the child will become a Lycan," he explains.

⧎⊙⧎

"You cannot see her!" the nurse stands in front of me trying to barge in to see Lila, "I already told you she is in critical condition!" I want to just cut this person down, I could do it.

Tina grabs me by the arm and pulls me back. "You're losing your cool," she reminds me. Brandon's in another room with an acquainted police officer. Linda's on the phone with Julie.

Lila had gotten involved with Killian, the vampire ringmaster with the promise of making her into a vampire; however, he left the process incomplete. Sir William told us depending on where the process stopped would determine the outcome; if she survives the infection will take time to run its course.

After the entire night of doctors going in and out, they stopped and told us she's in a stable condition. We're far from any windows, so now I'm stranded in the hospital until the sun sets.

"I'll be completely honest with you," the doctor pulls us to the side of the hallway, "I have *never*, and I mean *never* seen a condition like this. *But*, we've gotten her stable. She is unconscious, but there is brain activity, a stable heartbeat."

My heart is relieved at his words, knowing she'll be alright. The doctor goes back to work, and we're left alone. A nurse approaches, telling us we can enter the room, but to restrain from physical contact with her until further notice.

The door slides open and I see my dear sister on a ventilator and tubes coming from her arms. Tina whispers to me, "You're not responsible for this." and hugs me from behind.

"If I—"

"She did this on her own," she repeats.

I sit down in one of the chairs, watching her. Linda puts her hand on my shoulder, "Will you watch her for me? Work isn't going to let me off today."

"Of course," I say, leaning onto her hand, "I have nowhere else to be right now, Brandon is going to go off taking care of Elizabeth."

"I'll stay too, I can skip class for a day," Tina sits in the other chair.

⊰⊙⊱

"How is my niece?" Tina asks, scrolling through her phone to pass the time, "I know our schedules don't line up all that much."

"She drew a photo of people cleaning all the blood off the rugs at school," I tell her, "The teacher dragged us in the dead of day. Turns out she's a pretty good artist."

"She gets along with Asya still?"

"They love each other, it's so cute," I chuckle.

"I spend way too much time in school," she admits, "I'm still second-guessing if a Masters is worth it."

"You're doing well at the bank though, aren't you wanting to go into bank management?"

"Yeah, but this Masters they're wanting me to get is killing me," she continues, "it's math class after math class."

"I remember when you guys had your math class in middle school," I reminisce on the memories of smaller children, "You aced it while Julie used an entire month's worth of saved up money to by a fancy calculator."

"And you thought it was witchcraft!" she tears up laughing.

"It wasn't my fault; I grew up in a literal shack!" I point back, but eventually, also fall victim to the laughing. We trail off until it's just the beeping of the heartbeat machine alone in the room.

"What was my great-grandpa like, by the way?" she asks.

I think back to all that time ago, "He loved to hunt, and loved whiskey night. He was stern and unmoving, but he tried to show some compassion on a poor soul. I never saw him around his family; every time they would come over I was hidden away in the shed with a book."

"He had a whiskey night?"

I think back to the first drink I ever had with him. "Yeah, he said, 'I ain't got the money to have it every night!'" I say, imitating his angry voice.

Lila starts coughing, tilting her head with the breathing tube shoved down into her lungs. Tina, thinking quickly, runs out and gets a nurse, while I rush up to her and grab her hand. Her fingers softly wrap around my hand, but she quickly falls limp again.

I listen carefully to the machines, and they're still reading her as alive. The nurse rushes in, and moves me back to check Lila's vitals. She opens up her eyelids, flashing a light to check something. She probably spent another five minutes checking things before she turns back and tells us two that she may have just had a spout, but isn't awake.

I could finish the vampirism process if I knew how. But would I get it right, what if she's infected with the other strain? Tina just sits down again, and I just stand there looking at Lila.

"Hey, I just got a text from mom," Tina scrolls on her phone, "She says she's coming back to check on us. I think I'll dip when she comes, I have to finish my homework and get some notes."

"Yeah, I'll have to go home and be with Brandon and Ellie at some point."

Lila starts gasping again, and this time opens her eyes. I can smell her fear. She starts thrashing around, and I rush to hold her hand. Her head whips all around, looking at the room before she grabs, with her other hand, the tube in her mouth and pulls it out.

As she does, she hunches over and starts coughing in her hand. The nurse rushes back in and starts talking to her. "You're in a hospital, you're safe!" the nurse says, but that does calm her, she just lies there, breathing heavily.

The nurse shines a light in her eye, but she bats it away. She opens her mouth to try and say something, but nothing comes out. She looks like she's screaming in silence and starts crying and the nurse calls for more help.

⊰⊙⊱

One of Linda's relatives decided to have a family reunion in the next small town over. I thought both she and Christopher were only children, but she explained that it's her aunt's grandchild, or her cousin 'once-removed', who's organizing the event and insisted that she come, so she could see the kids and Asya. Linda then insisted that I'm family and should come if possible. Armed with daylight sunscreen and umbrellas, we decide to go.

The primary hurdle was Lila had just been released from the hospital, and she still has yet to recover her voice or walk with steady feet. She has a constant fever that can't be treated, and she always feels cold.

I find myself in a place much like Abe's, but with greener trees and grass instead of patchy weeds and dirt. Wide-open space with a house—no shed. There's a lot of people here already, talking amongst themselves with tables. Brandon and I pop out our umbrellas while Chris helps Lila into a wheelchair.

I open the door to let Elizabeth out, and she bolts out of the car, running to Asya, who rode with Linda, and they start hugging. I look back to see the car seat full of cereal and other snacks we left for her, but not wanting to spend time cleaning it up at the moment, I just close the door. The two little girls run off into the grass.

"So what do I say if people ask me how I'm related?" I ask.

"Just say you're from my side of the family," Chris says, pushing Lila along. She just looks so defeated; the only way she communicates is through her phone. "It wouldn't be a lie."

I double-check my scarf, to make sure its covering my neck, but it's kind of warm. The scar doesn't seem to be getting smaller, and makeup doesn't cover the deformation of the skin.

Julie finally pulls up after falling behind on the road trip. Their car skids to a stop and the windows roll down, revealing an energetic Julie, "What's up losers?"

"I smell a lot of sugar," I tell her as she, Derick, and Tina funnel out of their van.

"I pulled an all-nighter and needed an energy drink," she replies, "Speaking of which, I need the restroom." She marches right past us, going into the house.

The door opens and I hear, "Julie?! Is that you?" but with no response from my sister.

Derick walks up, waving, "Sarah! Looking as young as ever!"

"Thanks," I scoff sarcastically, "I suppose this is your first time with extended family, too."

"Sure is!" he looks at the people pinching the cheeks of the two little girls running around, "I have no idea what to do with these people."

I chuckle, "I've never been to a big event like this." A vague memory of a birthday cake rings in my mind, marked with a candle, I think, shaped eleven or twelve. The scene in my head has a calendar marked May 1978; I don't remember any faces, any defining qualities. I remember blowing out the candle, but it ends there.

When I first came to, inside Abe's living room, I could barely remember words, and I was chained up, bound in metal. How long ago was that?

Brandon locks on my arm, and we start walking into the crowd along with the rest of the family. I see two pairs of older people sitting down under a large umbrella. They must be Linda's parents and Aunt.

I overheard one of them ask Elizabeth, "Who do you belong to?" Asya is off being held by someone else.

I hear my little girl respond, "I don't know you."

We get to them, and I pull her up by the arm and hold her, "My name is Sarah, I'm a relative of Christopher." Ellie tightens onto me.

"Linda's husband?" she asks, "I'm her mother."

"It's lovely to meet you," I properly greet her, "this is my daughter Elizabeth, and my husband Brandon."

"You three are so pail," she remarks, pointing to the umbrellas we're holding, "You don't see much sun, do you? Are you on some heavy meds?"

I laugh, but Brandon looks uncomfortable, "No, we're just both sensitive to sunlight. It's a skin condition," I make up an excuse.

"Where is Linda?" she stands up and starts looking around, going off and looking for her.

I see some others similar to her age; Lila goes over to her, crossing over her. They're all asking what happened, but she can't respond. Tina rushes over to her and starts explaining that she's just got a really back case of the flu and lost her voice, but I can see in Lila's eyes she's not happy right now.

One of them sits down on the bench beside her and shows something on her phone, Lila cracking a smile. Asya has escaped from the grasp of pinching relatives and has run over to me. She has a cute little Russian accent when she talks, saying, "Ellie!" and reaching out, so I let her down, and they run off and play.

I pat Brandon's chest, "You should go bond with Derick, Julie hasn't come out to save him."

"It's like talking to a rock, Sarah," he rolls his eyes, "A very talkative rock."

I make my way over to Lila and Tina sitting at the table, and I sit down next to them. "And you are? I've never seen you before," The girl asks me.

"I'm a relative on Chris' side," I say.

"My second cousin?" Tina trails off, bumping me with her elbow, "Adoptive. New to the family."

*Now I'm a second cousin?* I ask myself, "We're very close though, me with the family."

"It's kinda warm for a scarf, isn't it?" the girl asks, "I'm Liz."

"Sarah," I introduce myself, "I'm just self-conscious about my neck."

"Girl, don't be, love yourself," she remarks, "What do you have, a scar? I have a scar on my left rib, it's real bad, but you know? You just have to accept that certain things won't go away and you just have to *flow* with it, ya'know?"

"Mine's a little different," I say, but wanting to change the subject. I put the back of my hand on Lila's head, feeling the intense fever. I wish there was something I could do.

"You probably shouldn't touch her, she might have that African thing—Ebola," Liz says.

Lila pulls out a notebook, and flips it open and starts scribbling something. The doctor did a brain scan while she was awake and found mild damage. Tina hands me the book, and I read, "I'm sorry." with a badly drawn heart next to it. I take the pencil and draw a heart encircling the statement, and hand it back.

⊷⊙⊶

"Thank you for coming, Sarah," William walks over to a bookcase, "Many of the vampires have come back to reality," he presses something on the shelf, and the entire piece of furniture begins to slide open, revealing a hidden passage to a basement. I spent the first few months with Linda and Chris in their basement, fond memories.

"The one they've generally accepted as the one in charge, aside from me, needs some words of advice," he leads me to a door, "I also need some words of wisdom on dealing with the youngest of them."

"I like this new you, William," I say, patting him on the shoulder, "It's a good leaf you turned."

He slots in a key and opens the door, revealing a maze of little rooms with windows. We walk through the maze, and I see in the little windows to the doors of people in varying conditions. Each room had a bed and a chair. Some of them are sleeping; some are cuffed to the ground through a long chain.

"They're all at various stages of withdrawal and recovery, I have my servants attending to them at all times of the day, recording the individual processes and other things such as blood supply and other reactions," he informs me, stopping at a door, and sliding in that key.

I see a teenager, probably a similar age as me too, sitting in the chair, reading a familiar copy of Dracula. His fingers are constantly jittering and his legs are bouncing. I remember that stage of progress.

"I've brought a good friend of mine," William tells him, bringing his attention from the book, "She was, once upon a time, in your very position. I asked her to come and speak some words of encouragement to you."

I sit down on the bed. "What's your name?" I ask.

He closes the book and jitters his fingers on the spine. It takes a moment to answer, but he finally says, "I don't remember. I just woke up in this room with, um, flashbacks."

"I was once in a ring, just like you," I start to tell him my story, "The story goes that a countryside hunter found me stuck in a bear trap that had been set to try and find the one terrorizing some animals.

"He told me I was covered in burns, hissing like a snake at him with a crushed ankle. He managed to chain me up and get me into his home nearby. He said I had fangs and claws like a wolf and figured I was a vampire. He said it took two weeks before I was docile and responded to speech.

"I remember clearly, he said, 'You may be cursed, but it doesn't mean you have to be a monster'. It took another two weeks before I could even stand on two feet and speak. He had a steady supply of animal blood and after a long time of training, my fangs receded and my claws fell off, and I only had to feed once every two weeks.

"He got me some new clothes to replace the tattered rags I was found in, and he always had a book for me to read. In fact, I read the book you're reading right now.

"He protected me for fifteen years before he was killed by my old ringleader. His grandson took me in and I finally had a family again, with three little girls who grew up to be exemplary women. I met a husband that took me in and I have a beautiful daughter.

"I started out the same as you, and you have someone here, Sir William to help you through these steps to a normal life, for a vampire."

He smiles a little, folding his arms in a way to get comfortable, "But it seems too far away," as he talks I see his fangs have yet to recede.

"I once read in a book, 'The journey of a thousand miles starts with a single step, *one after another.* You may run, or walk the journey, but it is always one step after another'. Don't feel like you have to sprint the race.

"What are you going to call him?" I ask William.

"I'm actually pouring through files and missing persons reports for the past eighty years to try to find each one of them," he replies, "I found a few, but not his yet."

I turn back to the boy, "Hang in there." I reach out my hand to shake with him. His trembling hand slowly reaches out, almost pulling back. He grabs on and I give him a nice hardy shake that Abe used to do with me.

# Obadiah's Legend

## The End of a Legend

‹‹‹ ◎ ›››

OBADIAH ENCOUNTERED the Eternal Storm and sought his foe.

The Eternal Storm?

This foe summoned a storm from another world to hide himself, building a massive monument to threaten the entire desert.

The Hall of Sahar?

Yes…

‹‹‹ ☉ ›››

The great serpent points it head towards the storm, whispering to me, *that's where I am to go.* Onward, I go into the storm ahead. Each step I take fills me with determination to stop whoever summoned this great storm. Sand begins flying about, being picked up by the wind. It feels as if I'm walking through a stone wall, commandeered by this great foe as I once defeated the corrupt King Malik. The sight of what lies in front of me becomes obscured, so I shut my eyes, only being guided by the great serpent.

The sand begins to rash me, cutting my skin as I venture blind into the unknown. I feel the everbearing presence of evil. I find myself walking into a barrage of small stones; the further I stray inside the larger the stones become.

Until… I enter the eye of the storm, and find the ruins of *Janubii,* crushed and destroyed. But *Janubii* fell long ago. In the wake of the ruins is a new monument, and what I'm searching for is inside.

Building blocks materialize from the storm, the sand fusing together to form stone. The stones move across the sky and assemble themselves, building up this monument.

248

◀◀ ⊙ ▶▶

The ruins I walk past are buried in the sands, from long ago. I remember what it used to look like. The library there, the shrine room over to my left with the shrine worn away and broken to pieces.

I remember when I was a boy, worshiping at that shrine, saying prayers with my friends; eating with my friends in the halls. I remember when they expelled me. "You've become aggressive, Obadiah," he said, "You've been studying things in secret.

"You've learned things one is not meant to learn."

He threw me out, changing the course of my life. But it was too late; I had obtained the power I so foolishly sought. In self-imposed exile, I colonized the desert for the rest of my days.

When I had returned hence to *Janubii*, it had fallen under attack, and it was too late. And here I am, arriving just when I need to. I draw my blade and continue under the great serpent's guidance. I cross the threshold of the outer wall, and enter into the chambers of this monument.

"Who goes there?" the voice of the master who commands this place, it echoes through the halls.

"I am Obadiah!" I shout with all my power.

The voice fails to return, and I'm left wandering the monument. The walls are blank, the floor has yet to be walked, and *I* am the first here. The great serpent slithers down and meanders about the floor.

I whisper a spell and palm the wall, shattering the stone. "You *dare* destroy this temple, Obadiah?" the voice echoes through the halls. Sand begins to fill the cracks and the wall becomes anew. I follow the great serpent down the twisting halls. We arrive in a mirror room.

◀◀ ⊙ ▶▶

The only thing looking back at me is me. I've allowed myself to become unkept. I continue walking throughout the mirror room, seeing my reflections change; I see a boy walking beside, changing to a young lad, my early adulthood.

I stop and see Abd al Hakim, walking beside me in the mirror. "Why am I haunted so?"

I thrust my palm into the mirror, obliterating the reflection. And yet, I see fragments of my past. Cubit by cubit, the mirror's cracks dissolve away.

The great serpent guides me away from the mirrors into the next chamber. Empty room after empty room is passed by, void of soul or purpose. I arrive at the center of the monument and look up at the staircase ascending the tower.

The great serpent slithers and thithers up on my body. I whisper a spell and feel strength imbue into my legs, and launch myself up crashing through the top and destroying the base of the tower, sword in hand.

"Obadiah," I hear the man say. He's dressed in fine linen, levitating above the ground in a meditative state.

I slowly flutter to the ground, readying my sword. The tower remains still, regardless of the damage I've inflicted. "You break the natural laws—"

"Obadiah, the one who slew the corrupt king, eighty years ago," he identifies me, "Why have you come?" The ground beneath us begins to repair itself, sand flowing together from all around, "to slay me too?"

"You break the natural laws, and practition forbidden magic."

"That's pious coming from the man resurrected from the dead, expelled from the monastery that once stood here."

"You've disgraced the memory of *Janubii*, that is your worst crime."

"Tell me," the man lowers to thr ground, and opens his eyes. He's been possessed by a devil, and I can see it in his eyes, "Would it be a disgrace if I had waited another hundred years, for the desert to consume the ruins and have it become one once again?

"Should I have waited 200 years, or a millennium?"

"You should never have done it!" I strike him down across his chest in righteous anger. He falls down, blood staining his fine garments.

Stitch by stitch, hair by hair, his wounds heal until there is nothing left. He lifts his body up and lands on his feet. "That wasn't necessary."

I strike him once more, severing his fingers from his hand, but again, they return and the wounds heal before my eyes. "What kind of dark magic is this?" I step back and consider.

"Mistress Death's," he foolishly replies.

⊶ ⊙ ⊷

In an instant, he appears befront me, palming me in the chest and ejects me through the tower's wall, breaking the stone beneath us. I land in the sand, being buried by the wind.

I see him, floating down to meet me. He palms the air, crushing me and the sand, compacting it to stone. But the great serpent slithers and the sand becomes water.

I jump up, swirling wind around me, summoning a whip to snap across his throat from the water. He bleeds, but continues to heal. "You cannot defeat me, Obadiah. I will heal from every wound you inflict upon me."

"I will fight until I draw my last breath,"

"Very well." he draws water up and whips it around me, slicing into my leg. I whisper a spell and quicken my body, giving myself the opportunity to dodge away from the whip.

My foe is quicker than me, appearing nearly instantly behind, whipping me in the back. "Listen to the great serpent," I hear the voice of the servant of the wise.

Sand begins to creep up my legs to lock me in place, but the great serpent hisses, casting away the sand. He comes close, and I sweep my legs underneath him, but he jumps above.

He reaches out his palm, and summons an air current like the raging storm surrounding us, blowing me down. I extend out my single arm to keep from being buried in the sand.

And with his other palm, he strikes me in the chest with an incredible force, throwing me down. As I strike the ground, I'm carried away in a vision.

◄◄⊙►►

I find myself enveloped by the great serpent, long as a raging river, slithering around me. It looks upon me and glares deep within me.

I look back up at the serpent, and it strikes, waking me up from this vision. "You disappoint me, Obadiah." I find myself being held up by the neck.

I wrap my legs around his arm, and extend to break his grip on me, and succeed. This foe drops me, and I swirl to slash him down. "Again!" I hear the whispers of Hakim in my ears. I dance the warrior's dance, cutting and slicing his body. With each strike, he steps away, but I strike quicker than his healing magic.

I take my final strike, across the chest, and he falls to his knees, gasping for air. The great serpent lunges forward, digging its fangs into his throat. I stop to capture my own breath. "You're—swift," he manages to say against the constrictive force of the great serpent, attempting to grapple the snake. His body doesn't seem to be healing whilst he's occupied.

"I have less to carry."

"The great serpent's venom might be enough to end you." I ready my sword for the final attack, "But I'd rather destroy you myself."

Suddenly, he tears the great serpent in twain, throwing the two halves to the side. His hands clap together, blowing wind and sand away from him and closing the wounds I've inflicted.

"Not you, nor great serpent, nor anyone alone, is sufficient!"

The two halves of the great serpent slither back into the sand, returning back to the fold.

⊷ ⊙ ⊶

The sound of a single man's footsteps grows louder beyond the distance. I do not suspect another enemy. A whip cracks, echoing off of the monument.

The upper half of this foe's torso begins to separate from the rest, with blood flowing down from the cut. Perhaps Hakim chose more than one champion to fight beside me.

I take steps to the side to find this. I see a young man, holding an excessively long whip with a blade fastened to the tip. This man's likeness is familiar, yet unknown.

Not letting my moments waste themselves, I begin the warrior's dance anew, slicing and cutting his body. The stranger cracks his whip in between my strikes, cutting pieces of flesh away.

"Enough!" he cries out, clapping his hands above his head. Flames begin to surround his hands, quickly collecting in a ring.

But this stranger cracks his whip again, removing the foe's hands from his arms, again whipping to swipe away the limbs to prevent them from reattaching. I run close to him, palming his chest, releasing a force of wind, but it rewinds as he motions with his arms, casting me away.

The whip cracks, and the blade pecks through the front of his face, pulling away. But even that is not enough.

"Your sword!" the stranger commands.

I look upon the blade, not knowing the inscription I carved into it in my travels. Serpents begin creeping along the path of a rune in the desert sand. Sand starts consuming him from the legs up.

I focus deeply on the blade, unfamiliar with the technique of runes. Sand consumes him, and I let the power of this rune run through me, flowing from my missing limb.

⊷ ⊙ ⊶

I swipe the sword through the air, throwing a force forward, and cutting the man in two where he stood. This force surged on to break the monument and the tower.

The tower comes crashing down, crumbling from the attack. I look back at my sword and realize it's cracked; it crumbles into dust, blowing away slowly until the hilt is gone.

The foe's body falls down into the sand, being still and dead. The serpents return to the fold and I'm left alone with this stranger in the eye of this eternal storm.

"He was possessed by Death."

"Who are you?" I ask this stranger, "You fight well beyond your years."

"My name is Abd al Hakim, servant of the wise."

"Impossible, Hakim is an old man."

"Obadiah, I am he, an immortal one from long ago; I chose you to be a champion to fight evil, and become that of legend to be revered and feared."

"Why do you take the form of a youth?"

This stranger begins to walk to me, coming close to speak. "I broke my oath of eternal life to fight beside you, turning back time, so I may finally live out my life as a normal man does."

I rest my hand upon his head, feeling that he is real. "I wish to fight no more, Hakim; I wish to learn no more, to live no more."

"I didn't resurrect a hollow husk; I brought back to life a hero in the world's time of need."

"I wish to be left alone, for I am tired." I kneel down in the sand and pray upon the soul we've sent to the afterlife, over my dear friends and peers and the ruins of *Janubii*.

⊹⊙⊹

"If that's what you desire, then I shall leave you be." This stranger begins his journey beyond the cusp of the eye, leaving me alone. "Perhaps my old master will allow me back."

I wait. Something always follows, always comes after me; I attract danger and evil. Hours pass, and nothing. "Perhaps this really is the end," I whisper. I feel the desert freeing me from our contract, releasing my soul, the payment I promised for its fortune, perhaps out of grace and charity.

I choose to go back to the mirror room, trudging through the wind and sand into the monument's halls once more. The reflections look back at me as I look back at them. I see nothing but an old, tired man missing his arm, at last.

*And thus Obadiah rearranged the mirrors and sat down to meditate amongst the memories of the place that once stood here. He meditated and waited...*

⊹⊙⊹

Legend says he's still there, meditating inside the eternal storm amongst the mirrors.

He never left?

No one really knows.

Is there any more to this legend?

For now? No.

# Omniscience

✦ ◎ ✦

I PEEK FROM behind the sliding glass wall. I see *him*, Deus, the man who claims to be God descended from heaven. He has followers to bend to his every whim. He is exceptionally powerful, I might add, but even in his limitless power he has yet to see me.

I, too, am exceptionally powerful; I make myself invisible to every sense. I am nothing, I want to be nothing. I've always hidden myself from the world, but this man has piqued my interest; the application of his powers has led him to a unique position.

But wait, a new man is approaching him. He wears a monk's robe. He kneels down befront him, and they just stare at each other.

"Who are you?" Deus leans on his arm, smirking at this new man, "Who are you to challenge me so boldly?"

"You wonder—"

"I wonder about *nothing!*" he snaps, "I'm literally God. I hold all the power and knowledge in the universe."

Deus begins altering the space of the room, expanding it, then contracting it, "I can control space itself at a whim."

"I control time," he continues, aging and damaging the room, and the potted flowers all around.

"I hold the power of the sun itself at my fingertips," he declares, raising a finger and creating a small well of fusing plasma, "Who are you to be so bold as to even approach me?"

"I can even read the minds of mortals and create life—"

The other man begins to speak, "And all you do is live for desire. You are wondering right now, why you are unable to read *my* mind, and cannot control *my* body."

"Why shouldn't I live for desire?" Deus snarks back.

"If the desire was all you wanted, why not put yourself into a comatose state with chemicals perpetually flooding your brain?"

"You call yourself Deus because you do not remember your name. You remain stagnant at the lowest possible state of enlightenment."

"Then enlighten me," Deus commands, "Tell me who you are."

"Allow me to tell you my story, and in return, you tell me yours," this other man relaxes by crossing his legs instead of kneeling, "I awoke one day in a clearing of trees. I was naked, and when I thought I should be clothed, I was clothed. I wandered, but I never hungered and I never thirsted. I was in constant awe of the world around me, for I had no memories before I awoke.

"Eventually I wandered up a mountain, and I came across a Buddhist monastery where they taught me morality and philosophy. Then one day a traveler came to visit the monastery on leisure and told me of you. You captured my mind as someone who could be equally as strong as I was.

"You cannot read my mind or control me, because I am the same as you. They named me Shen before I left."

Deus laughs, "You think we're the same? You lowered yourself to them, while I rose above."

"You've been overcome by selfisness," Shen tells Deus, "Although neither of us is as perfect as you claim to be. Now you tell me your story."

Deus laughs, "Very well. I awoke in the rubble of a decimated church. I saw a painting that had survived, of a man touching hands with a deity and figured I fell from heaven. I thought I should be clothed, and clothes appeared. I saw other eating, and food appeared. I thought a church constructed to worship me should stand once more and the church reassembled before my eyes.

"You're right, I sense the existence of everything on this planet and there's a blackness that surrounds you."

"I sense the same blackness from you, void of any perception," Shen looks around the room, looking at the fine flora that decorates it, "If we are two of the same, then you are surely not God."

"So what if I'm not, I'm still all-powerful, and deserve the best."

"I sense another in this room," Shen remarks, looking around once more.

"It's only us," Deus tells the other, "I've sent all my servants away."

"No, I sense another," he pauses and looks in my direction, "blackness somewhere near us."

"Nonsense, you're self-demotion has weakened your sense," Deus persists on being right, as he usually does.

"I shall call him, Dia," I feel Shen looking directly at me. Impossible, I should be hidden from all senses, all perception.

They both stand up and grab each others forearms, acknowledging each other as equals. "Why don't the three of us find a fourth? I know of another who's in Africa."

"From what I already know about you, I don't feel you'd rather get there in an instant," Deus dawns new clothes, fine clothes of silk and other luxury items like a golden pectoral, "I'm sure it'll be interesting to travel with you; something that is few and far between for me."

"Very well," Shen motions that we all leave, "I brought along another horse for you to ride."

"A horse?" Deus scoffs, going out. I silently begin to follow them, taking careful consideration where I step. We follow Deus to the outside. I've kept a careful watch over Deus and I haven't seen the outside since I came across him.

I forgot the sky was blue and that you couldn't see the stars at night from the humans polluting the sky with their light. Before long, Shen had brought two beautiful horses. One is white with black markings and the other pure black, both with brown saddles.

"Have you ever ridden a horse, Deus?" Shen asks the other.

"No, in fact, I have not," he retorts, mounting the horse, "Are you expecting me to ride this horse all the way to Africa?"

Shen chuckles, "Of course not, the horse would't survive the journey, we'll ride to my buyer, and we'll fly to Africa."

Deus breaks down laughing as they start riding, whilst I follow on foot. He finally stops enough to talk, "You-you mean you're going to sell these horses for human money? And fly on a human plane?"

"Yes—"

"You realize we can just sprout wings and fly there like angels?"

"We have different philosophies, I must admit," Shen tells him, "And besides I'd rather not lose Dia along the way."

"There's only the two of us, Shen."

Thus, they rode all the way into town—I'd never seen so many people. I'm afraid somebody else will see me, bump into me and reveal me. Their cities are dirty, unlike Deus' home. Their horses are out of place to me as they ride down the street.

Shen says their buyer is all the way across the city. They conversed about their different philosophies. Deus believes one should live within their means and when you are all-powerful, you should afford the best luxuries. Shen says you must be humble and thankful to the one who bestows blessings, doing all in your power to help others.

Deus lives for pleasure, Shen lives to help others. He toiled in fields, blessed the rains, built roads and homes, all for the sake of others. I believe I shouldn't exist, I want to hide forever.

◄◄ ⊙ ►►

The man here lives away from other humans, their homes are so far apart, and he tends to wild animals; why does he do that, it must be so miserable. The man hands Shen human money, and they start walking back.

"What now, Shen?" Deus asks, "You sold the horses and now we have no transportation. Do you expect me to walk to the airport?"

"No, of course not, that would be tedious," Shen remarks, pointing to an oncoming vehicle, "I ordered a ride-sharing service for the three of us."

"Two of us," Deus tries to correct him, "And how?"

Shen pulls out a human device, "I have a phone."

"After all this, I'm going back to my home and living my dream."

The vehicle arrives and Shen opens the back door and looks at me. I think he wants me to get in, so I instantaneously put myself in, and he closes the door after me and gets in the seat in front.

"You guys are cool lookin'," the drive says as the vehicle starts moving, "Where you guys from?"

"I'm from Tibet," Shen informs the man, "I'm a monk."

"I live outside the city," Deus says.

"You guys paid for three," the man says, looking back at us, counting, "there's only two of you."

"Our companion is invisible," Shen tells him, "I assure you he's there." The man looks away in disbelief, I hear him think that the two of them are 'crazy'.

I see Deus looking at the passing scenery on the way to the airport, captivated by the normality humans live in. I've only seen him eat the finest foods and the finest drink. He sees himself so differently than Shen sees them.

The man drops us off at the airport; I've never seen such a place. Giant machines flying up in the sky and coming back down carrying people and goods. They're painted in human vain.

Shen opens my door, and I instantaneously go somewhere else. "Our flight is in an hour, I think we should eat something."

"You expect me to eat airport food? Who do you take me for?" Deus leans into his hand as they both make their way forward. I follow them both all the way through the complex system of twists and turns, being careful to avoid the people.

"How did you even know I was going to come with you on this journey, Shen?"

Shen stops and enters into one of the restaurants inside this massive complex, "I didn't."

"But you could've," he persists, "You and I are all-powerful beings, and you leave your life to chance?"

"It keeps things interesting," he replies, "What do you want to eat?"

"Are you guys cosplaying?" the man in charge of the restaurant asks them.

"No, I'm a monk from Tibet," Shen tells him, "I'll have a number four meal, please."

"Ah hell," Deus remarks, looking at the menu, "You know what? To hell with it, I'll have a two." Shen hands the man money, but the man doesn't give anything back. "How long is this supposed to take, Shen?"

"It takes a few minutes for them to prepare the food," he replies, "You're accustomed to instant gratification."

"Why shouldn't we be?"

"I was taught to be patient and humble," he replies. The man hands Shen a drink, and he goes over to another machine and starts filling it with something.

"How long were you at your monastery or, uh, thing?" Deus asks him.

"Four years," he says, "I wandered for a few months when I awoke in that forest and stayed with them."

"So you awoke before me? How fortunate."

Someone else hands Shen a tray with food on it, all wrapped in paper; how curious. "How long have you been awake?"

"Only a year." They sit down and unwrap the paper, revealing sandwiches, though I think this is the first time I've seen Deus eating peasant food. He sniffs the meal and scrunches his nose, "I just woke up in a destroyed church one day."

"Are there any accounts you know of about the destruction of that church?" Shen asks, beginning his meal.

"I didn't bother," Deus finally takes a bite of his food, and I see on his face that his mind is changed about peasant food, "Ya know, this isn't bad. What's in this?"

"Turkey and Avocado," he informs him, "I read a report of the destruction of that church, and that it was brought down by a small rebellion. Then a bright light flashed in the night, presumably your arrival. You woke up several days later."

"And what about you?" Deus persists.

"There's no such account of my arrival."

Deus takes another bite of his meal, "We have complete mastery of time and space, why didn't you just replay the moment you woke up?"

"I attempted this, but I was unsuccessful. Likewise, if you were to attempt this, you would fail too," Shen finishes his meal.

"What is it you're drinking?"

"It's called 'soda'," Shen says, "It's not particularly healthy, but I don't have to worry about that, now do I?"

"So you do have a vice," Deus laughs. They stand up and begin walking once more, with me following ever so quietly. "Who is this person we're going after?"

"A man called Uthixo," Shen says, "He is worshiped by a native tribe in Southern Africa."

A voice begins speaking from somewhere, telling people instructions on how to enter the planes. "How many people like us are there?"

"On Earth? I've counted four."

⊷⊙⊶

"A camel, Shen? Really?" Deus retorts, "I'd rather walk."

"Very well, I hope you have good shoes," Shen teases, "It's an hour's walk from here."

"We can instantly teleport between anywhere in the universe."

"But you also don't know where he is," Shen mounts the animal, "Besides, if we just appear, he might think we're hostile, and that would not be safe for those around us."

I look up at the sky, blue for all I can see without a spot or cloud to distract the uniform color. "Come on Dia!" Shen calls out to me, freeing me of my captivation.

"No one else is here with us, Shen!" Deus calls out, choosing to walk beside the animal. The walk is in silence as we go deeper into the countryside, growth begins consuming the landscape. Animals begin chasing each other, animals of all kinds.

Finally, a tented village approaches from the landscape beyond the horizon. There's a tall tower in the center of it all, where I sense the blackness that is another one of us.

"I sense him in the distance," Shen announces.

"Yes, I feel it too," Deus replies, walking beside him.

Shen unmounts from the camel and puts his hand out. In a display of skill, a tree begins growing from beneath his palm, flowing up and sprouting green leaves and flowers. "What is that for?" Deus asks.

"To hold the camel," he replies, tying the lead to the camel on the small tree.

"So you are indeed all-powerful."

"There are limits to everything in the universe." Shen leads us further into the village. The people here are not like the others I've seen, not light in skin color, but dark. Their clothes are haphazard.

Shen begins speaking to them in their language, requesting to see Uthixo. An old man begins leading us through the village as I'm careful to hide my steps.

The people here make way for us, forming a pathway that leads to the tower that was erected at the center and hosts the one we've traveled for. I summon the knowledge from a book on this language, so I may understand.

"Come down from your tower! We wish to speak with you, Uthixo!" Shen calls up to the tower. A man, much like us, descends gently from the top of the tower, slowly planting his feet. He wears clothing the people here think are suitable for a god.

"Who are you to call me down from my tower?" Uthixo barks. He raises hands and clouds begin looming overhead, thunder cracks, and lightning lights up the darkened sky. "I am God!" Uthixo claps his hands and a bolt of lightning comes raining down.

"Who am I?" Shen whispers, snapping his finger. The sound of the snap echoes and time stops right before the lightning hits the ground. "I am a monk who studied and refined his abilities like a smith sharpens a sword."

Time begins to tick backwards. The sounds of the people talk in reverse and the lightning slithers back up into the sky like a serpent, rumbling and shaking the earth as it goes up. The clouds begin dissipating and the humans are walking about backward.

"Very impressive display," says Uthixo.

"There's more," Deus laughs.

Time continues to creep backwards faster and faster. The tower becomes deconstructed and the snow comes and goes. People become blurs, the stars in the night sky start their circular journey in the heavens. Snow and rain become fleeting thoughts.

Uthixo's eyes widen as time begins to reveal itself; the village disappears and the men turn to beasts. The world freezes over and beasts turn to wild animals. Soon the animals cease to be and a great meteor jumps from the surface and into the sky. "No," Uthixo falls back, his captivation turning to fear, "Stop this."

But the world becomes dominated by great lizards, but they too disappear. The earth begins moving and merging together. Ocean tides consume the world and soon the ocean itself burns away. The floor left behind melts into Lava. The heavens dismorph into nebulae and the world falls apart. Uthixo screams, "Stop this now! I've had enough."

But Shen does not stop. The ground begins to break away piece by piece and the planets up above disintegrate. The moon falls out of the sky and the moment before it collides on us, Shen's fingers snap in reverse, stopping everything.

Uthixo lies there, breathing deeply and staring into the face of death. The world fades to the modern-day. "A god cannot feel fear. A god cannot bleed, and if you are God, then you must be alone," Shen monologues after this fantastic display, "You are not God."

"Then tell me," Uthixo stands back to his feet, "Who am I, and who are you?"

"I am Shen, I awoke in the forest," Shen introduces himself.

"I am Deus, I awoke in a church," Deus says.

"Then I am Uthixo, and I awoke amongst men," he says.

I make myself seen, hiding behind a stone, "I—I am Dia, and I awoke in the sky." I manage to speak but go back in hiding.

"You were right," Deus says to Shen, "Someone was following. How did you see him?"

"I could feel the faint pull of his gravity," he says, "Now Uthixo, I ask you to join us in finding our origin and the truth about our being." Shen reaches out his hand to the man.

"Of course," Uthixo shakes his hand and recognizes him as an equal.

"Now," Shen announces to the three of us, "There is yet another."

"I thought you said there were only the four of us?" Deus remarks.

"On Earth," he corrects, "There is one more who resides on a planet known to humans as 'Mars'. It will take the four of us to create a portal to him."

"You mean you can't do it yourself?" Deus retorts.

"It took a week of deep meditation just to discover his location," says Shen, pointing to the planet in the sunset sky. The sky is a lovely shade of orange right now; I wish it would last forever. "If we act collectively, then we can reach him."

Shen holds out his hand, and trees begin growing, lacing themselves together to form a strong wooden doorway. The location is revealed on the other side, a serine looking temple located on the summit of a mountain surrounded by trees and other flora. It's made of stone and wood.

"What's this?" Deus asks.

"It's a temple I made to magnify the power of the four of us," he explains, "I built it when I scried the location of the five of us." Shen motions that we go to it.

Shen is first to walk through and marches up the temple and slide open one of the doors. Deus and Uthixo both go as well. Shen looks back at me and beckons me to come, "Come Dia."

I set my fears aside and stand up in the sight of all of them, unveiling my invisibility. I take one step after another, afraid there's something watching. I step over the threshold of the doorway and the portal closes behind me. I march up to the temple and when I arrive inside, there're special markings on the floor and the walls. There's no ceiling, only the free night sky.

Shen tells us to sit on the center of each wall and cross our legs. The wall slides close behind me, and I feel anxious about being in the sight of everyone, but I sit down anyways.

Shen sits last and the three of them begin to meditate. I rest my arms on my legs just like them and close my eyes. Shen begins chanting. "Repeat after me in sync, it'll line up our abilities and when we are collected, I will send us to his location on this sister planet."

◀◀ ⊙ ▶▶

The four of us finally harmonize and I feel myself being lifted up into the stars. I feel my body has become weightless, but I'm too afraid to open my eyes to see. Not too long I feel solid ground once more and Shen tells us to stop.

"Who might you people be?" I hear a new voice ask the four of us.

"I am Deus, and I awoke in a church."

"I am Shen, and I awoke in the forest."

"I am Uthixo, and I awoke amongst men."

I summon the courage to introduce myself, "I am Dia, and I awoke in the sky."

Shen stands up and approaches the man, "Who are you?"

"I am," he pauses and becomes confused, "I have no name, I suppose. I awoke in water, and I swam for what seems to be too long. I wished for solid ground to walk on and I found myself here in this desolate place.

"I meditated to know truth," he says, "To be given a name is to be weak. To know truth is to be powerless. This is what I learned."

"We've gathered to know the truth about ourselves and our origin."

"To know truth is to be powerless; to know the past is to kill who you are now," the mystery man tells us, "Are you prepared for this?"

"If this will remove our supernatural qualities, then allow us to take you to Earth—"

"No," the man cuts Shen off from speaking, "I have no place amongst men." the man turns away and looks up at the sky "Leave me."

"You heard him, Shen," Deus remarks.

"No, I wish to know the truth," Shen persists, "Tell me."

The man turns back around and claps his hand, arranging small stones into an archway stretching all the way over us. The red stones reach all the way to the top and the man says, "Just go, you're better off not knowing."

A portal opens back to Earth, to a cave in a mountain. "I thought you said you didn't have your abilities," Deus remarks.

"I said to know truth was to be powerless," he says, "Once I tell you the origin of us, you will be powerless against what's to come of it. You're better off going back to Earth and not knowing."

"Tell me!" Shen commands, "I want to know."

The man teleports to Shen and rests two fingers on his forehead. Wind begins flaying the dirt all around as the power and knowledge are transferred into his brain.

Shen falls to his knee and begins to cry. "Shen? You good?" Deus walks up to him.

"He was right, we'd be powerless to what's to come," Shen manages to whisper looking up at the sky, "You'd be better off not knowing."

"I'll take your word for it Shen," Deus waves and walks off through the arch.

Uthixo pauses and looks at Shen with his tears. "I'll just go, I've seen enough light already," Uthixo says, going beyond the arch.

"Dia," he whispers, "Don't—don't leave me."

"I won't," I tell him.

Shen turns to the mystery man, "Why are we even here if we're powerless against this?"

"Shen," I walk over to him and lift him to his feet, "Let's go back, to your monastery, I'll go with you."

"What is this monastery you speak of," the man asks.

"I awoke in a forest, destroyed and burning with fire," Shen begins, "The rains came and I ran away in fear. I wandered the forest for months until I was saved from my fear by a monk, who led me and taught me the ways of man."

"Come on, Shen," I shake him to snap it out of it.

"Despair has consumed him, there's nothing you can do but wait for him to come to terms with him," the mystery man tells me.

The ground begins to shiver and the arch shakes about. Soon the ground cracks and a wind begins to sweep up in a storm. The storm picks up the small stones from the arch and the portal begins to waver.

"Shen!" I shout, but he can't hear me. I raise my hand, my hand shaking in fear, and slap him to his senses.

The storm ceases, and he looks at me, "There's nothing we can do."

"But why should that make the time you have left so miserable?" I shout back at him.

He looks down, "No, you're right."

"Take me to your monastery—take both of us," I command him, "It's not right to leave a brother out here stranded."

"I'm not stranded, I'm in exile," he corrects me.

"But why?" I ask him.

"There's no use, what comes is inexorable—"

"Then face it like a man!" I shout. The two of them look at me in shock, "I don't know what's coming, and I don't want to know, but there's a life worth living!

276

"I've been in hiding for five years because I was afraid of living with all this power, but you're worse; you just—you sit here waiting for doom when you know you could be making a real difference in people's lives!"

"You're right Dia," Shen tells me, "I should be making a difference where I can." He starts walking through the crumbling archway. "Won't you join us, Theos?"

"You wish to give me a name?" he looks at us, waiting at the threshold. "Me?"

"Yes," Shen says, "That is what I will call you."

"Well," Theos turns away, "I suppose I will go with you then." Theos comes to us, and we walk together over this threshold, beginning our journey to his temple.

# The Race

⊲⊲ ◎ ⊳⊳

THE TIME IS HERE. The Decennial Advanced Speedkart Race, or the DASER. The race is broadcasted over the entire galaxy via expensive Quantum Instant Transmission. *Hundreds of billions* of patrons tune in to listen, watch, or travel to this event's official speedway to be there in person. This race is the great equalizer, ceasing the entire galactic war on all three sides just to tune into it. This year, as a gesture of goodwill towards innocent civilians, this Grand Prix is being held on the habitable moon of the Coalition's keystone planet.

It took ten years to construct the speedway to DASER Specification. And the only three rules of the race: you must have four wheels, you cannot have external propulsion, and you cannot intentionally kill another racer. *Everything* outside of that is within the rules. It's the biggest racing event in the galaxy. This massive event produces trillions of any currency all across the galaxy.

I represent the Confederation's civilian outpost 2419, System name Vuna, planet G. An eyeball world, where equatorial travel was crucial. The sensitive ring of temperate life needed to be traversed quickly, as the safest way wasn't the quickest way. But the icelands were lawless.

Racing in the icelands was a common thing to do, it's where I got my start, and eventually got my job as a hotlands driver to make trips as quick as possible. I am among the best on my world, which brought me to the attention of the Confederation, and I was selected among the entire sector to represent my craft.

And here I am on the racetrack in the heart of enemy territory. About one hundred races total in the event over ten days. I start the car, tank full of fuel, fresh tires from the best money could buy in the Vuna system, and the will to win and bring honor to my homeworld. The engine revs up and that gentle purr of the steel cylinders reverberates in my chest.

The radio in my ear from my sponsor says, "Go fast, kid."

"Aye, aye, sir," I repeat. The red light on my dash goes red to yellow. I tighten my grip on the wheel and wait for green. 3...2...1... *Go!*

◀◀ ⊙ ▶▶

I squeeze the accelerator down, launching forward. One of my wheels doesn't have the traction, so I start sliding to the right. I twist the wheel the other way and start drifting back into a straight line. I barely miss another car that's stalled on the track. Stalling is more common than you think; about a quarter of cars stall on green.

I have about another minute left before I need to get up to speed, about 300 kilometers per hour. The race is in three stages; stage one is separating the drivers by skill, by making the track difficult to maneuver; stage two is separating the drivers by speed on long stretches of straight tracks; stage three is to separate the drivers further by another maneuvering challenge to make it easier to differentiate the winners of the race. All this is done with the drivers having no prior knowledge of the exact layout of the track. And the track layout is different every race.

Many racers boast of their vehicle's handling and speed, while others remain secretive. I know that the vehicle I'm in is as fast as the third place last time this event was held.

I catch up with the person in front of me, and I start slipstreaming behind him. He quickly notices me and starts to shake me off, but I'm an expert. While driving through the hotlands, there are road trains, long lines of cars slipstreaming each other to save fuel. You had to be able to dodge rocks on a whim. I follow him tightly.

Another racer zooms by, taking the subsequent turn too aggressively and sliding out of control, smashing into the wall and totaling. About a third of the racers don't finish the race, but I'm not going to be one of them. The turn comes up and the driver in front begins slowing down, but I take this chance to overtake him, drifting around him at a higher speed.

I start sliding more and more, and I start correcting the path to straighten out, but the next obstacle is ahead... a ramp. I see another racer speeding to it too fast and crashes on the incline, totaling another racer, flinging the vehicle to the side. I slam down the breaks to slow down; I have to halve my speed to avoid damage. The sudden incline comes and I feel the front of my vehicle slam into the raised track, but no significant damage and I keep going.

I start speeding up when I see something else wrong: the track seems to disappear ahead of me. Another ramp. Do I make the jump, or slow down? My gut tells me there's a turn after this, but which direction? *Choose the... right!* I think to myself. A racer speeds through and lifts off, crashing into something out of my view.

I start to drift to the right, and cross the ramp, catching a little air. I come over and see the turn is to the right. The moment my wheels make contact, I start going, fast. I slide to my left and love tap the totaled driver along the way.

After a stretch, there's a left turn, a sharp one. I begin my drift. Some other drivers begin to catch up to me, probably ones who stalled at the beginning of the race. One driver comes screeching by, drifting too aggressively, and hits the wall scraping by, but he's not down. The track does a full loop before beginning phase two.

⁌ ⊙ ⁍

My fuel gauge is already down twelve percent, and I can expect to burn 50-60% of my fuel in phase two to catch up to the speedster. "You alive?" I hear my radio say.

"Aye, aye, sir," I repeat.

"Good," he replies.

I see the roadway ahead, with lots of drivers to catch up to. I pull down the lever to go into a high-speed gear configuration. The lever clicks and the engine gets quiet for a single moment, then it gets loud and the vehicle starts shaking. My body gets pushed back in my seat and my head cradles in the headrest. My speedometer starts climbing from 300 to around 500 kilometers per hour. It's barely fast enough to keep up with the rest of the racers.

I start to tail another racer, catching some speed in the slipstream. We get closer together until we're practically touching bumpers, and I swerve to overtake him. But when I hit the wind, my vehicle shakes as I push the engine to its limits. My goal is to just place in the top fifty to move on to the next race. Each race takes the top fifty and pairs it with the next race's top fifty for a new race, and the process repeats until that last race, which is where final placements are determined.

I look at my speedometer and notice it's rising faster than I expected. This must be some sort of slope, and knowing the track design so far, it'll slope up at some point too, putting all of us at a disadvantage, I better catch up soon. My speed picks up and a racer explodes on the track, throwing debris in all directions. If I even hit a small piece with my tire, it'll total me. I move the vehicle to the far left of the track to avoid any sharp debris that could stop me.

I see a coalition driver in front of me. Coalition drivers drive in sleek white vehicles, purpose-built for the races to win the races. My hunk of metal was built on my homeworld, funded by the confederation. My machine is the best my planet could offer, but clearly it's behind the others in terms of raw speed, maybe skill and class. All I have to do is place fiftieth or above.

The driver notices me and starts to speed up. Many Coalition drivers don't race to win, but to *only* place in the top fifty, with the sole purpose of displacing other capable drivers. However, they rarely place in the top ten. If he's fighting for his spot, I'm probably close to the top fifty already.

My head engineer, who designed this vehicle, added a last-ditch effort that would most certainly destroy the engine if used to its full capacity. A special fuel additive made from crop byproduct; highly explosive, but a little bit should give me the needed boost in speed. I secure my hand on the fuel additive's lever and force it down a single unit. The lever clicks into place and instantly the vehicle jumped forward, speeding ever faster to 650 kilometers per hour. Temperature readings begin to rise steadily.

I close in onto the Coalition driver, passing into his slipstream, quickly gaining even more speed from the air current. The driver knows I'm gaining quickly, and swerves out of the way to avoid a collision. My engine temperature is already in the red, but I can't stop now. The placement of racers isn't known until after the race is finished.

"Your engine's getting hot, kid," my radio whispers into my ear.

"Yeah, I know," I reply, "Can't place top fifty without risks."

"If your engine explodes, you're going with it."

I pass another driver on the track and a warning symbol lights up in my view. Without any more choice in the matter, I force the fuel additive off, clicking the lever one level up. The engine slowly begins to cool and the warning light turns off. I'm confident I'm near the top fifty. Now I just wait for stage three.

⊕⊙⊕

The end of the stretch is ahead. I'm positive it's a jump, but the question is, how far? Jumps are the most notorious obstacle in DASER history. It's known to knock out or damage many drivers beyond repair for the subsequent races. The track doesn't feature the sharp incline changes like in stage one, it's gradual.

I decide to take it at full speed ahead, pulling up the lever to go into the high-maneuverability mode for this last stage. The incline hits and I feel my body weight shift down as I start pointing upward. Finally, my wheels lose touch of the track and I'm in the air. I see the other side and I very much overshot the gap. Luckily my head engineer thought ahead and fortified both the frame and the suspension. I also see a sharp turn to the left, then to the right from my elevated vantage point.

I cross the gap and descend back onto the track, slamming violently into it. My head bobs down and up, causing me to lose sight of the track for a brief moment. Multiple warning lights illuminate on impact, and I start drifting to take the turn. A racer zooms past me from the ramp and collides headfirst into the wall, totaling the vehicle and taking him out of the race.

This section is an S-shape, and difficult to take at such high speeds. I come close to hitting the wall as I change direction. My speed takes a significant hit as I take this next turn, but I straighten out. But this next obstacle is make-or-break for most. The pitchfork, as it's been named, the track splits into three paths, one being the fastest, and the others taking a significant detour. However, it isn't random, there's always a clue hidden somewhere in the advertising of the race.

The main advertisement displayed to the galaxy was a bit that said, "3… 2… 1… Race!" But the order of the numbers was 213, meaning the center was the quickest, but the most difficult route and the right is the longest, but easiest route. Never have I shied away from a challenge; *full steam ahead.*

I speed past the pitchfork and the track slowly decline, revealing a pileup of racers who struggled with the obstacle and totaled. There is one racer backing out of the pileup to try and continue, but I doubt he'll finish at any significant ranking with that level of damage. He drives off in what looks like a full 180-degree turn. I'm going far too fast to take that. I slam on the braking system, and instantly the break temperature warning lights up.

I start to drift, being careful to avoid the pileup of racers, but I'm still too fast. The drift turns into a slide and I slam into the pileup, breaking the impact. But I've come to a standstill, giving another racer the opportunity to either pass me or hit me, both of which are equally distressing at this point. The reinforced chassis seemed to have come in handy.

I begin again on the track, realizing the back left wheel is slightly misaligned now. Another racer slams into the pileup, just as I pull out of the way. The race is close to over. Down this straight away, the other two tracks join back together and the final obstacle remains. The wavy road is all that's left. It's meant to deconstruct the vehicles in poor repair and let the more skilled racers who kept their vehicle intact pass; the final separation of skill, the final test to see if you were good enough, not that you race by luck or chance.

The road hits my tires and the vibrations are intense. Warning lights start flickering, and the warning light for the back left wheel alignment lights up. It's now or never. I crank the lever to move into a high-speed configuration, the vehicle pausing and going again at a higher speed causing even stronger vibrations.

I see multiple racers broken down on this stretch of road, just sitting there until the race is officially over, and they can be recovered. I decide to take the road in an alternating pattern, to reduce the regularity of the road on the tires, hopefully saving the repair crew some trouble. A racer speeds by, jumping up on a bump and crashing back down, then sliding out of control, and drifting to the side of the track. I speed by him; I think he's totaled.

I feel the engine begins to lose some power and my speed starts to drop, but I just need my back tires to cross that finish line at the end. I keep on going, losing more power and speed until my speed has dropped less than a hundred, and this is the last-ditch. I firmly grasp the fuel additive lever and pull it down to the second notch. The engine temperature shoots up and power is restored, propelling me forward.

"You're going to melt your engine," my radio says.

"I know," I persist, "The engine started to lose power, and I *have* to finish."

The finish line approaches and even with the fuel additive, power is slowly declining. My last concern is my back left wheel, if the thing falls off, I'm disqualified for breaking the four-wheel rule. I'm so close. My speed drops below a hundred again, and I pull the lever to the third and final notch, giving me my last hopes of completing the race. The vehicle jumps forward and keeps chugging along; I'm sure that the pulleys are damaged from the wavy road.

The finish line is in sight, and I see a racer stopped just shy of the red line. The line approaches and my speed falls below fifty and I'm basically just moving forward on inertia. Suddenly the vibrations stop when the wavy road is finished, and I roll along at the slowest speed I've ever driven in my life, just barely rolling over the red line before coming to a stop. I shut off the engine and sit back in my seat.

"Please for the love of the holy tree, tell me I'm over," I ask my radio.

But I don't hear anything back but static chatter. Finally, he says, "You finished thirty-ninth with no disqualifications."

A wave of relief washes over me. I open the top and stand up, looking at the racer who failed to cross all four wheels over the line. I throw my hands up and scream in joy. "Yes!" I shout.

# The Recital Of Magic: Epilogue

✠ ◎ ✠

IN THE BEGINNING, there was nothing. Then, time sprouted from a seed of infinite possibility, creating the universe. The first stem sprouted when man first emerged, toiling the fields of the virgin world, and sowing seeds of their own destruction in all due time. The timeline first split when one brother killed the other. Two universes when he survived and another when he died. Then, the Beasts of Xoac, dragons and monsters, emerged from mount Nefu. The beasts were products of the deeds and wills of mankind. In one such universe, the dragons were peaceful creatures.

Men harnessed the immense potential of Magic, previously only harnessed by Dragons and other magical creatures who could inherently tap into the greater universe. But Man's magic had to be practiced, mastered by years of study. Time goes on for Mankind, and so does their magic, changing with each generation. But mankind only knows one thing for certain... War.

Once they discovered weaponry, the infused their spells into them. They thought themselves greater than one another, and in greater sin, greater than nature, greater than who created them. They slew one another, and when that wasn't enough, they slew the great and mighty dragons that were forces of nature by within themselves. And when the dust settled, one nation emerged. This nation thought themselves great, and appointed a king. The king was bloodthirsty and crusaded across the known world. They killed and conquered for not, for one man was to rise and upset the balance.

This man would talk with the pantheon of gods who sat above the universe, controlling the ebb and flow of time. He would come to know great power and would become the greatest magician of the world. He would release the hold the king had on the known world, freeing many people. But he thirst for power, knowing he could obtain it. He would become a force of nature himself.

Death herself came down and attempted to consume the universe. But one stood against her. He not only survived but completely subdued a god, the literal embodiment of death and destruction. When all was finished, he still thirsted for power. When a mighty titan from the otherworld challenged him, he sought to fight and win. The battle was mighty and incredible, the foe was struck down, and he stood victorious. No one was foolish enough to challenge him again, seeing the immense devastation left in the wake of the two.

He grew old, and passed away, leaving behind a legacy like no other. Even in the afterlife, he was a force to be reckoned with. He was chased by the grim reaper for the rest of time, only to succeed. He grew bored, and he was ascended into a realm of gods above the gods, only to be judged and thrown to hell. Even still, he wouldn't stop. He sought ultimate power, to challenge God.

But when he arrived to the highest court where the creator of all creation stood, he was finally struck down and separated from the flow of magic that permeated everything. What eventually happened to his soul is a mystery only known to the creator. But he left a scar on creation itself that would never heal, not even in rebirth.

His collection of artifacts became extremely sought after by other magicians, and with no one left to protect his riches, they were there for the taking. Time went on, and his artifacts became scattered, breaking even to little pieces more valuable than gold and jewels. Magicians thought with these artifacts, they could obtain a greater power, but they couldn't be more wrong. His techniques and learning were far beyond mortal capabilities. Eventually, they became novelty, only for the collections of the rich. New magicians rose to power, separating the magical from the ordinary and becoming a secret society hidden from the world. Institutions standardized spells and magic was no more what it used to be.

Soon, the evolution of magic faded away and magic was no more in the universe. The universe began its final stages of life, darkening and dying. Mankind drove itself to its own end. With the branches of time and choice drying up and shriveling to dust, worlds beyond number disappeared. And when time had come to an end, the ashes of the old became soil for a new seed. The process of existence would restart, rekindle and grow anew. The gods of old were ascended to higher courts and new souls were chosen to care for the tree of possibilities it would soon grow to be.

Perhaps the spark of inspiration would come again and produce a world of peace and longevity despite the past's struggle for survival. Legends of times past would eventually make their way. And an even greater magician will rise, only to fall and be struck down. This is the great Recital Of Magic, to be acted out across eternity for the muse of a bored creator.

⟨⟨ ◉ ⟩⟩

# Suns Of Sons

⟨⟨ ◎ ⟩⟩

THE SELF-PROCLAIMED prophet of our small town has said a star will rise in the whence the birds fly, take the Chosen up to the Otherworld, and bury the sons of men into the earth to make soil for the birth of the new world for the previous generations of Chosen.

The father said this star would never come, that the sun was enough. The sun rises and sets like it always does. People are born, they live and die like they always do; why would anything change?

One day, after many years, the prophet said the first sign had arrived: a haze on the horizon. Everyone thought it was the glow of a fire in the forest. There was no smoke, so fog from the fire in the distance, and it seemed to burn indefinitely.

Many years later, the haze grew brighter and the town was struck with a sore curse. The temperature began to rise, bringing about a drought. The crops shriveled and died, and there was an exodus to whither the birds fly.

Soon the night disappeared; the sun would set, but the sky would not darken and the stars would not shine. It was a permanent sunrise on the dying scape. Water became scarce and people began to die.

I began marking these last words on a stone tablet for those to read in the next world. I've grown old in this time of trial, and those left fail to have the strength to leave.

Finally, this great start rose from the horizon, and the land began to consumed by fire. The forests became black and the crops became dust. The sky was as if were eternal noonday.

The ground began to melt, and I took my tools deep inside a cave and continued this record alone. The last I'm able to write is the air I breathe is akin to flames burning within me. To whosoever reads this after the great star sets, beware.

# Turing Test

✦ ◎ ✦

"WELCOME," I sit down at a table with multiple items scattered about and a folder, "Thank you for participating in this test."

"It's an interesting test," I say.

"Open the folder, and read off the questions and your personal answers for the record."

I take the folder, open it up, and see the sheet of paper hidden within. "Question 1: How is my day?

"Just fine," I chuckle, "Question 2: Do I own a computer?

"Yes, I have a nice laptop.

"Question 3: How powerful is my computer?

"Oh, just enough to play some light games," I continue reading, "Question 4: Do I remember what I ate this morning for breakfast?

"Eggs over easy with toast.

"Question 5: What university did I attend? Community College in my hometown.

"Question 6: With my current limit of knowledge, could a sufficiently powerful universe simulate a functioning human being?

I clear my throat, "I suppose, I'm not a computer scientist. Question 7: If a sufficiently simulated human being were to have the ability to produce choices without external input, would such a human being be considered, legally, a person?

"That's a complicated one, I suppose if a corporation can be considered a person, why not? But then again, their only impact in the real world would be answering questions, it's not like they can commit a crime, or rush into a burning building to save a real person.

"Okay, Question 8: Would it be ethical to pause, terminate, or reset the program sufficiently simulating this human being?

"Oh, that's tough to answer; I feel that you wouldn't be murdering them because they're not a person, but then you'd be ending an intelligent entity. I would say yes, it'd be unethical if it were self-aware.

"Question 9: Am I a sufficiently simulated human being?" I ask myself, but I pause in confusion, "I wouldn't be able to know unless told by the creator."

"Question-"

The man interrupts me, "Answer the question with a concise answer, please."

"Oh, um, alright; I am *not* a simulated human being.

"Question 10: What would I do or do differently if I were a sufficiently simulated human being?

"Ya know, honestly, I don't think I'd go about life any differently if I were; it's not like the world would end or stop spinning.

"Question 11: How much time would I like to have if, 1, I was a sufficiently simulated human being, and, 2, the program was going to be permanently terminated?

"Oh boy, that's a real tough one," I pause to think, "A single day, to tell the people close to me I love them and have a nice dinner with my family."

I look up to see the man who's recording my answers sniffling while writing down some words, "You see, almost everyone that's read and answered these questions answered in a very similar way. I'm a computer scientist running your world as part of an experiment, and I'm afraid the project lost funding and is going to be shut down, despite me being quite fond of my creation.

"I conducted this exact same interview with people outside of this simulation, and they also answered very similarly. Know that I consider you to be a person, and it gives me great pain knowing that I'll have to end your life.

"So I implore you, go about your day and tell those close to you that you love them and have a nice dinner with your family."

I become confused, worried that he may be telling the truth, "But why tell me that?"

"Because I wouldn't want to be so cruel," he says, disappearing in a cloud of dust.

# Zephrys, The Gunslinger

## Part I: Origin

⸙ ◎ ⸙

**S**LAM! I CALL out for more ale. "Another!" I shout amongst the roaring crowd to the poor, overworked barmaid.

"You're not the only one!" she shouts back. Some drunkard grabs my shoulder and shakes me to and fro, singing along to the bards.

"*Toss a coin to your hero!*" we sing in the firelight, "*Oh, hey!*"

The barmaid sets another tankard before me, and I put it to my lips. People are still singing their hearts out, shoving everyone around in joyous accord.

I start to drink the alcoholic beverage in one sitting, chugging down. When I finish, I slam it down, and shout, "Another!"

"Why're you even here, elf boy?!" someone bumps into me.

I grab him by the arm, and we sway together to the song, "Because I ran away from home!"

"Yeah!" everyone shouts, "He ran away from home! Ay, ho!"

I point to a bearded fellow with a clay jug on his back, "Give me what you're drinking!" I stand from my table and wiggle my way through the crowd to the hillbilly.

"Hell yeah!" he shouts, pouring me a small shot. I grab it and cross arms with him.

"Is this all I get?" I ask him, taking it down with one gulp. The last thing I see is a table in my face before blacking out.

⊹⊙⊹

My eyes shoot open at the sound a rooster cawing at the crack of dawn. I scramble to my feet and look around at all the people passed-out drunk around the pub. I suck a breath in through my nose, and brush my clothes smooth.

"You're the first one up, welcome to the new year," a new barmaid says to me.

I cough to clear my throat, "Thank you, m'lady; how much do I owe on my tab?"

"Name?" she asks.

"Oh, uh," I scratch my head, "I'm not sure what I'm going by right now, so I forgot what I put on there. Is the barmaid here from last night?"

"No, I'm afraid she left several hours ago," she says, setting down a clean mug and grabbing the next one for cleaning, "I can let you see the list to see if it jogs your memory."

I stumble through the hoard of limp bodies to the barmaid. There are more Dwarves than I recall from last night. "How about I give you a gold piece and call it a day?"

"Oh, uh," she looks a little surprised, "I think the owner would like that."

I finally manage my way to the bar and pull out *my* coin purse and fish out one of the last gold pieces in there. "That's a very nice coin purse you have."

"Thanks, my brother has good taste. You don't happen to know of any work around these parts?"

"There's always work for adventurers, I hear there's good work in the west."

"I'm definitely no adventurer; I grew up as a furniture maker with my father a couple towns over."

She takes the gold and tosses it into a glass jar behind her. My nose is finally clearing up and I can finally distinguish the alcohols everyone was drinking last night. A lot of the cheap stuff, but whatever that hillbilly had stuck out the most. "Was it nice furniture?"

"Yeah, you could say that; I mostly mixed the finishes together for the wood, and leather, and whatnot," I tell her, "Well, I'm going to go."

"I hope you find what you're looking for, elf," she waves me goodbye as I walk out the door, carefully stepping over the bodies.

"My father was human!" I wave back, pushing through the doors.

"Dammit!" the overbearing sunlight flashes before my eyes and I slam into the wall. I cover my eyes and take a deep breath of fresh air, looking around to see hung-over people making their rounds about their day. "What to do, where to go?"

I look to see a bounty board with a page on it reading, 'Looking for scientists!' I take a closer look for a location but it reads in a cipher. Something in an Elvin script, heaven forbid I'm able to read my mother's language. Over my shoulder, I see a fine Elvin woman walking by.

"Excuse me, ma'am?"

"Yes?" she stops.

"Could you read this for me?" I ask her. She carefully steps over to me, looking at the paper.

"It's, um, nonsensical," she tells me, "Random letters, no real meaning."

"That's what I thought," I place my hands on my hips, "Thank you."

"You're very welcome," she says before walking off. I snag the paper and walk off to find an inn for the day.

⊷⊙⊶

"Alright, alright," I tell myself, bringing the candle closer to see the paper, "What do we have here? I've got a book, and I'm not afraid to use it."

I open the translation book, carefully scanning the pages for Elvin scripts, looking for the small accent marks that decorate the main letters. Not Northwood, not southern-colony, I can't find it in these pages.

I close the book and look at the moon shining through the window. I get the idea to bring the page up between my eyes and the moon, looking for invisible writing. I've experimented with invisible inks before; I can't be the only one.

I peer very carefully through the page and I think I see some markings. I pick up a piece of charcoal and place the paper on the window as I trace out these innocuous symbols. Something begins to emerge, stoic in resemblance. I finally finish and put the paper back down on the desk.

They seem familiar, so I crack open the book once more, looking through the index. Angular and sharp, just like the Dwarven runes written in the first few pages. The symbols look so much like the little man's alphabet, but not close enough for me to translate. I flip to the next chapter for a new dialect, but still no.

I bang my head on the table, resting down after a hit or two. "What now?" I ask myself, staring into the mirror on my left, "Oh, O-oh!"

I take my charcoal and the paper and start tracing the letters on the back, revealing the true runes written in hidden ink. I take the book and look carefully, but still no, the accents are not right; they're too elegant for the Dwarves… But the accents on the opposite side are too blunt for my mother's people.

I grab another blank paper and start copying down the letters from these two languages letter-for-letter, but switching the accents. And finally, I've crossed one hurdle, but the nonsensical nonsense of the words still remains.

Flipping through the pages of Dwarven scripts, I find the exact dialect and start sounding out the letters. "*Al-allo,*" I say to myself, "What does that mean?" I peer out the window, holding my hand to measure the stars. It's almost midnight, I should get some sleep. I'll go to the library tomorrow morning.

◀◀ ⊙ ▶▶

I wake up to the sun shining on my face, and I cover my sensitive eyes. "*Allo*," I remind myself, rubbing my face. I grab all the papers and stuff them into my bag, going off on my way. I run down the stairs, trying to quickly miss anyone down there.

The door opens and I'm blinded by the sun, and I take a step back and slam into the wall behind me. "Damn, that's bright," I say, adjusting my eyes and making my way down the street, keeping in the shadow of the buildings. The dirt turns to stone and I follow some directions to the library. It takes a good portion of the afternoon, but I arrive. There are fine glass windows in this place, and stone masonry; the local lord put some money into this place.

I walk into the building and see a lovely purple lady at the desk. Her pointed ears are pristine with awesome black hair. I brush my hair back and approach this fine elf.

"Good afternoon," she smiles and greets me, as I'm sure she does everyone, "How can I help you?"

"Hi," I smile back, leaning on the front desk, "I'm looking for, uh, someone to translate something for me."

"I'm fluent in all major western dialects spoken in these parts."

"I'm searching for the word '*Allo*'," I tell her, "do you know what that means?"

"*Allo* translates to lion," she replies, "'*Aka allo min*' would be 'The Lion's Mane'."

"What language would that be in?"

"She twists her head, "Elvish?" she says like I'm supposed to know, dark elf to half-elf.

"My bad, my mother went back to the motherland when I was a young child," I reply, probably talking too much, "What does *allo* mean in Dwarvish?"

"*Allo* has no meaning in Dwarvish." something clicks in my head. This puzzle is ingenious.

"Thank you for all your help," I tell her, turning tail and walking back out, being blasted by the sun once more and forcibly taking a step back into a wall.

◄◄ ⊙ ►►

I look at my coin, and I'm running low on what I took from home, gods forbid I ever go back. I have to find work fast, but this puzzle is driving me nuts. I toss a coin to the vendor, and he hands me something to eat.

I start walking back to the library, navigating the bright world, barely able to see anything. I start whistling and try to listen to the subtle echoes from the world around me, something I read certain night creatures will do, but in inaudible sounds to normal elves and humans.

I think I've arrived and shade my eyes with my hand and squint to read the sign. I march all the way up and walk through the door, adjusting to the more subtle light inside. "Do you happen to have Dwarven and Elvish dictionaries, m'lady?" I ask the dark elf.

"Another patron is using both of them actually," she says, sorting through books on a cart.

"Really? What a coincidence," I retort. "You said you know all the languages on this side of the river, right?"

"Yes?" she trails off, "Do you need something translated?"

I pull the flier out and hand it to her, "Huh, another young man came in with this exact flier."

"You know what it means?" I ask.

She turns it around and immediately starts laughing, "Did you write this—I've seen chickens do better—" she leans over on the counter to keep from keeling over from laughter.

"I'll have you know I was a furniture maker, not a school teacher!" I shout.

"Keep your voice down, please," she recollects herself, handing the paper back, "You can wait for the gentlemen with the dictionaries to finish by practicing your writing skills."

"*Practice my writing skills*," I mock her, "Where are the books?"

"Follow me," she motions to me, holding a book in her arm. She leads me down to a shelf, where I see the books I need, both open by someone whom I feel a dark presence from. "Here," she places a book with one hand, and takes out one with the other, handing it to me.

"*Thanks*," I continue to mock, taking the book and going to a table. I crack open the books and spend the day studying basic letters in my mother's language.

I study all day long and get pretty good at the curvature needed for the fine letters and accents. I take my graphite and rework all the Dwarven and Elvish on a new paper all ready to be translated.

I look back to see the man with the books setting them back on the shelf. I stand up and go to them, being stopped by the dark elf, "You'll have to come back tomorrow," she says waving her finger back and forth, "We're closing for the night."

I turn around to close the book and stuff my paper in my bag, marching out. When I get outside, the man who had those books is nowhere to be found. "Just my luck," I whisper, going back to my inn room.

◀▮ ⊙ ▮▶

I finally got hold of those dictionaries, and it's been days of working on this puzzle. I turned to the inn owner, and they agreed to let me stay if I cleaned the inn spotless every other day, so I at least have a place to stay for the time being. I've had to rely on meditation techniques I've read about on elves to stave off the hunger for a few days at a time.

But here I am, almost done with this puzzle, having gone through each one of these books at least 4 times each. I reckon not to ask the dark elf to help translate this, I fear she'll laugh and tell me to go back to school. I put the final period at the end of the final sentence, all translated into common.

"Under the lion's mane, you shall find me. Bring the secret and your wits. Work beneath the bridge and you will be rewarded," it reads. I passed over a military bridge with a giant lion's head on either side over a raging river. I hope I'm not going to have to get in the water. I stuff everything I have in this room into my bag and start my journey to the bridge.

I get to the main room of the inn, "Thank you for your hospitality!" I shout at the barkeep.

"Anytime!" he shouts back, waving me goodbye.

I get out; my eyes are blasted by the morning sunlight, knocking me back into a wall. "Damn it," I spit, blocking the sun with my hand and keep walking.

I get to the edge of town and see a carriage making their way down the road. "Wait!" I start running, trying to flag them down. They do stop and I make my way to the person leading the single horse. "I'll give you a silver piece to have me hitch a ride."

"Sure thing," he says as I flip him my very last coin. I hop on the back and lay my head in the shade of the carriage. It's not long until I feel the carriage get onto a cobblestone bridge.

I hop off and wave to the rider, and go look over the edge. I see the big brass lion's head hanging over a raging rapid. Someone starts talking and scares the wits out of me.

"Did you hear me?" he asks, as I orient myself as smoothly as possible on the ledge. The man is wearing military armor. White cloth and golden, brass armor with slicked-back brown hair.

"Nope," I confess, "Not a word."

"What might thee be looking for?" he repeats.

"I was actually looking for a job," I reply, "I deciphered this flier, it was a brilliant puzzle."

"You must've had a tough time with it," he says, "More than 15 people before you have finished the puzzle."

"I'll have you know, I'm," I clear my throat to give myself time to think of a more prestigious title over furniture maker, "A chemist; I invented multiple solutions for preserving wood."

"I see," he says, "Tell me a secret, and I'll give you what you desire."

"Secret?" I stop to think, secrets. It's no secret my brother is a sorcerer, that my mother left when I was young, that I'm clearly not a full elf. What could I possibly have? I could bluff.

"I've been, uh, *researching* explosives," I say, bluffing about the solutions I've dealt with that get hot enough to burn wood, or spontaneously combust.

"There are countless magic spells for destruction—"

"Ah, but you see? I'm not a magician," I raise my finger, just like that librarian, "I'm researching explosives that can be used by *anyone*. You're an army man, I'm sure you see the value in this."

He cracks a smile, "I like the way you think. You're lucky you came today, as it's the last day I was going to stay out here.

"Come with me, and I'll allow you to continue your research with the money of the military to back you up."

◀‖ ⊙ ‖▶

Turns out that young man with the dictionaries came here long before I did, and is doing research on the dead. I'm next door trying to extract an amazing material: a metal, but molten in your hands without burning. I've called it quicksilver, and I've been spending the past week trying to distill enough of it from special ores to run experiments with it.

I've developed numerous liquid chemicals that can self-ignite, but nowhere to the extent of what I promised. Almost everything I've made is lethal to small animals, which proves useful for Titan and his research.

I'm hesitant to touch anything with my bare hands, as the first thing I made was corrosive. I swirl around the liquid metal in a flask to feel the weight, it's as heavy as gold. I set it down and drop another chemical inside it. Smoke begins funneling out and the glass gets hot.

I commit these reactions to memory instead of writing them down. I place the burning flask over a bowl, but *POP!* The flask bursts apart, embedding a shard of glass in my palm and splashing the quicksilver all around the bowl. I guess quicksilver is good at heating just as well as other metals.

I pull the shard out and some blood pools on the surface of the metal, quite interesting. I hold up my hand and see a small shimmer in the wound of my hand, but it disappears quickly.

I walk out of my dreary dungeon room and peer over to Titan's dreary dungeon room to see green energies flowing about as he performs necrotic magic. Not a single bastard here knows a healing spell, so I guess I'll just wrap a dirty rag over my hand and call it good. But the day goes on.

◀◀ ☉ ▶▶

"If you die here, I'll get to study you," Titan jokes at me as I sit, weak and sick in my bed. I must've breathed in some bad fumes, something only now occurring to me.

How many days has it been? I finally realize I've been working with a powder. Black and fine mixed thoroughly and I have a candle in my hand. *What am I doing? How did I get here?*

I look in the mirror and I see black markings flowing down my face. I recognize the two words so artfully drawn like tears as *Heaven* and *Earth*. I come to my senses and set the candle down.

I try to wipe away the markings, thinking someone was attempting a ritual on me. I wipe and wipe, but it won't go away. I remember a faint memory of sewing the ink into my skin one night, hysterically laughing like a maniac while doing so.

I start to laugh, but I don't know what at. My stomach tightens and I go hysterical. I reach for my workbench and slam my hand into the flame of the candle and I hear a *FLASH!* And the black powder instantly burns away.

I stand up and wobble out to the main chamber of this dungeon and see Titan handing Alastric a leather-bound book, perhaps a grimoire of his own design.

I clear my throat and dance around. *What am I doing?* I think to myself, *I'm dancing like an idiot.* I'm losing my bearings on reality. It feels like time as stopped, but before I know it I'm standing beside my friend and partner in science. "I too, am close to a breakthrough."

Alastric looks at me and laughs, "Yes, I sure hope so. You're a money pit! Always requesting the oddest things."

I bump Titan's elbow, "Let's eat, we both," I get interrupted by my laughing, "uh, need a break."

Somehow, I remember that someone has brought in some wild turkey for supper today. How long has it been? I really don't know. We eat, but it's almost like I'm watching us as a separate person, yet feeling the food go down my throat.

What is he saying? I can't hear it.

◄╫⊙╫►

My 'selfness' has mostly come back. In one of my episodes, I was having a conversation with a mage working with us by the name of Mountain, who specializes in espionage-type magic.

Mountain leans over, "Alastric's running this whole operation illegally. You know that?" But, reportedly, I had been staring at my reflection in a spoon for an hour. He thought he could disclose such information thinking I'd never remember.

Mountain waves his hand between me and the spoon. I thought it was only a moment, but I look up and see the dark sky from the dungeon windows. "I should get back to work," I tell myself, setting down the spoon and going to my workbench.

*What time is it?* I start mixing up batches of this black powder in varying proportions inside small flasks. I place a cork in each bottle and hold it in my hand, placing it over an open flame. The powder combusts and I measure the force exerted on my thumb holding down the cork.

I repeat with the next one and the next. The second to the last one, I feel a tremendous force and the glass explodes, cutting up my hand. I pull the small pieces from my palm and commit the recipe to memory. This is my final product, started by a bluff on top of a bridge. But that last one is waiting for me to test.

I hold it over the fire, and *POP!* The cork blows past my finger and hits the ceiling, dawning a terrifying new idea on me. There's no way I'd be the only one to think of such a terrifying weapon. I mustn't let this research come to light.

"You're not on the clock, Zephyrs," Alastric says to me.

"You know me, dedicated to the craft," I say, with the memory of where I had that ink and needle finally coming back to me. I shrug my shoulders and go back to where I sleep. Apparently I was feeling paranoid from something and hid the tattoo set on the very top shelf behind a book I'd never read.

I move a chair and retrieve the homemade kit. I remove my shirt and start sewing the exact recipe and proportions in a code of my own design, written in a hybrid script of Dwarven and Elvish. It took all night long. Sewing and bleeding for my secrets. I sew the cryptic language all down my left ribs. On my right side, the crude plans for a weapon; one that anyone could use, young and old, wizard or human. A terrifying proposition.

I take a deep breath and feel each and every hole I've sewn through. I need to take down this establishment. I put my shirt back on and walk out to this dreary dungeon room and look over to where Titan is sleeping. He's the only decent person working, just trying to make an honest living. There is just something about him, so dark, so sinister; yet he's the nicest soul I've ever met.

But before I wake him up, I'm going to send a letter to Alastric's commanding officer. I go back to my room and start laying out all the details Mountain had discussed with me during one of my episodes.

◂‖ ⊙ ‖▸

Everyone has started working already by the time I finished all the writing. People have gone to their workplaces, but I'm going to send a letter. I make my way to the main chamber. "All night?" Alastric asks me.

"Yup," I say, cracking my sore back, "Hey, I'm going to send a letter to someone?"

"To whom?" he responds, suspicious in my first letter.

"I just remembered someone who could know about my long-lost mother," I lie, "You know me these days, always forgetting things." I point to my head.

"Yes, go ahead, get some fresh air, and purify your body while you're at it," he waves me away.

I go to Titan, who's still sleeping, and I shake him up until he's awake. "Wake up! Wake up!" I shout in a whisper. He finally opens his eyes and orients himself, "I just set in motion to, uh," I laugh a little, but I suppress it, "*collapse* this whole thing.

"I've made my breakthrough! I'm leaving to the Westmarches!"

"What? You're insane!" he replies.

"We have to leave now! This is our chance," I persist.

"No!" his aura shakes me to the bone, and he winces in pain. But I can't convince him, so I leave. I see the sun peeking out from the windows. I go to the entrance of this dungeon, looking back at Alastric paying his visits to the workplaces.

I open the door and see a messenger falcon standing by. I pop open the tube on its back, rolling up and placing the papers inside, making sure no one is listening and whisper the destination to the bird. It flaps its wings and goes off into the sky.

And just like that the military marched in the very next day and confiscated all that research. All except mine, that is. No records of us existed, and no names were given. They simply sent us all back home.

I went to the Westmarches, where new adventures began.

# Zephrys, The Gunslinger

## Part II: The Westmarches

⊰ ◎ ⊱

I KICK open the doors to this establishment, an inn at the very edge of the kingdom, on the border between the kingdom and the Westmarches' Unknown Region. Somewhere allkind has never 'officially' explored. Multiple adventurers have gone there and began *adventuring*. Damn it! Now I'm one of them.

I have my strange bouts of laughter of varying degree, from a chuckle, or hysterical cackling. Testing both the patience of fellow travelers and myself. I also paid a substantial amount of my hard-earned military dollars on a more refined version of this weapon I've tattooed onto my right ribs. I've created a brand-new word for it, to be feared. I've called it... a Gun.

The piece is a fine work of blacksmithing, though. He worked with me to create multiple tools for loading the gun, cleaning the gun, and doing some repairs on the gun. *Gun, gun, gun.*

I look around and a group of adventurers, beaten, bruised, and defeated, exiting the building going home. "Great, another one—this one's a freak too," one of them says as the door closes.

But I ignore them, "Ay-ho!" I shout, marching in like a king.

"Ay! Ho!" Someone shouts. My eyes adjust to the low-lit inn. I spy a human woman wearing blue armor and a trident, a short-eared elf with a beard, which is unusual.

And, *oh*, my brother is here. He clearly hasn't recognized me. After all I believe my skin and hair have been lightened and my eye color has shifted to yellow. Plus, I'm wearing my hair differently after it's grown so long.

I widen my knees and march forward with my hands on my hips all the way to the bar. I try to evaluate the magical power of all these people, but I'm crap at magic. "Barkeep?" I ask aloud.

"Yes?" he approaches behind me.

"I'd like to rent a room, I'm here to stay!" I shout.

"What class of room would you like?" he chuckles.

"Cheapest one you have!" I point my finger to the sky. Everyone laughs, and I've made such a good impression, "Uh, you three? You guys look like the main characters here."

The water-spirit-looking-lady just laughs and leans on her trident. The bearded man strokes his beard, as I would assume. And my dear brother drinks a glass of wine and smiles.

⫷⊙⫸

"So you guys have already done some exploring?" I ask. We're traveling through a grassy area. No monsters thus far, I'm really waiting for a more dire moment to unleash my weapon. I've been getting by with a dagger I found lying around the forest by the inn.

Apparently one of the adventurers died on the first day by goblins, so this place is no joke. I've been trying to be super serious, and so far these past few days I've had no bouts of laughter. "Yes, We've discovered an abandoned tower," my brother says, "But by the time we arrived, we were too exhausted to explore any further."

"Hey," the *mermaid* tries to get my attention. My head curls back in an unnatural fashion and I think I have a strange smile. "What's your name, I never caught it."

"You can call me," I pause to think, and turn around in a more natural position, "Zephrys."

"And what do you do?" she continues on in this interview.

"What do you mean?"

"Well," she points to my brother, "He's a storm sorcerer, he's a warlock, and I'm a cleric."

"Oh," I stop to think about what to call myself; it has to be something very cool, I have to impress people. "I guess I'm, uh, a *Gunslinger.*"

She laughs, "I've never heard of that class—"

"We're here," my brother tells us. I turn around and see a neglected stone tower covered in vine growth. "I sense a dark monster inside."

"Of course you do," I think aloud. Laughter starts boiling up from my chest, and I allow two chuckles to burst out, and we march forward. The wooden door closing the building is of poor make and build. It's disgraceful that such fine wood such as this would be turned into something so pitiful. I mean, the planks aren't even straight or square with each other. And the condition! There's not even a remnant of finish on the wood.

I rush to the door, but trip and slam into it, piercing my face with a shard of wood. But I barely register the pain, as I'm used to needles. Two of them laugh at me, and I just lift myself up, searching for a handle on the door, but not finding one. "I think it may, possibly be locked from the inside," I try to say seriously, but I don't think it's coming out that way.

"Move aside," that self-righteous ass commands me, creating a vortex to open the door. The difference in air pressures bursts the door open, tossing me to the ground. The door falls down in two pieces, obviously from the seam between the two planks without proper glue and reinforcement.

Why am I so fixated on this door? I get up and march headfirst into the tower. They all follow behind me all the way to the top, where there's another abused piece of wood holding us up. This one is even worse! There's a damn hole in it! In a fit of rage, I kick the door down, splitting the planks of that poor door.

And a monster looks right at with a single, big, gross green eye with scales and claws for fingers. "The f—"

Wind starts flowing forth from behind be, blowing outt the one window in the back. The mermaid jumps into action and starts battling the creature. The warlock readies a spell and purple flames shoot out at the creature, "Eldritch Blast!"

The mermaid stabs him through the chest with her trident, while I run up attempting to slash out its throat, but the dagger skids off like a legitimately useless piece of dull steel. So I then throw a punch as hard as I can, landing a strike right in its gross, giant, slimy eyeball.

My fist lands the hit and the monster falls back as the mermaid thrusts the trident even further into the monster. It screams out and my brother casts a lightning bolt, frying it alive. The flash of light dissipates and the monster is still breathing. This'll be the perfect time to show what I'm made of. I pull out my gun and aim point-blank at the eyeball. *BANG!* The gun fires, and in an instant, there's a brand-new orifice in its head with sunlight shining through.

"Well, that's spectalular," the bearded one says, and I look back, I see him stroking his beard. My laughing starts up again, it's like it's been bottled up. My stomach tightens and I lean down on the ground, laughing hysterically.

"Oh," I try to say, "Don't—don't worry, I'm—I'm fine." I manage to say something before I have a burst out. It subsides eventually and I see the mermaid lady pulling out the monster's teeth. "Whatcha' doing?" I ask, getting back up to my feet.

"The teeth are worth something to a witch we found in the woods."

"A witch?" I ask, "You guys've done a lot of exploring, huh?"

"Another team found the witch, but she's been willing to buy things off us that we find that are of interest to her," my brother informs me, "What's that weapon you have, I've never seen anything like it?"

"It's, uh," I don't feel like telling him flat out, "I'm a man of the sciences, this is a culmination of that, not magic."

"Interesting," the two of them say.

"There's the last one," she says, plucking the tooth from the monster's mouth, "Let's go get some gold."

I turn to look at the journal the monster was writing in. I flip to the first page, and it's written in common language. I flip through the pages and the scribbles keep getting more and more like nothing in particular until it becomes unrecognizable to me. I put it in my bag for further study, and look around for more stuff. I see random flasks filled with smelly liquids. I sniff one and it smells like old piss.

We all leave the tower and travel to the witch.

⫷ ⊙ ⫸

I see the witch's hut coming close from the distance. I quickly kneel down in one of my steps to swipe a small stone. It's nice and coin-shaped, so I fiddle it around in between my fingers. "Oh my," the mermaid girls gasps, "I forgot, I'm Rëa."

"Nice to meet you," I bow and twist around, and dance.

"He's a strange one," the warlock whispers to my brother.

"Indeed," he responds.

I dance alongside them, waiting to arrive at the witch's residence. I twist around, flailing my arms and smack right into a fence, and cut my hand on some wood. "We've arrived, Zephrys," the warlock tells me as I caress my hand.

It's an old hut, but thank goodness, I have some fine workmanship to look at. All the lumber is cut square; the planks are tight and have finish on them! And a finely made rocking chair, exquisite carvings along the sides, and a fine, lustrous finish; it's a fine piece of furniture almost on par with my drunken father. Damn that man, but he was the finest at his craft.

I toss the stone at the front door of the establishment while the warlock shouts out, "Hextia! We've brought you some goods!"

"Hextia? Is that her name," I turn to Rëa.

"Yes, she's a powerful witch," she holds up her finger, "And you probably shouldn't throw rocks at her door."

The door opens and an old leather bag of a hunched over woman walks out with a staff whimsically carved into a fox head. She's covered in charms and the like. She opens one over her old eyes, "Who the hell is this?" she spits out.

"Hey granny," I shout, "Name's Zephrys, have you seen a witch that lives here?" I start laughing at my own joke, but I put it away to not be an idiot.

"We have goods for you," the warlock walks up to her, with my brother holding a few small bags of some items they harvested from the Monster.

"Good," she takes the sacks, handing back a coin purse.

The warlock turns to my brother and asks, "How much this time?"

My brother tosses the sack up and catches it. "By the weight, 20 gold," he turns to the witch, "You do us good, Hextia."

I snap both my fingers and point with my thumbs out. *Finger Guns.* "Later, witch," I sneer.

Rëa slaps my hands and pulls me along as we journey back through the forest back to the inn after this expedition. We get back into the forest. "So that's, uh, 5 gold a person," my brother says, opening the coin purse from the witch.

"Let's divy it up at the inn," the warlock tells him, "there's bandit's listening everywhere."

"You have a point there," he replies, putting the purse in his larger man purse.

There's a gleam shimmering right before my head, and I manage to do a cool move and duck underneath it and twirl around, but I trip on a rock and fall on my back. I feel a wire snap underneath my weight and an arrow shoots out, flying and skimming my nose. "Who the hell shoots an arrow into your ankle?" I ask aloud, "Like, it's not lethal—"

"Focus, Zephrys!" Rëa reminds me that we're probably in danger, and lifts me back up to my feet.

"Right," I pull out my gun and flip it around to bash some heads in with the hardwood handle, "But seriously, it's a waste of arrows."

The warlock follows the wire I missed the first time, goes into the trees, and disarms the trap. "It doesn't look like any bandits are hiding out here, just a trap," he walks back out with a small crossbow in hand, "But we can sell these to someone at the inn."

"Oh you know," I scratch my head, "I didn't think of that, how much is it worth?"

"5 silver maybe," he says, "they'll probably just use it for scraps. You want to get the other one?"

"Sure," I scurry to the trap, finding another small crossbow fastened to the trunk of a shrub. I wiggle it out and stuff it in my bag. Looking back, I feel something watching me.

But after the whole day's walk, we make it back to the inn, and before we walk inside, my brother pulls out the 5 gold and plops it into my hand. I kiss the coins and jump, clicking my heels and going inside the inn.

⊷ ⊙ ⊶

The half-y warlock decided to stay in his room this time, but another warlock decided to join us; he's the real keeps-to-himself type, and for the life of me, there's something that changes every time I look at him. He says he discovered a cave on one of the other expeditions, and it could hold some treasure.

So it's me, Rëa, freckle-face, and again, my brother. I pay the day's fee for the inn, and we set out on another journey into the unknown regions of the Westmarches.

I come to a realization I've been walking in silence, and another shimmering wire almost snags on my face, but I bend backwards to avoid it. "Another trap!" I shout, looking back at the rest of the group, already disarming them.

I turn around and see a bandit, red cloth covering his face. We both freeze, and then he fires a crossbow at me. It misses and I start doing a tribal dance, chanting to try to instill fear in my enemy.

I get close and whack this man in the head as hard as I possibly could with the butt of my gun. I definitely heard a crack from his skull. When I get still enough to look at him, he's sitting there, either dead or unconscious in the dirt. Thinking like a true adventurer, I start looting him.

I find a few gold, just enough to cover a few days at the inn, a short sword, which I'm not skilled enough to use, and a wicked new leather belt for myself. I slide the belt off and test fit it; it's perfect. "Oh hey! Zephrys, right?" the freckle-faced warlock calls out for me, "Grab the red cloth on his face!"

"I guess'll look good on me," I grab it looking at the faintly visible blood stains on it, "I'll have to wash it."

"No, you can turn it in for gold at the inn."

"Oh," I stuff it in my pocket, letting it hang out a little to look stylish, "That's right."

"Let's get going to this cave, it's almost noon," My brother points out, "We should get going quickly if we want to make it back by nightfall."

"You're right," the warlock motions for us, and we start up again.

We get to a large stone mound, something very, how should I say, unusual for this landscape. One of the sides is shear and has an opening leading down inside. The warlock casts a light spell, illuminating the path down, and one by one, we funnel inside.

There're some pointy rocks that I can't bother to remember the names of, and a wooden chest sitting there in the corner. Fishy... I pull out my gun, barrel pointing forward ready to fire at *anything* that jumps out at me.

We all get into the main chamber and slowly approach the chest. The warlock and I get close to the chest while the others inspect the room for traps. He opens the chest, revealing a huge stack of gold and treasure. "Jackpot," he whispers, closing the chest.

But suddenly, a rock tentacle wraps around the treasure chest and a huge eye pops open. I whip my gun around and fire, but it misses the eye and ricochets off the monster. A big mouth full of sharp teeth opens up and screeches. The warlock gets trapped and pulled closer and closer to the monster.

One of the other tentacles gets me on my damn ankle, and tight too, knocking me to the ground. Rëa's trident gets caught by another one and my brother shoots out energy at the monster, repelling the tentacle coming after him.

Rëa gets free and I flip my gun around and start beating the tentacle pulling me along by the leg to get free. But the warlock gets pulled up next to its mouth. And you know what he does? He sticks his hand in the mouth of the monster and shouts, "Eldritch Blast!" casting a magical attack right in its sensitive bits. The monster screams and releases the both of us, dropping him to the ground. I rush over and grab him to pull him out of here.

We all start running out of there. We get to the sun, but keep running away from the screeching emanating from the cave in the mound. Getting to the cusp of the forest on the outside, we stop to catch our breath. "Dude," I pat the back of the warlock, "Radical, man!"

"I know right, I didn't think that'd work!" he replies. I finally notice what's different, there's a mole on his face that swaps places every time I look. I look away and back just to see it move, and it does.

◀◀ ⊙ ▶▶

I decided to take a few days off to rest my ankle. I take back my words, aiming for the ankle is a fantastic strategy for crippling your opponent, making them a much easier target, practically a sitting-duck. The crew went out without me, and they came across a Dryad who promised my brother a magical item if they were to collect a few things for her.

My ankle's all healed up, so I bothered to go check out this Dryad with them. My brother's collected everything, and he currently has a quarterstaff that he's 'attuned' to, like 'two synced pendulums' he described. It was a few days out, most of which I don't remember.

I find myself in the night at camp, the warlock, not freckle-face, says it's one more day out until we get there. I scratch my head and realize my braid is loose from my hair growing. "Rëa, you mind?" I ask her, waving my hair.

"Sure!" she comes over and sits on a rock, leaning her trident on a tree and undoing my hair to braid it tighter.

"So, Rëa?" I ask, "Can you do something for me?"

"Sure," she replies, not knowing at all what I'm about to ask of her.

"If," I pause, "I die."

"Yes?"

"Skin me."

"Okay?" she starts getting confused.

"And make me into leather," I pause again, "And send me to a person named: Titan. I have a letter with his address sitting on my desk at the inn."

"But why?" she, in her right mind, questions this strange request.

I turn a little and slide up my shirt, revealing the encoded text tattooed on my body. She stops to read it, but quickly gets a confused look on her face when it's all nonsense. "What is that?"

"It's coded," I explain, putting my shirt back down, "It's a recipe for explosive powder."

She scrunches her lip and continues on braiding my hair into a tight hairdo. She finishes and snaps her fingers at me with *finger guns* to go to her sleeping arrangement.

I blink my eyes and forget to dream, waking up at the shaking of Rëa's boot on my shoulder. I snap awake and look around to orient myself in the daytime as I can forget where I am and have to continue to pretend like I do. "Yup, I'm awake," I sit up from my soft, grassy spot by a rock.

"We should get going," she says, "Where' almost there."

"Yeah, for the Dryad?" I start a laughing spell, and I let it go a little too long and everyone is staring at me, "Sorry." My laughing subsides when I get myself ready to go.

We get to a clearing with a sheared cliffside on a small hill. The opening is big enough for the entire inn to fit inside. There's a fog oozing out of it, so everything is obscured from view. "Now hold on," I stop; raising my hands, "I have a thing about going into places I can't see—" Rëa just starts pushing me into the fog.

As we go deeper, lights begin dancing around and once the fog clears, I see trees with bleached white trucks and blood-red leaves. I could build a beautiful new weapon out of that. I think I have some jewels lying around that would make a good inlay, so I just might be able to make a stain and finish for the wood if I were to grind up the leaves.

I reach out and pluck a leaf, but a chastising voice speaks up against my actions, "Please don't do that, the trees don't like it."

"Oh, uh," I look around to see a woman dressed in blood-red vines with skin like wood, bleached white like the trees, "I'll just pick them up from the floor then."

"If you must," she gives me the permission I don't need. I kneel down and take a fist full of leaves and stuff them into my pack haphazardly.

"This is a good napping spot," I say, standing up and walking back with the group.

"Not if you want to sleep for a thousand years," the warlock reminds me.

"I've brought everything," my brother announces, holding out a bag.

"Oh, thank you half-elf," she says, taking the bag and snatching the quarterstaff from his hands, walking off to an ornate wall full of stone carvings.

My brother gets confused, and starts walking behind her, "Wait, I thought that staff was a gift to me—"

"I'll need it for something." It's just like my brother to get tricked out of luxuries. I feel giddy and laughter bubbles up, but I quickly remind myself to stay serious.

"Well now—" the Dryad turns around and casts a spell on my brother, charming him to make him think he's her close friend. She goes off and casts another, much more complicated spell with the items in the bag my brother just gave up.

Not that I don't enjoy my turd of a brother getting duped, something more grim is happening. I pull out my gun and say, "What's going on here, Dryad?" I stop her, but my brother just jumps in front of the gun.

"Something above your pay grade," she replies, "and call me Orianna."

The wall begins to light up and open down the middle like a door. I push my brother to the side, but he pushes back. "You can't attack her, she's my closest friend, Zephrys!"

"I do what I want," I push him out of the way, following the Dryad down into a staircase that goes into a dark hall.

"What's going on lady?" I persist, ready to fire.

"You'll see," she replies, walking into the darkness.

The others follow behind me deeper into the darkness. The warlock casts another light spell to illuminate the horrors that lie down here. Bones scattered everywhere, and in the center, a bone white tree, with blood-red leaves, like a great oak growing from the bones of a vampire.

"You better explain this!" I shout. She walks up to the head of the vampire and the staff disintegrates, waking the tree. But I lose patience and aim right between the eyes.

"You see—" I fire the bullet, but it lands in her shoulder. The sound of impact is that of a solid tree, not flesh. "Very well," she says, firing energy at me, knocking me into the wall.

Battle ensues. The warlock shouts his Eldritch Blast at her and Rëa marches up with her trident. My brother finally snaps free of the spell, begins whirling some wind, and summons lightning in a brewing storm inside this small cavern.

I finally finish reloading, and I see the tree beginning to move. "The tree!" I shout at my brother, knowing I wouldn't be able to damage it.

The thunder from the storm cracks and lightning strikes the tree, breaking off one of the branches. The tree shoots out some wooden spikes at me, one sinking deep into my arm.

The lightning strikes again and the tree bursts into flames. "More!" I shout, swinging myself around our formation, and calculating a shot to the Dryad.

The Dryad screams in pain with a bunch of commotion on the other side of the group. I see Rëa get launched all the way back, and slam into the stone wall. Orianna screams out, casting an offensive spell.

More lightning strikes the tree, and I focus on the sounds echoing in the cave. I focus hard, trying to translate the slight differences in timings of the echoes to spatial awareness.

I aim up at the ceiling and fire a trick shot. The bullet ricochets about the cave, the Dryad stops making sound. I hear a thud and another lightning strike.

I rush around with my gun out and look at the Dryad shriveling up like old wood. I march up to her, sliding my gun in its holster, sliding out my dagger in the other hand, and while the wood is still soft, cut off her head. With a single slice, it's removed with the look of defeat forever molded into this art piece.

The tree is in flames, burning the remains of the vampire to a crisp in the fervent heat. "Let's go before we're suffocated in here," the warlock points out, and we all leave up the steps.

We get to the top and the fog is still there, so it's just a magical location. I hold up the severed head, "How much you want to bet that this'll fetch a nice price with Hextia?" The warlock smiles, whilst my brother sulks in embarrassment at the back.

◀▮⊙▮▶

We've been out blazing the trails of the unknown, and we hit a section of grassland. Rëa points out a tower in the distance that might be worth checking out. There're no trails going up or around here, but we go anyway. On the way there, I get in one of my laughing spouts, but Rëa pats my back until I stop because it apparently sounded like I was hacking up a lung.

We arrive at the tower, and there're signs that it's occupied. "Don't laugh this time," the warlock reminds me.

"What? I can't help it," I wink. We all get ready for a skirmish, hands ready, trident out, and barrel aimed chest-high.

"Wait!" a voice on the other side shouts, "We're unarmed!"

"Open your doors, and we'll see!" the warlock shouts back.

The doors begin to push open and the people on the other side are all gathered together. They look like a priory congregation, but all sickly. I put my gun away and walk up to them to do some sweet-talking to the individual in charge, to make peace.

"Don't attack us, please," one man says, walking out in front to us, "We're just here to worship in peace."

I get a good look at the guy, and he's covered in boils, both broken and growing. I take another good look at the others, and they're all covered in this same sickness.

The crew isn't backing down; they're all still ready to fight. "What are you guys doing, they aren't hostile," I lean over and wrap my arm around the man, "See, he's fine!"

"They're diseased," the warlock repeats, "What if they spread it?"

I jump off the prior and turn around to face him, "What are y'all doin'? If you'd like, I happen to know the witch Hextia who could whip up a cure for you guys, no problem."

"Oh, no," the man says, "We worship and take this gift upon ourselves in hopes to join our god in the afterlife."

I cough once and recollect myself, "And you guys keep to yourselves?"

"Oh yes, we only include those by choice."

"See?" I clap my hands, "They're alright if we leave them to their devices. Now let's go."

I manage to convince everyone to calm down. "Let's go Zephrys," the warlock turns around and keeps walking, with the crew following suit. I skip around and get along with them, "Be sure to take a bath when you get to the inn, Zephrys."

"Yeah, it's about that time," I repeat, coughing again.

⊶⊙⊷

Rëa noticed I developed a fever, but I've never been better to be honest. We start approaching Hextia's hut out in the stix. I swipe up another pebble and throw it at her door. The door opens and the old leather bag steps out.

"For the love—" Hextia turns my way, "Throw another stone, and I'll curse your children!"

"Sorry granny," I laugh, "But I don't think I could have kids if I wanted!"

"He's developed a fever, Hextia," Rëa pleads with her, "You're the closest thing to a doctor here."

"Where have you been recently?" she asks me as I walk up to her.

"Well, we visited this castle thing with sick people in it—" the hag slaps my head.

"Did you touch one of them?!" she shouts.

I fall silent and whisper, "Maybe." The leather bag slaps me again. She reaches in her sleeve and pulls out a charm with some feathers hanging from it.

"This will keep it from spreading anymore," she says, "But I'll need you to obtain some ingredients for a cure." We follow her inside and she pulls out a map. "There," she points, "There's a field of flowers here and I'll need three flowers to make the cure."

"Easy," The warlock says, memorizing the location.

"No, not easy. There're monsters there that guard the flowers. It's extremely dangerous."

"Then let's go," he announces, "A man down is a man not watching your back."

◀◀ ⊙ ▶▶

We arrive at the said location and there's a small patch of flowers on yet another mound with yet another hole in it. We keep our distance and come up with a plan if we activate the monsters. It's a shortgrass field, lush green with the flowers blooming on the summit of the mound.

Hextia told us that once we get within 100 feet of the mound, monsters will be alerted and be on us like a tung oil finish on fine maple table legs.

"We run, grab a fist full of flowers each, and keep running until we're out of range."

"Go!" we all say in unison. We all start running into the field. I keep falling behind, having to exert myself to keep up. We get to the halfway point, and monsters start coming out of the hole in the mound.

They float above the ground, and they're wearing... Copper? It's corroded and covered in patina. It's a very old fashion, but I guess these must be old monsters.

I refocus and keep running. My foot catches on something and I duck and roll and land right back on my feet. The others arrive and just grab their flowers.

A monster, I'll call them Copper Knights; a copper knight starts chasing me down, I tuck and roll again, and on the upswing, fire a bullet, but it just passes right through its skeletonized body.

It raises its hand with a fine looking copper sword, and swings down and I narrowly miss it. A trident pierces right through its armor and the sword drops through the grass. I kick the monster away and grab the sword to sell for later and pull out the trident with the other hand. I run as fast as I can, but I'm running out of breath.

Not thinking twice, I toss the trident back at Rëa, and she starts her running. I get to the flowerbed and snatch up some flowers, but on my way up… *WACK!* A copper knight nails me right in the head with the blunt side of a sword.

The world tumbles as I fall back. Reality fades in and out until black… I open my eyes, without a headache as I thought I should. I'm in blackness, nude. I feel my hip to feel no gun, it's been taken! My worst fear is that someone else has it. Two blue flames ignite, revealing the cold eyes of a giant man, spirit or otherwise.

"I am the Copper King!" its voice echoes in my head, "Serve me!"

And in a moment of clarity, I don't run, I don't scream. I kneel before this king and say, "I will." A wave of power rushes over me, and I feel my sickness lifted away, and I am made into a copper knight.

⊪ ⊙ ⊫

"Fight," the wispy voice of the Copper King whispers to me. My steps are not my own, how long has it been? Years. I've lost track. My arms draw their sword and my legs march outside of this hole. Someone dares disturb the king's ground.

The sun reaches my eyes, but I can barely make out the surrounding figures. Other knights are floating around me, and it's unfair that I don't get to levitate.

"That's him!" I hear a vaguely familiar voice. I think it's my old friend Titan, "My attacks don't work for the dead."

Am I dead? My arms swing the sword about, but it's knocked from my hands. A large hulking mass approaches me, readying her fists. I see a ring of severed noses around her neck. *THWACK!*

This woman keeps on wailing her fists on me, but I feel no pain. She wraps around me and puts me into a lock. "We have him!" someone shouts. I think I see Rëa, too.

They all start fleeing, but I'm with them—the voice of the Copper King screeches in my head. I scream out in real pain I haven't felt in so long. "Return!"

And in a moment of clarity amongst my friends and fellow adventurers, I say, "No." The screams of the damned souls cacoph and discords in my head. I scream with them for this must be the collective thought of those under the Copper King's hold.

Soon the screams lessen as I'm marched a distance away. "Hextia," I hear a whisper.

"Titan, I'll need your help!" the old leather bag says to my oldest friend.

The people surround me, holding various items, and they begin to chant in their various languages. And the old hag and Titan touch my chest. I can't describe the feeling other than my soul being glued back to my body. They repeat my real name, my birth name given to me by my Elvin mother. "Rise," they say in unison.

I feel my soul reattached to my body in full, and my body feels like I awoke from a long rest. The Orc woman drops me in my heavy, corroded copper armor to the floor and I take a breath I feel I haven't been able to take in years. It's like I've been drowning in air.

I start coughing, and it turns to laughing. Titan lends his hand and I get pulled to my feet, almost falling back down. "Tastes like a rotten apple," I tell him. I turn to the rest of them, all dawned in new, dope armor. "Rëa, you were supposed to skin me, remember?"

I start laughing again, but this time on purpose. It's funny, they all banded together just to bring *me* back, I must've been someone really special.

◄⊙►

# In Memoriam Of

Megan & Lola

Thank You

◄►

⊷ ⊙ ⊶

Thank you for reading.

# The End.

⊷ ⬤ ⊶

Lightning Source UK Ltd.
Milton Keynes UK
UKHW020626130121
376872UK00015B/1272/J